She heard her name, a whisper, a breath of sound

"Karen."

Her heartbeat drummed in her ears. The figure coalesced in her vision as her eyes grew accustomed to the dark.

"Karen," she heard again, and he approached, his face terribly pale against the black of his clothing, his eyes... They held hers, two glowing embers piercing the night. And then he was standing over her, his face all beautiful angles and planes and yet ravaged.

He stood there above her, and she knew he wanted her, and she became abruptly aware of her own involuntary response, the hot rush of blood through her veins.

The moments stretched out, each one a separate, tumescent entity. She saw the flare of his nostrils, the way in which he drew in her scent. This was who he was, *what* he was, at the very pinnacle of his power, and yet it was also the bottom of an abyss, his singular brand of hell.

ABOUT THE AUTHOR

Carla Peltonen and Molly Swanton, the writing team of Lynn Erickson, enjoy a challenge. "We have always been interested in archetypes," says Carla, "the basis of mythology. We wanted to use that concept in one of our books." *Out of the Darkness* successfully manages to merge the worlds of shadow and light. Carla and Molly have created a tortured vampire who earns our human sympathy, and a good woman who finds him worthy of love. "We think the story is very sensual," Molly says, "even though it isn't sexual." Another challenge.

Both Carla and Molly live in Aspen, Colorado, with their families.

Books by Lynn Erickson

HARLEQUIN SUPERROMANCE

Don't miss any of our special offers. Write to us at the following address for information on our newest releases.

Harlequin Reader Service
U.S.: 3010 Walden Ave., P.O. Box 1325, Buffalo, NY 14269
Canadian: P.O. Box 609, Fort Erie, Ont. L2A 5X3

Lynn Erickson

Out of the Darkness

Harlequin Books

TORONTO • NEW YORK • LONDON
AMSTERDAM • PARIS • SYDNEY • HAMBURG
STOCKHOLM • ATHENS • TOKYO • MILAN
MADRID • WARSAW • BUDAPEST • AUCKLAND

ISBN 0-373-70626-X

OUT OF THE DARKNESS

Out of the Darkness

CHAPTER ONE

MIGUEL RIVERA Y AGUILAR crossed the deserted avenue, slipped into New York's Central Park, avoiding the illumination of streetlights, and let darkness gather him to its bosom.

It was November, and a light rain was drifting down onto the park's winter-brown expanses, but Miguel Rivera paid the icy drizzle no heed. The cold he felt came from deep within, and the warmth he sought in the raw black night would come from no fireplace.

The park was empty or, to the uninitiated eye, it appeared to be. But Miguel knew that somewhere, perhaps huddled beneath a gracefully arching bridge or stretched out on a bench in the bowels of this emptiness, there would be life, a single beating heart from which he would extract the warmth.

He moved with purpose, his passing no more than a fleeting shadow, as all the while the demand grew within him. His thirst became excruciating, a pain that had been growing for a very long time now. Yet even as it intensified, his soul writhed in torment over the act he would soon commit.

Near the reservoir he stopped momentarily, his senses sharpening. Yes, Miguel thought, he could just make out the scent of a human, though still some distance away.

He began moving again, the night shadows embracing him with aching familiarity. He cursed his awful craving and his lack of courage. He cursed himself for the knowledge that he could, if he had the will, end this unnatural existence. All he needed to do was await the dawn, turn his face into the rays of light and he would wither, an agonizing death, of that Miguel was certain, but death nonetheless. Death and peace. Others before him had ended it, Miguel thought, but they were far braver than he.

The scent of human life caressed his nostrils then, and the painful craving filled him again. He moved across a path, through a stand of bare trees, the fog that swirled around his legs obscuring his strides, making it appear as if he were gliding through the night. On the far side of an embankment he stopped abruptly, the rain dripping slowly from his long, dark lashes. He stood motionless, the human scent very close. Flesh and blood. Ah, yes, blood. Salty, thick, warm. So warm. A feral gleam ignited in the blue of his eyes as all his senses tuned to the moment and his body quickened with the longing. Over there, yes, his prey.

It was a woman. An old, bent, homeless creature who was seeking shelter on a bench, a tattered blanket wrapped around her hunched shoulders. Alongside her sat a grocery cart, crammed full of her worldly possessions.

Pathetic, Miguel thought as he stood there in the darkness, one still shadow among many. He could feed so easily on this one, and no one would be the wiser.

Pain tore through him as he remained motionless not thirty feet from the crone, pain both familiar and terrible. His eyes glowed, and he could hear the pulsing of blood in the old woman's veins. So easy...

And yet... Hadn't he sworn that if he ever fed again it would only be on the blood of a criminal, that he would exact a peculiar kind of justice from the dregs of society? Surely somewhere in the park even now a crime was being committed!

But the sad old woman was right there, huddled against the rain only a few feet away, soon to die, anyway, by the looks of her.

He tilted his smooth ivory face up to the blackness and felt a cry of agony erupt from the depths of his being. Oh, God let the torment end! Where was his courage, his dignity, his humanity? He could end this nightmare of existence, end it for all eternity. But still, the scent of the crone swirled around him, beckoning, promising that ecstasy of fulfillment.

The wind and rain buffeted him, tore through his dark hair, and with it came a groan of misery. The old woman. She was suffering. Alone. So alone. Ah, he knew that loneliness only too well! He could help her, end her pain and sorrow. It would be over in a minute.

Miguel stood on the embankment and rocked back and forth, a part of him already tasting the woman, a part of him recoiling in shame. And then suddenly, with a swirl of his long black coat, he was gone, a flitting shadow in the night, the agony driving him, making him insane, enraged, making him swear vengeance—as he had done so many, many times over the centuries—on his old nemesis.

THE YEAR WAS 1481, and Miguel Rivera y Aguilar was thirty-five years old. His life was good. He had spent eighteen years in the priesthood in Zaragoza, Spain, and he was the pride of his family.

Like most men in the priesthood of post-Moorish Spain, Miguel had been born with his destiny laid out before him. His older brother was married with two surviving children of the six his wife had borne him, and his younger sister, though widowed, had two strapping boys. Miguel's father was dead, having succumbed to a lung infection many years before, but his mother, Elena, lived on, a healthy woman of fifty-three. Indeed, no other path had been offered Miguel except the priesthood, and he'd entered the monastery happily, proudly, an inordinately intelligent, handsome and pious young man. It was even said in Miguel's home village that one day he'd see the Vatican; after all, he was thirty-five and could expect to live till his forties, and even beyond that, God willing.

Indeed, Miguel had made his family proud. But that was in the spring of 1481, when newborn lambs gamboled on hillsides and the grapevines sprouted new leaves. That was before the coming of Baltazar.

It was that same autumn that word spread in his province of a strange wasting illness that was sweeping the land. Dozens were falling to a scourge that seemed to drain the body of its lifeblood. Physicians were at a loss—even the church examined this sudden and inexplicable illness that had taken hold of its followers. Rumors were sprouting that the devil's hand was at work.

It was on the morning of October 21 that the news was brought to Miguel. Dressed as always in his coarse brown robes, he was crossing the courtyard of the monastery, his morning prayers still held peacefully within, when Brother Armando approached him.

"Your sister has fallen ill and calls for you, my brother," Armando whispered to him. "The abbot bids you leave."

And so Miguel left the monastery, going on foot as swiftly as he could to be at his sister's side that night. By the next morning she was dead, a wasted, ashen shape lying on the cot in their mother's modest house, not a drop of blood left in her body, or so the village physician declared in awe. She was buried quickly, as no one knew how the terrible malady was contracted.

Within a week, Miguel, who'd stayed to comfort his mother, began to notice the paleness in her cheeks and the flesh all but falling from her bones. Oddly, too, there were bruises on her neck, for which she could not account. On his eighth night in his mother's house he was awakened by her screaming and found her thrashing around on her pallet, her eyes wild in madness, her hands clutching her throat. The next day she was raving, rambling on feverishly about demons and a pale-haired man. Once she even lunged for Miguel, pulling him onto the bed, tearing at his robes. She died at midnight. And it was that next day that Miguel first heard of Baltazar, the tall, fair-haired stranger who lived at the edge of the forest. It was said—in fearful whispers—that the man roamed the woods and village at night with fire in his eyes.

"Tell me," Miguel demanded, taking hold of the neighbor who had first spoken of Baltazar, "tell me what you know!" Then, that evening, assailed by a sense of impending doom, Miguel set out from the edge of the village to discover the truth about this man.

For the next five centuries Miguel would always recall that fateful journey. The October evening had been warm, the surrounding hills gilded softly with late light. For some unfathomable reason he'd paused and glanced up, his painful and confused musings momentarily put aside, and he'd watched the sun setting over the hill, its golden rays striking the blue of his eyes, blinding him. He'd felt an enormous, overwhelming sadness as the sun slipped away, but he'd gone on, striding purposefully to his destiny.

THE RAIN IN CENTRAL PARK was letting up, but a fine mist clung to every blade of grass, every barren branch. Miguel slid in and out of the fog, silent, the rawness seeping into his soul. It had been more than a year since he'd last fed, and the craving had been building within, a bitter thirst that could no longer be denied.

He was weak and had not even ventured out into the night for some weeks now, fearing his terrible urges, cursing the inevitable need for sustenance. Every sight and touch and scent had taken on a unique texture, that of blood, red and smooth and oily, warm, so warm, with the special odor of copper.

He moved eastward through the park now, sensing more human life—the homeless seeking shelter, using the seclusion of the park as protection. They would be safer with their brethren who sought shelter in the subways or public buildings, for there the crowds protected them, but these isolated souls—did they not know they were in peril?

He had not actually felt the presence of Baltazar in this city, not yet, but it was becoming the perfect home for the creature, a place that was crime-ridden, a place where so many lived in hopelessness. Yes, New York was ready for Baltazar's special touch; he fed on anarchy.

They had not met in fifty years, but a confrontation was coming, he knew. Sooner or later Miguel would read or hear about people who had died in unusual circumstances, drained of blood, and then he would know his nemesis had arrived. Most revenants killed only when they had to, discreetly, carefully. But Baltazar killed with terrible violence, the victims bitten all over, not only in the neck. Oh, he would know when Baltazar began his killings here in New York.

The cry came to Miguel as he was passing behind the row of fine museums. The scream hung eerily on the mist, muffled by it, and he stopped short. Somewhere close by, a person, a woman, was in trouble. Again a scream drifted on the fog, and Miguel, at ease in the blackness, moved toward it.

Even before coming upon the scene, Miguel Rivera could sense three beings: the woman, whose cries were weakening, and two men whose curses filled the air. Her attackers? Then he saw them, in some bushes near the edge of the park, directly off a lighted path. The men had the woman down, one trying to clamp a hand over her mouth, the other holding her struggling legs.

Rage rose in Miguel as he paused, assessing the scene. And he took action, swiftly breaking the cover of night, then, with inhuman strength, lifting one man and tossing him into the brush, where he lay stunned.

"What the . . . ?" The other man stopped his attack on the female and stared up into the fire of Miguel's eyes. "My God . . ." he croaked, but it was too late.

"You will not dare venture into the night again," Miguel whispered harshly, and he was on the man swiftly, mercilessly, with the precision of a surgeon.

That cold rainy night in Central Park Miguel fed, filling his soul, feeling the beating of the man's heart as he drank his fill. The warmth that spread through his body was searing, jolting him like a shock as the liquid penetrated every fiber of his being.

The man did not die. But then Miguel had never intended to take his life. And when he was done, his thirst abated, he lifted his head and was vaguely aware of the other one scrabbling off into the night, and of the woman still lying close by. But at the moment nothing mattered to him except the sensations that rippled through him—the sweet blessed warmth, the return of strength, the all-consuming satisfaction.

For a long time he crouched beside his victim and remained motionless, his handsome head tilted upward to the night, mist shining in his dark hair, glistening in his long lashes, illuminating a single ruby drop at the corner of his mouth. *Oh, yes, yes,* he groaned inwardly, pleasure coursing through him. And then finally his surroundings came into focus once more, and he twisted his head to stare down at the female.

She was no street person, of that he was instantly aware. She wore a white uniform of sorts—was she a nurse, venturing home after a night shift? How foolhardy, he thought, still crouching beside her, crossing Central Park at this hour.

He stayed next to her, weighing the situation. Clearly she was dazed by the attack—perhaps she had hit her head, been stunned. He wished she would come around. As it was...

What was he to do with her? Miguel knew he could not alert the police or take her to a hospital. There would be questions. He turned his head and glanced at his victim. The man still lived, as Miguel knew he would. But half his blood was gone, and there would certainly be questions. No, he could not take the injured woman to the authorities. He would have to leave her, then, hope she awakened and could make her way to safety.

He stood and felt the strength coursing through his limbs, so unfamiliar of late, so satisfying. And as he'd sworn, he had fed on one who deserved what he had gotten. Miguel would wager that the man, once recovered, would think twice before preying on a helpless woman again. Unusual justice, but justice nonetheless. It was unfortunate, however, that the woman was harmed.

He stood over her and frowned. She moaned but did not open her eyes. "Wake up," he said. "Wake up, woman, for God's sake, you cannot stay here in this cold rain." She only moaned again and shifted a little, her torn white uniform hitched beneath her, riding high on her white-clad legs.

Miguel emitted an irritated sigh and bent over, trying to adjust the thin brown coat that was spread beneath her. She would freeze to death. After he had rescued her from the scum who had attacked her, she would perish if left out here.

"Wake up," he said again, commandingly, and then he tried touching her, his long-fingered hand on her chin. He noticed then how pale she was, how plain and pale, her delicate features drawn in pain. After a minute or two her eyelids finally fluttered a little and she sighed raggedly.

"There, there," Miguel said, relieved, "wake up now. You are all right."

And then she seemed to come back to her senses all at once and sat bolt upright, flailing out against him.

Miguel held her arms with ease and told her that it was he who'd come to her rescue. "It is all right now," he said over and over, "you are quite safe."

Safe, yes, he knew, but terrified and obviously not in her right mind.

"Can you stand?" he asked, but her struggles, which had stopped, had weakened her even further. "You must try to stand up."

It was no use. After a time he helped her up, but she sagged against him, and he knew he had to at least get her out of this park. The rain had started again, too, a thin, cold drizzle that soaked them both. Of course Miguel had not felt the effect of cold or heat or rain in five centuries, so he stripped off his heavy black overcoat and draped it over her thin brown one.

She leaned against him, and he began to steer her along, back to the path she'd been on, back toward the western edge of the park. Perhaps there he could find a bench, sit her down—eventually someone, even at this late hour, would come along. A taxicab. A police vehicle. Or, Miguel thought grimly, another thug or two.

They reached Central Park West and he cast about, but there was no one in sight. A single car streaked by, splashing oily rain from the street onto the sidewalk, and then its taillights disappeared, shimmering dots of red.

He stood there and tipped her face up to his, rain dripping off his sleek dark hair onto her pale brow. He stared at the droplets dumbly for a long moment before he realized he must act. "Where do you live?" he asked, but she only huddled closer to him and moaned something he could not comprehend.

He thought again of a hospital. There were several not far away, but there would be those questions: Name, address, workplace, questions he could not answer.

An alien sense of frustration swept over him. He was saddled with this woman. Unless she came fully awake, he had only one option.

They started across the street, Miguel moving quickly, the female pressing herself to his side, stumbling along so that he had to half carry her.

He did not like it, and had no idea of how to react to this ludicrous role of protector he'd somehow taken on. And yet she was hurt, out of her head, relying on **him. What irony!** Crushed to his side, a woman, a flesh-and-blood mortal whom he had rescued. It was unthinkable.

Miguel steered her into an alley, across another street. Into another alley. A car or two swept past them. A cat cried forlornly from behind a trash

Dumpster. On a corner two drunks lingered, passing a bottle between them, noticing the drenched man in the black turtleneck sweater with the woman bundled against his side. Miguel eyed them as he passed, and the two quickly turned away, frightened.

He walked on into the night, the rain dripping from eaves and gutters and puddling in the alleys, the female warm and oh so close. He moved rapidly and with a curious ease, the mist closing in behind him, the shadows ahead a beacon of comfort.

CHAPTER TWO

THE FIRST THING Karen Freed saw when she regained her senses was a high, elaborate pressed-tin ceiling that didn't look in the least familiar. Her eyes traveled down to dark wood paneling and bookshelves filled with volumes and volumes of leather and gilt. My God, where was she?

Her eyes traveled to lead crystal lamps and vague shapes of furniture that were draped with white sheets, like somnolent ghosts. To dark green walls, a faded Persian carpet, a veined marble mantel, hunting prints on the walls.

She tried to clear her head. What had happened? And how on earth did she get here? Wherever here was.

Karen realized she was reclining on a sofa; she tried to sit up, but she seemed to hurt all over. Panic began to curl inside her in tiny hot licks of flame. A heavy black overcoat lay on top of her, and she pushed it aside, suddenly claustrophobic. Then she looked around again, finally realizing that she was in a strange Victorian library, dimly lit, old-fashioned and dusty, but elegant in the overdone style of the turn of the century.

She put a hand on her side—it was sore, bruised—then looked down and saw that her nurse's uniform was ripped, her slip protruding from a long, jagged tear. Panic grew hot in her belly, but she was alone in the ornate room.

And then, as if a switch had been thrown, it all flooded back into her brain like a rush of scalding water: the park, the shortcut she knew she shouldn't have taken at four in the morning, those men with their dirty hands and sour breath.

And then another part of her memory fell into place. Yes, a man had saved her, a man who'd appeared suddenly out of the darkness and frightened away her attackers. Who was he, this rescuer? She had only an impression—medium height, dark hair, a mustache, strong hands that had held her up when she'd felt so terribly faint, very white hands. But that was all; she had no memory whatsoever of his face or if he'd said anything, or if she had.

Was this where he lived?

Karen sat up and swung her feet to the floor, wincing. She put her head in her hands; she felt so awfully disoriented, her head pounding, her stomach nauseous. A concussion, that's what she must have. The symptoms were all too familiar, but Karen's experience had always been with other people's injuries, not her own.

She fought the nausea and dizziness down and pushed herself off the sofa to her feet. She felt weak, but she was sure she could get home. Maybe she should call a cab and leave, or maybe just leave without even calling... But where was she? And how long had she been here?

Her coat was torn and muddy, nearly soaked through. Ruined, completely ruined. And the stranger—her eyes fell on his heavy black coat lying on the sofa—had bundled her up in that. She put a hand out to touch the fabric. It was soft and luxuriously heavy, a rich cashmere, slightly damp. Her own cheap, threadbare one shamed her. She'd been meaning to replace it, but such things had little importance for Karen; after all, who was there to notice her? But now, someone *had* noticed, and he'd had to give her his own coat, probably getting soaked himself in the process. Oh, God.

Her purse. Gone. Her few dollars, her license, her credit card, her hospital ID. Gone. She set her jaw. She'd asked for it, walking through the park like that. Stupid.

It came to her then that perhaps the stranger had spoken to her. She thought she recalled a voice calling to her: *Wake up, wake up.* But she hadn't been able to answer. And she vaguely remembered someone holding her up, but it was very unreal, a dream memory. Then again, she might be imagining all of it, but in that case how did she get here?

No doubt she should thank this stranger, but he wasn't here. She was alone, entirely alone in this elaborate, dusty room that looked as if it hadn't been lived in for decades.

Karen put her hand on the carved wooden back of the sofa to steady herself. Yes, she could make it home. Then she could rest. By tomorrow she'd be fine. She told herself this despite the training that was issuing warnings she wasn't in any mood to acknowledge; namely, that a concussion, even a slight one, could be dangerous. The patient should be observed while sleeping and awakened every hour for twenty-four hours. She should go to the hospital, but she knew she wasn't going to. She just wanted to go home.

A strange noise intruded on her consciousness, and she tensed. It was a hollow, scratching sort of sound, as if someone were drawing fingernails across a blackboard, and it made her skin crawl. The window. Yes, it came from the tall, heavily draped window. She moved shakily across the room and pulled back a velvet drape. Naked black fingers reached at her through the glass, and she drew back with a gasp. Then she saw that the fingers were only tree branches that were rubbing against the window, and she chided herself for her irrational fear.

When she turned back toward the door a stranger was there, a glass of water in his hand. Karen gasped. The man's face was startlingly pale save for the darkness of his mustache and his shadowed eyes. A palpable stillness surrounded him.

"I am very sorry if I alarmed you," he said then, and Karen discerned a faint accent in his words, a vaguely foreign cadence. "My name is Miguel Rivera y Aguilar, and you are in my house. You had an...um, accident, you might say.''

"Those men," Karen whispered. "Were you the one who...?"

He nodded somberly, a graceful inclination of his dark head.

"Thank you very much," she said breathlessly, feeling terribly self-conscious in her ripped clothing, with her hair hanging in damp tendrils on her neck. "I appreciate it. They didn't...I mean, you aren't hurt, are you?"

He waved a hand, as if the notion were of no consequence.

"Oh, I'm glad. I wouldn't..." Why couldn't she finish even one sentence?

"And you," he said. "The more important question is if *you* are uninjured."

"I, uh, well, I think I must have hit my head, but I'll be fine." Her hand fluttered at the side where her uniform was ripped.

"And there?" The stranger gestured toward the tear.

"Just bruised. I'll be...Oh, I'll be fine."

"The men did not...harm you in any other way?" he asked.

Karen felt herself flush. She looked down before answering. "Uh, no, they didn't do anything."

He took a gliding step into the room. "Here is some water—I have nothing else to offer you. I am so sorry."

"Oh, I don't . . . really need . . ."

"Please sit down. You appear very pale. Perhaps you are hurt more than you think." He hesitated then. "How should I call you? I forget my manners."

"Oh, I'm sorry. I should have introduced myself. I'm Karen Freed."

"Well, then, Mrs. Freed, please seat yourself." He moved closer and indicated the sofa.

"Miss Freed," she said automatically while she moved around to sit primly on the edge of the crackling, horsehair-stuffed seat.

He handed her the glass of water, and she took it in both hands, as if it were some sort of talisman.

"So, Miss Freed," he said, sinking soundlessly into a white-shrouded chair, "please tell me, only to satisfy my curiosity, why you were in the park at such an hour?"

She looked down at the glass of water. "It was stupid," she replied. "I'm a nurse at Upper Manhattan Memorial Hospital, and I'd just finished my shift. I know better, but I'd missed the last bus home, and it was shorter to walk through the park to the subway."

"I see," he said. "You are a nurse. Um, I understand."

His voice had a certain timbre to it that resonated inside her. That accent, the formal English, made her relax a little. She knew instinctively that he was a gentleman, a foreign, very commanding, gentleman, and that she was safe with him. It occurred to her to wonder at this knowledge, because no one who lived in New York ever trusted a stranger. But this man...

She took a sip of the water and swallowed. "Well, I should be going," she said.

Gazing at her intently, he said with apparent reluctance, "Rest for a little while. You have had a shock. I will call you a taxi in a short time, and then you can go."

It struck her then. A taxi... Oh, Lord, she had no money, not a penny. "I...I don't have any money. My purse is gone. Oh, dear, do you think the cabbie would wait while I go up to my apartment to get a check or something?"

"Please, do not worry. I will pay the fare. It is of no consequence."

"Oh, I can't ask you..."

"Consider it a loan, then."

"Oh, yes, I'll pay you back, Mr. Rivera."

"Please, it is not important, truly. Rest for a time. Do not concern yourself with trivialities."

"Well, that's very nice of you. But, really, I don't want to be a bother. I hope I'm not disturbing you. I mean, it's so late...."

He bared his teeth in what was obviously meant to be a smile. "I am always up at night. That is when I do my best work."

"Oh, I see." But she didn't see at all.

"Where do you live, Miss Freed?" he asked.

"Oh, the Upper East Side," she said vaguely.

"Not so far, then."

"No, not far, but at night..."

"Yes, of course, I see."

"And cabs are so expensive, so I usually take the bus." She was blathering on with her usual inability to make conversation with men, she realized ruefully.

She stole a glance at him. He sat there in perfect repose, without nervous mannerisms or unnecessary movement. A very handsome man. There was the hint of a slender but taut physique under his dark wool trousers and black turtleneck sweater. His hair was very black, silky, longish and damp from the rain outside. His unblemished skin was as pale as alabaster. His eyes were dark—dark blue, not the brown she'd first supposed—and fringed with long, beautiful dark lashes. His nose was curved, his nostrils flared imperiously. There was something about this Miguel Rivera that was very unusual, very different. It must be his foreignness, Karen decided. Yes, that was it. Nervously she sipped at the water, feeling more inconsequential than ever.

"You're sure," she began, "um, I mean, are you sure I'm not keeping you from anything important?"

"I'm quite sure. My time is entirely my own. I am at your disposal, Miss Freed."

She looked down in confusion. "You're just being polite. I'd prefer you to be frank with me. If you just show me your phone, I'll call a cab."

"Soon."

"But..."

"I would rather you took your time. It would be unconscionable of me to send you out into the night, not knowing if you were recovered. Call it selfishness on my part if you will."

Karen sank back against the sofa. Her head ached, it was true, and it was so warm and pleasant in this room.... It was easier to stay, just for a little longer. "All right," she said, "but just for a few minutes. I don't want to impose."

"Will you report the...ah, attack, Miss Freed?" he asked carefully.

"Call me Karen, please. I mean, we're practically old friends now that you saved my life...." She stopped, not sure if she was making a fool of herself.

"Karen, then. Will you?"

"What? Oh, report the attack?" She knew instantly what he was getting at. "No, I don't think so. After all, I have no idea who they were. I couldn't even give the police descriptions."

"It is a shame," he said, "that it was too dark for me to have seen them, myself." He paused. "Do you need to report to the police the loss of your driver's license, that sort of thing?"

"No," she replied. "I only have to request a duplicate. And the credit card company will automatically replace mine with a new one—new numbers, you know. I don't think I'll bother with the whole police routine. What would be the sense of going through all that? My goodness, there must be thousands of crimes like that every night in New York. They're never solved."

He nodded gravely, and she could tell he preferred it that way. Obviously he was a bit eccentric and would hate newspaper coverage or questions from the police.

"Oh, I'd never get you involved. You don't have to worry about that," she assured him.

"Your concern is appreciated," he replied, his blue eyes fixed on her.

She'd never known a man who spoke as he did, so courtly and polite and obviously well educated. Even the doctors at the hospital didn't sound like Miguel Rivera.

"Are you from...um, somewhere in Europe?" Karen asked, searching for a topic of conversation.

His gaze bored into her like the beam of a lantern. "Originally," he said, "I was from Spain, but I have lived in many places in the world."

"How interesting," Karen said. "I've always wanted to travel. I went to Bermuda once."

"It is not always interesting," he said in an odd tone.

"Oh, because you have to travel for business," Karen guessed.

"You could call it that," he replied dryly.

"What is your business? This house is so old and so lovely. Well, it's none of my business, I know." She gave him a small embarrassed smile. "Just tell me to pipe down, like my father does when I get nosy."

"You are not nosy," he said. "I consider your question fair, but I cannot answer you in detail. My affairs are far-flung and complicated."

"Oh, please, forget I asked," she said, fluttering her hand as if to wave away her questions.

He shrugged. "In truth, I am retired. I have an agent here in New York who handles everything for me."

"That must be nice," Karen said before thinking.

"It is merely... convenient," he replied.

She always said the wrong thing. Or if she did say something acceptable, then her manner was wrong. And this man was so urbane, so elegant, like a character from a wonderful movie. She was embarrassed at her own awkwardness and inability to respond cleverly or intelligently. No wonder she was single, no wonder she didn't have dates very often. No wonder her mother nagged her constantly about getting married. Here she was with a handsome man, a nice man, someone who'd rescued her heroically, romantically, and all she could do was stumble over her tongue, stutter and make dumb remarks.

She sat there, damp and miserable, unable to think of a thing to say, afraid even to meet Miguel's gaze, and suddenly she wanted to disappear. She wished she didn't have to deal with the social amenities; she simply couldn't do those things well. She was a plain woman, good at really only one thing in her life, and that was her work. She was sure Miguel Rivera recognized that in her and was only being polite, gentlemanly. She swallowed, feeling a lump in her throat, and her head pounded hollowly.

"You are not feeling well" came Miguel's voice, as if from a distance.

"No, no, I'm all right," she murmured.

"You do not look all right."

She finally glanced up. "I think I should go home now."

"That might be wise," he said. "I'll phone for a taxi."

"Thank you," she whispered, looking down at her hands still tightly clasping the glass.

"Please excuse me while I arrange it," he said, and she was aware of him rising and moving silently toward the door.

He was back in a moment. "The cab will be here in ten minutes," he said. "Will that do?"

"Oh, yes, of course. You're awfully nice to do this. I mean, not many people would bother. Chasing those men away in the first place... Why, you might have been killed."

That humorless smile again. "Do not concern yourself. I was in no danger at all." He spread his hands, and Karen saw that they were very fine boned and as pale as ivory. "What was I to do, leave you there on the ground?"

"I don't know," she said quietly. "Most people wouldn't have interfered. You must be very brave."

"Not at all. In truth, I am the worst sort of coward," he said.

She was surprised at the fervor in his voice. "Oh, no, you can't be, not after what you did."

His eyes met hers, and she saw a spark in their sapphire depths. "I did only what needed doing at no cost to myself."

"And for your troubles you got stuck with me," Karen said, trying for levity, achieving only pathos.

"It is my pleasure," he said smoothly, and she knew he was lying.

When she finally heard a knock at the door, Karen was nearly overcome with relief. She stood and pulled her ruined coat around her while Miguel went to answer it. She followed him, out of the library, down a bare hallway to where he stood, holding the front door open.

"He is waiting for you," Miguel said. "Can you manage?"

"Oh, yes, of course. Thank you. I can't ever repay you—I mean for your help, for saving me. I will repay the money, though. I hope you know how much I owe you, Mr. Rivera."

He stood in the open doorway, his features shadowed. "You owe me nothing," he said. "And do me the favor of calling me Miguel."

She tried to smile. Cool, damp air came in through the open door, and she pulled her torn coat around her more tightly. Outside dawn was at hand. A cold, gray, empty November dawn.

"I apologize for not seeing you safely home," Miguel said, looking down at her. "But I have some affairs that keep me here."

"Oh, that's okay. I'll be fine, honestly. You've done too much already."

Miguel glanced out and stepped aside from the open door, moving back into the deep shadows of the hall-way. There was an air of distraction about him now, Karen thought. No doubt he was dying to get rid of her. "Well, I'll be going now," she said.

To Karen's surprise, he took her hand, his fingers smooth and cool, and in a charming, old-fashioned gesture, he raised it to his lips. She felt the touch of his skin, the tickle of his mustache, and a shiver ran up her arm as she gasped in frightened delight. Then he raised his head and said something that threw her into a state of stupefaction. "Would you care to go to din-ner this evening, Karen Freed?" he asked.

"What?" she finally managed to say.

"But, of course, it was only a suggestion. Indeed, you may have previous plans...." He let his words trail off eloquently.

"Dinner?" she repeated stupidly.

A corner of his mouth quirked. "Surely you must eat?"

Karen stood there on the threshold of this courtly, mysterious stranger who'd saved her life, a thousand emotions battling within her. Then one achieved su-premacy, and everything was abruptly clear and simple. "Yes," she said, "I'd love to go out to dinner with you, Miguel."

"And how shall I find you?" he asked.

"I'm . . . oh, in the phone book."

"Tonight, then," he said. She could only nod and make her escape, but when she was in the taxi she braved a glance back toward the stately brownstone that was now emerging from the darkness. He was nowhere to be seen. Not a light shone from the building, and for no reason at all, Karen felt the chill of dawn deep inside her.

CHAPTER THREE

THE LONG BLACK LIMO glided through Upper Manhattan's traffic, its tires hissing in the puddles that lay like dark mirrors on the streets. Inside, the plush interior muffled all sound, and Miguel sat motionless, heedless of the sirens and horns blaring around him, of the screeching brakes and changing lights. He rarely noticed these mundane details. He'd lived in too many cities for too long to pay any mind to the crush of humanity.

Tonight, however, there was a difference within him. There was caution and something else, something to which he had not yet been able to put a name. When he'd awakened that evening, after the light had left the city, he'd thought that this so-called date—this rendezvous—he'd made with Miss Karen Freed was eliciting some faint stirrings of... He'd tried to dredge up the memory of those long-lost feelings and could come up with only the nebulous idea of pleasure. But that was quite impossible. He was only anticipating this meeting because it was different from anything he'd ever done. In over five hundred years, this was at last a new experience.

He must be quite mad, nevertheless. All these centuries of unbearable loneliness and self-loathing, of exile from life and the sweetness of human companionship—and now this, a flesh and blood woman. A dinner engagement! What could possibly come of this farce? He shuddered to think, and put the notion aside. He did not want that from this woman. He would never allow it.

The long car finally pulled up to the curb alongside an ordinary graystone apartment building that had a rather shabby appearance. But then, so did this entire neighborhood.

"Would you like me to get the lady, sir?" came the driver's voice over a speaker.

But Miguel would not hear of it. "No, I shall fetch her myself," he said, and then climbed out into the night.

He rang the buzzer on number 121 and waited, wondering again why he had chosen this particular female as a partner for the evening. In his interminable days he had seen the beautiful women of Europe and Asia and Africa, and had appreciated in his own way their grace and fine, chiseled features, the glow of their hair and cheeks, the slim whiteness or duskiness of their hands and necks. Yes, he could appreciate beauty, just as he appreciated art and music and the perfect orb of a full moon. But the pale imitation of passion he felt at these things was so far from human that the chasm was immeasurable. He was *in* life, but he was not *of* life. He could not partake of the actual physical essence of the beauty he saw; he could not taste food or feel the beat of his heart or the sweat of his brow; nor could he love the women. The closest he came to humanity was in the cerebral appreciation of line and color and texture of art or the swelling of notes in music.

But Karen Freed... What was it about this one creature that had piqued his interest? Why such an ordinary woman out of the scores of beauties he'd observed in his lifetime?

When she answered the buzzer she told him she'd be down directly, and he wondered if she had not invited him up out of embarrassment over her meager lodgings or because of modesty. Of course, Miguel had little notion of modern women's true feelings, but he did know that, in this century, modesty was in short supply. So this small mystery of Karen's was another curiosity.

As far as her circumstances went, he did not give a fig one way or the other. He knew how unimportant money was; he knew it could never buy peace of mind, yet he had to admit its power. Without money he'd be neither more nor less happy, although he would certainly be less comfortable.

Then Karen appeared, practically running down the stairs, breathless as she opened the door for him, smiling. What a sweet, shy smile! She was wearing a plain, chestnut-brown knit dress that did little to flatter her as it clung rather shapelessly to the extreme slenderness of her limbs. Her hair, which was practically the same color as her dress—perhaps a shade or two lighter—was curled tonight, held back from her pale brow by two dime-store clasps.

"Good evening," Miguel said, smiling back at her, taking her coat, the same one she'd worn last night, carefully cleaned and mended, and draping it over her shoulders. "I should have brought an umbrella," he said.

"Oh, are we walking?" she asked.

But he only gave a humorless laugh. "No. I have a car." He led her out to the sleek black limousine that purred at the curb, its wipers swish, swishing in the rain.

The driver had come around to hold the door for them as first Karen and then Miguel slid into the plush interior. Miguel was amused by her sudden speechlessness.

"Your first ride in a limousine?" he asked as she ran a hand along the butter-soft tan leather seat.

"Oh, yes," she said. "It's...magnificent. You really didn't have to go to all this trouble. I mean..."

"Put your mind at rest, Karen," he said. "I always travel by hired car."

"You mean you don't drive at all?"

"It is inconvenient for me to get to your driver's license bureau," he said smoothly. "And this is certainly far more pleasant, don't you agree."

"It sure is," Karen said, shaking her head in wonder and delight.

Miguel studied this mortal quietly for a moment. She was not at all like the women he saw on television or in the late movies he attended, nor was she like the women he saw on the streets of the city as he wandered. There was an air about her, a simplicity and a lack of pretension, that was not the norm these days. She could have been from a previous, less complicated time; he could see her in the dress of a gentlewoman of the century in which he'd been born. Yes, a long brown dress of linsey-woolsey.

He could see she was embarrassed by his close scrutiny, though. "Is something wrong?" she asked.

"No, not at all. I was merely looking for... uh, bruises from your unfortunate encounter last night."

"Oh. Well, I guess I was lucky, because nothing really shows, but I sure have a sore spot on my head, a real knot, and my ribs are black and blue."

He frowned. "You are in pain?"

"Oh, really, I'm okay. It's not bad. I slept practically all day, and I just took some aspirin."

"This outing is perhaps disturbing your rest, then."

"No. I feel great." She smiled again, shyly. "After all, a girl has to eat."

Miguel thought of some he knew who did not, but he replied, "Yes, certainly," and attempted to return her smile.

Miguel directed the driver to a favorite spot of his, a quiet little French restaurant that was hidden off the lobby of a midtown hotel near Gramercy Park. Of course, not a morsel of food had passed his lips in fifty decades, but he gleaned pleasure of a sort from watching the diners and the fine service of a good restaurant—it was all rather like a work of art when done properly. And as for his appetite, no one had ever commented on his untouched food—a well-trained waiter would never mention such a thing.

Oh, it was not so difficult duping people. The secret was not to stay in one locale more than a decade; then no one would take note of his perpetual youthfulness. Miguel had already almost overstayed his sojourn in New York, in fact, and soon his agent, who held his power of attorney here, would notice the thickness of Miguel's still-dark hair and the smooth skin of his face. Soon, he knew, he had to leave this vibrant city. Perhaps he would travel for a time. Or perhaps he would muster the mental energy to once again continue the search for Baltazar.

Karen seemed to take instantly to the small French restaurant, sighing over the rich red-and-black velvet interior, the lovely subdued lighting of chandeliers, the crisp white linen on the tables. She smiled as the maître d' helped her into her chair.

"Good evening, Mr. Rivera," the man said, bowing slightly. "It's nice to see you again."

"I am afraid it has been too long, Maurice," Miguel said, seating himself.

"Ah, everyone is so busy nowadays."

"Yes, very," Miguel agreed.

The French menu was incomprehensible to Karen, and she said so, asking Miguel to order for her, which he did with ease. He thought that she was a unique female, possessing a ready intelligence and yet a delightfully fresh naiveté, as if every sight and sound and smell were new to her. While they awaited the Caesar salad, she touched the tiny glass rose petals of the centerpiece so delicately that Miguel found he could not take his eyes from her hands.

"Aren't these beautiful," she was saying as he watched her slim index finger move over the fragile glass. "Imagine, someone made each little one of these."

"It is truly an art," he agreed, his eyes still fixed on her as if he'd never observed the grace and tenderness of a lady's touch before.

They ate their salads or, rather, Karen savored hers while Miguel pushed his around the plate. After a time her gray blue eyes lifted to his and she asked guilelessly, "Aren't you hungry, Miguel?"

"I fear I recently overindulged," he said easily.

"It's delicious, though, isn't it?" she said, and he inclined his head in agreement.

She was an innocent, he decided, possessing a rare humility and patience. She was the exact antithesis of his five-hundred-year-old weariness and bitter cynicism.

She dabbed at her mouth with her napkin and then whispered, "You don't suppose I could ask the waiter for the recipe for the dressing? I mean, my mother's a great cook, and I know she'd love this." And then

Karen dropped her hopeful gaze. "How silly of me," she said. "The chef probably guards it with his life."

"It will be yours by the end of the meal," Miguel said softly, his eyes roaming over the delicate lines of her fine-boned face. He noticed the way her light brown lashes formed perfect fans against her cheeks, the slim column of her neck, where he imagined he could see the pulse throb. Oh, yes, Miguel fixed his gaze on *that* tender spot.

Dinner arrived, lamb for Karen and duck for Miguel. He often ordered duck, savoring the heavy, oily aroma that mingled with oranges and lemons, recalling, even after all this time, his mother's table set for a feast provided by his father's successful hunt. Miguel could still summon memories of his human existence, and he could still ache for that stolen life—for the stolen lives of his mother and his sister. And certain settings, certain aromas and sights and sounds, brought those memories back with stark clarity. He could not experience physical pain, but there was an agony in his soul that never abated.

With Miguel watching her intently, the way she chewed, swallowed, sipped on a glass of wine—a deep red wine—Karen finished her meal. And when the chef entered the dining room to check on the guests, Miguel quite easily extracted from him the recipe for the salad dressing. But then, too, Karen's obvious delight would have accomplished the same thing with the man, and Miguel suspected the world could be hers if she but knew how to ask for it.

Over coffee he questioned her about her work, curious that so delicate and gentle a woman could abide the horror she must be witness to every night in that hospital emergency room.

"Everyone asks me that," she admitted. "Maybe it's just because I look... Well, you know, fragile or something. I can be as tough as anyone, though. And, well, I love my work. I save lives."

"But all the crime," he said, "the results of violence. So much—bloodshed, shall we say, must touch you in ways I cannot imagine."

"It's sad, but it's reality. And then there's always the one life that's worth saving, like a child in a car accident or someone who's truly a victim."

She looked down at her coffee cup shyly, and the gesture stirred Miguel in an unfamiliar way, as if something inside him had given way just a little. He gazed at her as she added, "You know, well, I'm not a person who brags, but I really am a good nurse. I have...uh, a sort of talent." Her eyes met his, and they were filled with the essence of sincerity. "I help people. I touch them with my hands, and they feel better."

"That is a gift, Karen," he said.

"Um, well, I always wanted to be a nurse. Even when I was a little girl."

"I understand that, yes. You have a calling."

She cocked her head. "It's rewarding, you know? The rest of my life... Well, it's pretty dull. Except for tonight, that is," she said, her eyes lighting up. "This has been the most wonderful night."

"Has it?" he asked quietly.

"Oh, yes," Karen said. "I feel as if I'm living in a fairy tale."

And she queried him about his life, too, which was a subject he had to handle with great care. "I have traveled quite a bit," he told her, and then he went on to regale her with a small portion of the sights he'd seen. Still, he must have told her a little too much, because she said, "My gosh, how old are you? You don't look more than thirty-five."

He laughed. "I am in my mid-thirties," he said, "though I feel at times a great deal older." Then he tactfully turned the conversation back to Karen. "And you?"

"Oh, I'm in my mid-thirties, too."

"Never married?"

She shook her head as if it were of no consequence. "Haven't had the time, I guess. My mother says I'm an old maid."

"I see," he said.

"Have you ever been married, Miguel?" she asked abruptly.

"Once," he told her before realizing what he'd said.

"Oh," she said. "Divorced?"

"Completely," Miguel replied, aware of the bitterness of his tone.

She let the subject drop, though, and he was grateful. Married, he thought. Yes, to the church, to a life of pride and dignity—and peace. Oh, he had most definitely been married once. "Tell me more about Paris," Karen was saying, and he had to force his attention back to the present.

"Ah, Paris, yes," he said, "a lovely city, a museum unto itself." He spoke on, and Karen listened raptly, sipping her coffee, her blue gray eyes fixed on him. But as he told her of modern-day Paris he couldn't help remembering another age, a time when Europe was in upheaval and filled with darkness.

Baltazar had been there.

It was the decade preceding the French Revolution, almost three hundred years after Miguel had first left post-Moorish Spain on his initial quest to find Baltazar, the fiend who had murdered his mother and sister and turned him into a bloodsucking monster.

For Miguel had not died from Baltazar's ministrations. No, Baltazar had saved him from death for his own perverted purposes, although it had taken Miguel years to realize what they were. And when he did he shuddered with the horror of it, for Baltazar chose those he transformed carefully, always the special ones, the best of humanity. So, Miguel had recovered, or thought he had, and returned to the monastery, mourning the loss of his family, at first only vaguely recalling that fateful walk to the edge of the forest.

For months he had tried to live piously, as before, but his prayers had been difficult and meaningless to him. And then there had been the restlessness at night, the inability to stay awake during the day. His appetite had left him, too, but in its place had been born a different sort of appetite, a lusting thirst. Often Miguel had found himself roving the countryside without direction—always at night—and he'd been overcome with this thirst. And then, one cold, bleak night in the forest, he'd come across a dying deer. And he'd fed.

Miguel had returned to the monastery, but his calling, his life, his very humanity, were gone. And he gradually recalled the night he'd confronted Baltazar. The man had sunk his teeth into his flesh and Miguel had felt a curious pain that was somehow not pain, then weakness and loss of memory and the subsequent emptiness of his soul.

For a time Miguel had tried to exist in this other world, going about his duties, though he had told the abbot that he was more comfortable performing nighttime tasks. The abbot and his fellow penitents began to look on him with curiosity and no small measure of wariness as Miguel's strength seemed to come and go. How could he tell them of his night forages into the bowels of the black woods? How could he tell them of his loss of faith?

Over the months of the following winter he secretly read church doctrines, stealing silently into the abbot's private library when the monastery slept. And it was then that he learned of men—creatures—like this Baltazar, who apparently had roamed over the earth for many, many centuries. The secret writings told of these undead beings in vivid, horrifying detail, of their hideous thirst, of their dark deeds. And yet there was little in the manuscripts to tell Miguel where he might seek them out, for apparently they existed in secret, hiding among men and women, seen only at night. And as for any theory as to what might be done to stop them, there were many superstitions, but none seemed truly efficacious.

Spring touched the land once more and Miguel found himself physically and mentally isolated from his surroundings, and he finally realized that he must leave the sanctuary of these high walls that had been his life.

He told no one that he was going. He simply gathered his meager belongings and one night walked toward the woods, never to return.

Ah, yes, on this initial quest to discover what he'd truly become—to perhaps locate and destroy the one who'd done this to him—Miguel had discovered the northern reaches of the known world, the magnificent cities of Europe, and the disease and squalor, too. He saw the good of humankind, and he saw the evil in men's hearts.

He took jobs when forced to for sustenance, always working at night. He despaired often, wondering what the future held, but in Genoa, Italy, in 1553, the Black Death struck. Miguel took a job collecting corpses by night, stacking them on a cart pulled by a spavined horse. He, of course, never caught the dreaded disease, although people died around him. Why? he wondered. Why did he not die, too?

Then one night he found two gold coins in a dead man's pocket just before dawn, a fortune in those days. He knew what he had to do then: carefully and slowly he bought some land, rented it out and reaped the landowner's reward. He was intelligent and educated, and in a time of unparalleled growth wealth was not difficult to come by. His small fortune grew, and the decades went by. His initial investments became very valuable, and one day he realized he was a rich man.

He learned much that first century—the cynicism and bitterness had not yet set in. But always, no matter where he roamed, he was one step behind Baltazar. It was not until the next century that Baltazar allowed him to catch up and initiate their first confrontation. It was only after regaining his strength that Miguel realized Baltazar had been toying with him all along.

"The Louvre," Karen Freed was saying, "it sounds so wonderful. How lucky you are to have lived in Paris."

Miguel forced his mind back to this century, to the female who sat across from him, listening to his tales. It was impossible, but there seemed to be a certain easing of his loneliness in her presence. She had spoken of healing hands—had this woman's power somehow touched a place in his dark soul? The notion was unfathomable.

He looked at her closely, guardedly, the deep blue of his eyes fixed on her cheeks, where there was a blush brought to the surface by wine. A flesh and blood woman. He stared at her for a very long time and put from his musings the notion of her taste against his cold lips. Yes, he was acutely aware of her being, of the fresh scent emanating from her, of the fine structure of her bones and the hint of pink that tinged her skin.

He put those dark thoughts aside and instead dwelled on the absurd fantasy that he was a mere mortal dining with this rare creature. He'd take her home, most likely to her apartment, and there he would make love to her, their naked bodies joined in the age-old rhythm of which he knew absolutely nothing.

That wasn't to say that he'd never been touched by those base, carnal yearnings. Certainly as a youth before joining the priesthood Miguel had known the stirrings of a man's loins. But he'd always been able to put that singular temptation aside, knowing that his calling and destiny were of greater importance. Pleasures of the flesh were never to be his.

What irony! Miguel took in the details of Karen's face and felt bitterness writhe in his soul. He had denied himself so much, so very much, and look at the hand fate had dealt him—*eternal* denial.

God, what he wouldn't give for the courage to one day walk out into the brilliance of the sun and end this agony. Would there be a moment of redemption in those warm, gilded rays that he had not set eyes on in so long? Perhaps, if ever he were to vanquish his old enemy, Baltazar, perhaps then he'd find the courage to face the end.

Miguel paid the bill in cash, as he always did, and they left the secluded little restaurant.

In the limousine Karen said, "I really can't thank you enough, Miguel, for such a super evening."

"The pleasure was all mine," he replied as the sleek black car moved into the traffic.

"You know," she said, "I love the way you put things. It's so...well, old-fashioned. And when you were talking about all your travels I could almost believe..." But then she faltered.

"Believe what?" he prompted.

"Oh, it's silly."

"Nothing you say is silly to me."

"Well, when you were telling me the history of Paris, I could see you there, living it. I could even see you in the dress of the times, you know? I guess it's just the way you speak, it's so...impassioned."

"Impassioned?" He wanted to laugh.

"Yes. You seem to feel things very deeply. I've never known a man who could describe things with so much emotion."

"I see," Miguel said softly, though he did not comprehend in the least.

The traffic was heavy on the avenue as the limo headed back uptown, but neither seemed aware of anything except the atmosphere in the hushed interior. They talked a lot, mostly of the city. Miguel knew New York as a place of fine arts, theater and opera, while Karen saw so much of the ugliness, even though her heart appeared pure and innocent.

"You've never been to the opera?" he asked, aghast.

She shook her head, and in the red glow of taillights he stared at the place where her pulse beat beneath the paleness of her ear. "Never," she said.

"No theater, musicals?"

"Once. I went to *The Sound of Music* when I was little."

"And how did you like it?" He forced his gaze away.

"It was magic."

"Yes, magic indeed." He thought a moment. "Perhaps sometime you would allow me to take you to the theater." But the instant he'd spoken, Miguel regretted his words. Confusion gnawed at him.

"I'd love that," Karen said. "The theater..."

He truly was going mad, Miguel thought. He had no real interest in this woman, in any woman except for the liquid fire that pulsed in her veins!

No, he told himself, he dared not even think those thoughts. He would never allow himself that assuagement, not a woman, not an innocent of either sex. Never. And yet he had just initiated another appointment with her. What else could he be seeking?

Miguel was relieved when the driver pulled up to Karen's building. He stepped out and waited for her, not taking her hand to assist her, fearing the sensation of warmth in her fingers, knowing he would feel the flow of her blood through the fine sheath of flesh over her bones. He would not allow it.

"...a lovely time," she was saying at her door. "Thank you so much, Miguel."

A slight drizzle still wept from the night sky, and he felt the icy drops light on his brow and in his hair, saw the way the mist collected on her cheeks and upper lip as they stood outside her building.

And then she shook his hand. "Well..." she said, smiling tremulously.

"I will telephone," Miguel said, not meaning it, aware only of the sweet warmth of her hand clasped in his.

"My goodness," Karen said, "you're so cold. You'd better get back into the car before you freeze out here."

"Yes," he said, and she removed her hand from his, a severing that shocked him.

They said a trite goodbye, and he watched as she disappeared inside. The rain embraced him as he stood utterly still, and a low fog coiled at his feet. Still, he could not force himself to move. Instead Miguel remained there, feeling the phantom touch of her fingers lingering on his hand. So warm. And abruptly he was speared with an agony for what had never been and could never be.

CHAPTER FOUR

OVER THE NEXT WEEKS, as winter descended upon the city, Karen's life took on a new dimension. Her shift in the emergency room remained the same, but that was all, because the rest of her life had turned into a fairy tale. She lived for the evenings, three or four times a week, when Miguel would take her out, and those nights that they didn't see each other, when they would speak on the phone.

She drifted in a bedazzled state that was utterly unfamiliar: she hardly slept, her appetite was gone, she dreamt and thought of Miguel obsessively. She was blissfully happy. Words of songs went through her head, oddly disconnected phrases of love songs that she'd heard in the past and finally understood.

It was fortunate that Karen worked the night shift and slept during the day, because Miguel was always busy then, and the only time they had together was in the evenings before her shift, or on her nights off, when they would dine late or go to a show or the ballet or the opening of a gallery.

"Please, Miguel," she said one evening as they got their coats at the Savoy, "you don't have to take me out to such expensive places all the time. I could cook something for you, or we could..."

He held her shabby brown coat for her as if it were a full-length ermine. "It is my pleasure, Karen. You work hard enough as it is, and I would not dream of asking you to do a thing for me."

She slipped her arms into her coat and turned to look up at him. "Why are you so good to me?" she asked.

"Because it pleases me," he said gravely. "And because of all the many souls I have known in my life, you alone deserve it."

She couldn't help smiling. He was always saying things like that, things that burst inside her with ineffable sweetness. She accepted all these pleasures because she believed, perhaps naively, that Miguel really did derive happiness from them, and because she wanted to be with him so desperately that she didn't dare analyze this new relationship. She certainly didn't dare ask herself—or him—why this polished, handsome, wealthy man had chosen her.

"Did you want to go to that nightclub in Soho, the one I told you about?" he asked.

"The jazz group?"

"Yes, they are considered fine musicians."

Miguel steered her out of the restaurant and into the cold night, and Karen breathed in the fresh air. "Do you want to very much?" she asked.

"I wish whatever you prefer."

"Would you mind if we just went home? To my place or yours. I'm perfectly happy just talking, Miguel," she said.

They usually ended up at his brownstone on Riverside Drive, which Karen had come to love. It was on a corner lot, three stories high, with granite copings and a fanlight over the shiny black front door. There was a flight of white marble steps ascending to the entranceway, which was also faced in marble. In the middle of the door was a huge brass knocker, and on either side were exceedingly tall windows framed by black shutters, fronted by wrought-iron grilles in a lacy design.

Inside it was old and dusty, but so elegant, so roomy. Miguel had told her he'd purchased it furnished some years before and had not changed a thing; he had selected the neighborhood because it was private and quiet, almost like a small town, removed from the frantic pace of the rest of Manhattan.

Miguel was an enigmatic man; Karen recognized this despite her lack of worldly knowledge. He was kind and gentle, with a dry, sardonic wit. She knew without asking that he'd had some dark episode in his past, perhaps the divorce he'd mentioned. He was absolutely proper, never touching her, never holding her hand, never kissing her good-night. And yet she knew he liked her very much, and she was often puzzled, thankful at times, slightly disappointed at others.

He was so beautiful, so smooth and perfect, his clothes immaculate, always in dark colors, his voice low and hypnotic. He spoke softly in his slightly accented English, and Karen knew he also spoke Italian, Greek, French, even Mandarin Chinese, because he always ordered in those languages at the restaurants they frequented.

They talked about many things, and Miguel knew so much about every subject. Art, music, dance, theater, business, politics. Karen realized how narrow her interests were, and she tried to learn, to absorb all the beauty and culture and knowledge that Miguel had at his fingertips. She told him about her family: mother, father, sister, brother, nephews and nieces. Such an ordinary family. Miguel, on the other hand, spoke little of his relatives, telling her only that his mourning had not abated since the day they'd died. A strange man, touched by tragedy, she thought, but she would never, never pry or press him for more information.

He ate nothing when they dined out, merely toyed with his food, telling her he'd spoiled his appetite at a business lunch or some such excuse.

"Then don't take me out to dinner," she said. "If you're not hungry, we could stay in and order a pizza. There's no sense in wasting all that good food."

"I enjoy taking you out," he told her. "I enjoy your pleasure. Please, Karen, humor me."

A strange man. Mysterious and certainly different. Oh, God, she was so fortunate to have met him!

On the bus going to work one night, Karen idly picked up a newspaper left on the seat. She glanced at the headlines, then read an article about medical research funding that caught her eye. On one of the inside pages she noticed an article because the headline was odd: Man Drained of Blood in Central Park.

She read on. Several weeks ago police had found a man near the reservoir in the early morning hours. He was unconscious. In the hospital he was found to need five units of blood. A small injury was discovered on his neck, but he couldn't remember what had happened to him.

How weird, Karen thought, and something made her shiver inwardly. Was that the night she'd been attacked near the same place? My goodness, she thought, maybe those men who'd attacked her had done this as well. Maybe she should have gone to the police.

Well, it was too late now. That poor man...

Miguel called her at six the next evening, the usual time. He would never phone earlier, he explained, for fear of waking her.

"I wish to take you to the Manhattan Gallery this evening. There is a showing of a very fine new artist I particularly want you to see," he said.

"I'd love to, Miguel. Um, will it be dressy?"

"Not at all. Come as you are, Karen."

She laughed. "I'm in my old bathrobe, Miguel."

"Oh, I see. Yes, something a bit more formal than that," he said, and she wasn't sure whether he was teasing or dead serious.

Miguel came for her at seven that evening, and she was already waiting by the mailboxes, wearing a black skirt and a white blouse with a round collar under her brown coat. Clothes were becoming a problem, because she had no wardrobe for evenings out, and Miguel always dressed impeccably. She knew her own garments were cheap and plain, and she was self-conscious. Miguel, however, never seemed to notice.

"Hi," she said as he came into the building, and she was so glad to see him that her heart leapt with joy.

"Karen, you are already waiting. Am I late?"

"No, no, just on time. I was ready early."

"Shall we go, then?"

The limo sped them silently downtown. "Tell me about this artist," Karen said, sitting next to Miguel in the cavernous back seat. He sat close, but not touching her, and she wondered if, under his sophisticated veneer, Miguel was shy. Or was it something else? She suddenly realized Miguel was speaking.

"His name is Jay Hamish, and his medium of preference is watercolor. Scenery, but impressionistic. He has a fine touch." And Miguel went on to describe the way this newly discovered artist used color and line, the way he had experimented with realism when he was younger.

"You know so much about painting," Karen said. "Have you studied it, I mean in school or something?"

"School? Ah, no, I am merely interested. I attend the gallery exhibits."

As soon as they entered the gallery Karen knew her clothes were all wrong. The women wore black velvet pantsuits or bright flaring long dresses or tights and fringed, beaded or sequined tunics. She set her jaw and stayed close to Miguel, who was to her mind the handsomest, best-dressed man in the elegant throng. Beauty is only skin deep, she reminded herself, and it didn't matter how she was dressed.

They sipped champagne and ate canapés, or rather Karen did. Miguel was not hungry. They strolled among the beautifully lighted canvases, and he pointed out to Karen the way Hamish had executed each piece. She listened, rapt, and studied each painting, learning from Miguel's knowledge.

Still, she was always aware of the female attention Miguel drew. It didn't matter if they were at dinner or a show or strolling through a museum, women noticed him. He had a certain magnetism that radiated from him, although he never, ever seemed the least bit aware of it. When Karen used the rest room, she returned to find a gorgeous black-haired creature trying to latch on to him, and, as always, she felt uncertain. Maybe he'd rather be with that woman. Why wouldn't he?

But Miguel saw her standing there and quickly moved to her side.

"Who was that?" Karen couldn't help asking, and then she hated herself. What a mouse she was!

"No one," he replied. "There is no one here but you, Karen." And he gave her that reassuring smile, a mere tilt of one corner of his mouth.

They left the gallery after an hour, and Miguel asked if she would have time for a late supper.

"After all those little things I ate?" She laughed. "I couldn't manage another bite. But if you're hungry, I'd be glad to go anywhere you like."

"No," he replied, "I am fine." He touched his stomach with those slim white fingers. "A late lunch, a board meeting."

They walked this evening—the gallery was not too far from Miguel's house and he'd sent the limo away. Karen kept expecting him to take her arm as they strolled. It seemed such a natural thing to do. She craved his touch constantly, even found herself tapping his arm or brushing his sleeve, any excuse to be near him, but he didn't respond. Yet she was forced to believe that he found her attractive—Lord knew why—and she fell back on her native patience. He was just too much of a gentleman, she supposed, to press her.

"That was a wonderful show," Karen said as they strolled.

"Yes, it was. I am so glad you enjoyed it."

"I want you to know how much I appreciate all these places you take me. Sometimes I feel, well, that I don't really fit in, you know. These people, the ones at the galleries and all, they're so sophisticated, and I'm..."

"What, Karen?" Miguel stopped short and faced her. "You feel unworthy?"

"Well, uh...I'm not like them. I'm not like you."

He shook his head. "You are a human being, so are they. The differences between you are nothing, a length of cloth, a few words. They mean less than nothing. You are a better person than all of them. They are not worth your little finger."

"Maybe I'm not worth so much as all that, Miguel. How do you know?"

"I know."

"You have a high opinion of your own judgment," she said lightly.

"I have had quite some time to develop it."

"Well," she said simply, "thank you. I think you're very nice, too."

"Nice," he said, and that corner of his mouth lifted in gentle self-mockery.

He began walking again, and Karen felt a chill fall between them, a coolness that hadn't been there before. "Did I say something wrong?" she asked after a minute of strained silence.

"No, not at all. I am, perhaps, unused to compliments."

Relief flooded her. And then she couldn't help saying, "I'm not the only one who thinks you're... attractive, you know. Women seem to..."

But he put up a hand. "I am not interested in that," he said gravely. "I would equally enjoy the opera or an art show if the places were entirely empty of spectators."

Karen gave him a curious sidelong glance. "I guess we're alike in some ways," she said. "Not very social." But, still, his statement made her wonder.

They walked on, along Eighty-fourth Street, the one also called Edgar Allan Poe Street. Karen commented on it. "I wonder why they named it that." She shivered. "His stories are so scary, spooky. What an imagination."

"His stories frighten you?"

"Yes, oh gosh, they're so weird, and everyone always dies in strange ways."

"You do not like eerie stories?"

Karen laughed. "Give me a happy ending, a wonderful love story. That's what I like."

"Happy endings are so rare in real life."

"All the more reason to have them in books and movies, then." She felt Miguel's weighty gaze on her, although he said nothing.

At his house she had a cup of coffee. He'd gotten some things in his kitchen, she noted, so that he could offer her a drink or a snack. He poured himself a cup, also, but when hers was finished, his cup was still full.

"Tell me, Karen," he said as they sat in the library, the room he seemed to use most often. The sheets had been removed from the furniture, and he'd started a fire in the fireplace. Shadows leapt on the dark green walls of the room, on the rows of books, on the heavy leather chairs and sofa, glinted off the glass teardrops of the lamps.

"Anything," she replied.

"Are you free Saturday night? Do you work then?"

"I'm supposed to work, but I could switch with someone."

"Ah, it is too much trouble."

"What? Come on, tell me."

"There is an opera I wish you to see. At Carnegie Hall."

"An opera," she breathed.

"Mozart. *The Magic Flute,* a favorite of mine."

"I'll switch with Alicia."

"This is not a problem for you?"

"No." Karen shook her head. "I've worked for her lots of times, whenever she has a date. She owes me."

"I will acquire tickets then, if you are quite sure you can arrange the night off."

"Oh, yes, Miguel, I'd love it."

Late the next afternoon, when Karen arose, she knew she had an important task to accomplish. She had to go shopping, buy herself some clothes, make herself presentable. The opera. Men wore tuxedos to Carnegie Hall, didn't they? Well, sometimes, anyway. Oh, yes, she could picture Miguel in a tux. He'd be devastating.

She dressed quickly, checked her savings balance and shook her head. Well, she'd just have to spend some of it, and never mind that Mexican trip she'd been saving for. This was far more important.

She took the subway to Brooklyn, where she knew the stores better, all those discount places her mother constantly told her about. She'd have to hurry, too, because they might close before she was through.

The stores intimidated her with their vast arrays of clothing, racks and racks of dresses and skirts, tables of sweaters. It took a long time and four stores, but Karen got back on the subway with several shopping bags. She totaled the items in her mind. She'd spent too much, but it couldn't be helped, and, after all, the coat had been an incredible bargain, only ninety-nine dollars, half price.

She'd bought a midcalf-length black skirt for the opera, and a pink satin blouse to go with it, two dresses, a pair of black heels, a plaid pleated skirt and a white silk blouse. Pearl clip earrings, leather gloves, hose. It had cost a lot, but Miguel was worth it. She wanted so very much to be worthy of him.

On Saturday he picked her up precisely on time, as always. And he did have on a tuxedo, and a black cape lined in scarlet satin. He was as splendid as any king.

"You have purchased a new coat," he said when he saw her.

"Yes," she said, abashed in the face of his magnificence.

"It is most becoming."

"Thank you." Was he just being polite, Karen wondered, when her plain gray coat was so obviously inferior to his cape? Well, she wouldn't let it bother her, because this was a special night—she was going to the opera with Miguel Rivera!

He'd gotten them seats in the orchestra, close to the stage. Wonderful seats. Inside, Karen was quivering with excitement. The beautiful people, the hall itself, the atmosphere of refinement and culture and beauty.

"You are comfortable?" Miguel asked.

"Yes, thank you. These seats are fabulous."

He was the perfect companion, charming, attentive. And here she was, all dressed up in new clothes with the best-looking man in the place, the best seats. Her heart was so full she was close to tears. She couldn't help it; she squeezed Miguel's hand and said, smiling tremulously, "Oh, Miguel, this is so wonderful." And then the house lights dimmed as the orchestra began the overture, and Karen never even noticed that Miguel's eyes were not trained on the stage like everyone else's, but on his hand where she'd just touched him.

It was during the intermission that Karen began to notice the other women's clothes. Long gowns, sweeping skirts with gold lamé jackets, jewel-toned dresses with plunging necklines. She caught a glimpse of herself in a mirror and saw instantly that her outfit was all wrong, tasteless and unbecoming, the pink blouse childish, the skirt dowdy. Her new pearl earrings paled in comparison to the chunky jewelry many of the women wore, and her hair was too plain, hanging straight and all but colorless. Her happiness drained away in some measure, even though she told herself fiercely that it didn't matter.

They were returning to their seats, and Karen knew she'd been too quiet, her mind fighting the small nagging sadness.

"Is something wrong?" Miguel asked as they seated themselves.

"Oh, no, no, really. Everything's wonderful. The music, the seats . . ."

"You are very quiet."

"Sometimes I get that way," she said. "Do you mind?"

"Of course not. As long as nothing is wrong."

Karen straightened her back. "It's the most wonderful night, Miguel," she said, and she meant it.

He leaned his head down close to hers, and he said in his hauntingly modulated voice, "You realize you are very lovely tonight."

Her heart lifted, soaring with the music as the opera began again, and she sat there next to Miguel, a smile on her lips, suffused with joy.

CHAPTER FIVE

KAREN WORKED THE NEXT TWO night shifts. It was odd, but at work, when her hands were busy, she never consciously thought about Miguel and the amazing changes that had come into her life. She concentrated only on the patients, the sick and injured who poured in in a never-ending flow through the emergency room doors.

She had an amazing experience on her second night. A child of eight, a little girl, had been shot by accident; her older brother had been playing with a weapon that should have been locked up. The trouble was that the girl was a bleeder—her blood didn't clot well. She was brought into a trauma room while doctors rushed to attend her in a frantic attempt to stop the bleeding. Karen rushed to supply the team with everything they required. The scene was bedlam to the uninitiated; to Karen and the doctors it was routine.

They must have worked on the pretty little child for a full half hour, but nothing appeared to help. Outside the curtains the parents wept and prayed, and an attendant had to prevent the terrified mother from entering the trauma room. Finally the lead doctor rocked back on his heels and shook his head, and the frenzy above the inert body ground to a halt.

"It's no use," he said, stripping off his gloves and pushing his mask down.

And then something happened to Karen. Later, when she tried to describe it to the team, she could only say it was intuition, but she knew it was more than that. It was the gift that she'd been granted, the gift to heal. It came to her sporadically, and she always felt as if her body was being controlled by some outside force. She never fought it; she was too grateful for the ability to help.

"May I?" she asked as she moved to the child and threw away the gauze packing over the injury.

Blood pumped out, gushing, hopeless, and Karen placed her hands on the wound, pressing gently, something in her brain willing the flow to abate, willing life back into the still body of the little girl.

"What in hell . . ." one of the younger doctors said, but Karen's superior stopped him, while the entire team looked on in wonder.

A minute went by. Two. And then someone whispered, "My God, it's slowing!"

And it was.

The team instantly went to work again and Karen moved aside, coming back into herself, shaken, awed, thankful.

The girl lived. Oh, she needed several units of blood and would be in intensive care for a week, but she was going to pull through.

The next night at Miguel's, Karen told him about the experience. She'd talked him into staying home, and, in blue jeans and an oversize white sweater, she made soup and sandwiches in his kitchen while he looked on quietly.

Karen stirred the pot on the big commercial-sized stove in the cavernous kitchen that Miguel never used. "I know you'll think I'm crazy," she said, averting her gaze, "but it's like it's not me at all when I work that way." And then she colored. "I shouldn't have told you, Miguel. You must think I've flipped."

"Flipped?"

"Gone nuts, insane, you know."

"Because you have a talent, a gift?"

"Well, you've got to admit, it is a little hard to believe."

Miguel looked up at the tall ceiling, and with a twist of his lips, said, "There are more things in heaven and on earth..."

But she only sighed. "Do you really believe that?"

"Oh, absolutely," he said, still smiling sardonically.

They ate at his kitchen table, which Karen had scrubbed clean of the dust and grime that looked as if it had been there for a hundred years. "Do you have a housekeeper?" she asked, ladling the soup into bowls.

"Infrequently."

"Um," Karen said.

She ate her soup and sandwich while, as always, Miguel barely touched his. He was not a small man, and she continually marveled at his pitiful appetite; she'd even wondered if he had some sort of metabolic disorder. She had no right to ask, of course, but she sure was becoming concerned.

After a time she raised her gaze to his, her hands now clasped nervously in her lap. *You're a nurse,* she thought, *it's not prying, so go ahead and ask.* "Miguel," she began, "I know it's none of my business, but I worry about how little you eat. Have you had a checkup recently? I'm sure there's nothing wrong, but it never hurts to look into things."

"A checkup with a doctor, you mean."

"Yes. Your appetite..."

"I have not seen a doctor in ages," he said smoothly. "And though it would be difficult to convince you, I assure you, Karen, my appetite is quite hearty at times."

She accepted his statement, though it left her puzzled. Later, though, when she was doing the dishes, she was even more disconcerted to catch his impenetrable deep blue eyes riveted to the neckline of her sweater. She turned around abruptly, but the image of his eyes, the way the light seemed to kindle in their depths, refused to leave her. And yet he never touched her.

Karen felt uneasy that entire evening. It was as if every event in his huge house was dramatically important. She heard every creak of beam and stair, the rich, haunting chime of the clock in the entryway as it struck eleven times, the crackle of logs and hiss of sap in the fireplace.

Outside it had begun to snow. Karen could even hear the tiny muffled taps as snowflakes dashed against the windows and the hollow scratching of tree branches when the wind bent them toward the house. All sounds were muted as the snow amassed on the trees and bushes outside, and it seemed as if his house with its unkempt back garden was set apart from the throb of the city.

Every moment, every sound, was significant beyond its normal implication. Karen felt oversensitive, her hearing, her sense of smell, her skin, all ready to receive some kind of signal, but what?

It was as if she awaited some word from Miguel, a message, some profound information he was about to impart. Yet he said nothing. He looked, he turned away, he was silent.

Feet tucked beneath her on the Victorian sofa, she looked up from a book she was glancing through and saw him standing by the tall window, gazing out at the snow, apparently lost in contemplation.

Her heart quickened as she watched him, the pitch of his head, the breadth of his shoulders, the curve of his buttocks beneath the fine wool of his trousers. He was the most attractive man she'd ever laid eyes on. His features were flawlessly masculine, generous, imperious. He had beautiful teeth, too, she'd noticed from the very first. White, perfect, revealed when he gave her that thin-lipped, cynical smile.

She wanted to hold him when he allowed her to see that side of his nature. She wanted so very much to hold and comfort him and to feel the pressure of those lips, the tickle of his mustache against her skin, cheek, neck, shoulder, breast—oh, how she longed to feel the touch of his hands on her! They'd been out together almost a dozen times, and not once had he even held her hand.

Oh, but he looked at her, Karen knew. Just as she'd caught that gaze boring into her in the kitchen tonight, she'd often felt the weight of his stare. And she'd swear it was desire she'd seen in his eyes, a yearning, hungry look that scorched her flesh. She knew he'd be a wonderful lover, giving, taking, tender and violent all at once. Yes, she could feel his body clasped to hers, his hips rising above her.

So why hadn't he laid a finger on her!

Okay, so he was the consummate gentleman, old-worldly, sophisticated, in complete control of his urges. But enough was enough.

"Did you say something?"

Karen's eyes flew up. Had she spoken aloud? "I...I didn't say anything," she managed to say, too aware of the throb of her pulse.

He'd turned toward her, the drapery long and heavy behind him, the snow tapping the windowpane relentlessly. And she saw it again, that look in his eyes, a flame that consumed her, craved her. Even the stillness of his body was somehow erotic.

"Miguel," she whispered, caught up in his passion, mesmerized by his eyes.

For a long time they both stayed motionless, gazing at each other, the tension in Karen's body overwhelming. In the end it was Karen who rose, as if driven by an unseen force, and slowly, slowly she went to him. When she reached up boldly and put her hands on his cool cheeks he remained completely still, so still, though the flame danced deep in his eyes.

She turned her face up to his, her neck arching. And then at last he moved, ever so slightly, his head bowing toward her, a groan escaping his lips as they parted, brushing her cheek, lowering—so cool on her flesh—lowering, grazing the skin of her neck, finding the hot, quick pulse there as blood raced through her, heated by his closeness, wanting him, needing him. His arms went around her slenderness, forcing her back to arch against his forearm, his cool hand on her throat, his teeth at her pulse...

And then suddenly she was being pushed away! And he was groaning, turning away from her in a rage, clasping the curtain in his fist as he moaned, "No, no, not like this. No!"

Karen was stunned. Shocked and helpless, so humiliated.

What had she done?

MIGUEL CALLED KAREN at six the following evening. She had barely slept in the past twenty-four hours, and her thoughts were muddled. But even as she answered she knew it was him. It had to be him. And despite the abject misery she had wallowed in all day, she allowed him to talk her into going to the brownstone.

"I can explain," he said. "It was not you last night, Karen, it was me. Please take a taxi over and allow me to explain."

She didn't catch a cab. Miguel would have insisted on paying for it, and, as confused as she was right then, she wouldn't allow it.

She walked. It was a good hour's walk, too, through the streets of New York. But the brittle air felt good in her lungs, and the sting on her cheeks was invigorating. Everywhere she looked, the city was cleaner from the fall of the fresh snow. She began to feel better, somehow.

Miguel had built a fire by the time she arrived, and he stood near the hearth looking solemn and devastatingly handsome. There was that air of world-weariness about him that she'd seen so often before, that tugged at her heartstrings and made her want to hold him to her breast and stroke his hair. She took off her coat and laid it over the arm of a chair and thought: how could she have been so upset with him last night? How could she have faulted this kind and beautiful man for his gentlemanly ways?

He was watching her quietly when she sighed, drew in a deep breath and said, "Miguel, I'm sorry I ran out last night. It was all my fault, and you don't owe me an explanation.''

He said nothing, only kept watching her, his expression unchanged.

''I'm not, well, experienced when it comes to relationships, with men, you know,'' she went on, fumbling. ''I've really only had two since nursing school and both times...''

But he put up a hand. ''You do not have to tell me these things,'' he said. ''To me they are of no account. I am with you, Karen, because your company brings light to my life. It has been a very long time that I have been alone.''

Again her heart swelled with the need to comfort him, to understand him. ''Miguel,'' she said softly, wanting to close the distance between them, yet sensing he'd rebuff her again. ''I wish I understood you better. I feel as if I could help you in some way, but I don't know how.''

''Help?'' he said, and he arched a dark brow above the blue of his eyes.

''I said that badly. I know you don't need help. I meant that sometimes I think you're lonely, and I want to be your friend. We are friends, aren't we?''

''Of course,'' he said.

And then she braved it. ''I'd like someday to be more than your friend, too.''

For a long moment Miguel merely stood there by the hearth, his face an inscrutable mask. Finally he said, ''I, also, would like that, Karen, a great deal.'' But somehow, although his words were sincere, he'd sounded as if their future together was an impossible dream.

Then Miguel opened up a part of himself to Karen that he'd previously kept hidden. As he led her up two long flights of stairs to his attic she wondered about that. It was as if he wanted her to understand him better, and yet he spoke with such uncertainty about the future. What did Miguel Rivera want from her?

At the top of the landing Karen waited while Miguel opened a door for her and then stepped aside so she could enter. Instantly upon entering the attic room, she was assailed by the strong odors of turpentine and linseed oil, and then she saw the canvases, dozens of them, stacked everywhere, leaning against sloped walls, on easels, some finished, some not.

"Wow!" she said softly. "I never knew. You did all of these?"

"It is a hobby," he said from behind her.

"Some hobby. It looks like a warehouse, Miguel. So many paintings." She turned and looked at him. "Can I...?"

"Of course," he said. "Though do not expect too much. My talent is meager."

Slowly, with Miguel negligently leaning one shoulder against the wall, his arms folded, Karen began to browse through his work. It was mind-boggling. So many canvases. He must have been painting every day for his whole life, and the subjects he'd tackled—everything from serene, bucolic scenes of rivers and gently rolling hills to seascapes, violent waves crashing against jutting rocks. There were paintings of bouquets and fruit bowls on tables draped in velvet cloth. There were cityscapes, too, European-looking.

Karen cocked her head at one. "London?" she asked.

"Yes" came his voice from across the room. "My rendition of the previous century."

"Interesting," Karen said, moving on, turning one, then, another canvas toward the overhead light. She was no critic, though he'd certainly been trying to train her eye, but still she had to admit to herself that while some of his painting seemed inspired, other canvases seemed somehow...wrong.

It was the light, Karen decided, the light and shadows in some of his work just seemed off, especially in the pastoral settings.

There were other works, too, that were so far removed from her experience that her breath caught. While most of his paintings tried to capture a serene mood, others were dark and disturbed. Hideous faces peered out at her from infernal settings. One painting was ultramodern, geometrical, colors slashed wildly all over the canvas, while another was pure Renaissance, floating angels and devils and rivers, cathedrals, storm clouds—good and evil in a never-ending struggle.

She shivered. The mind that had created these...

"Reminiscent of Bosch, wouldn't you say?" Miguel said in a sardonic tone.

"I don't know who Bosch is," Karen whispered.

"Hieronymus Bosch, late fifteenth century. Some said he was heavily involved with witchcraft."

"I can see why," she said. "This isn't my favorite."

Karen moved on, only quickly scanning these darker works. She wished she'd never seen them.

She found several portraits, all of which appeared to be renditions of people from a time long gone by. There was a beautiful woman... "Who's this?" Karen asked before thinking. It could well have been a lady from his past, a medieval portrait of her, anyway.

"That was my mother."

"She's... lovely, Miguel, so sweet."

"Yes, she possessed a heart of gold."

Karen moved on, uncomfortable. His paintings were so personal. She felt as if she were invading his privacy. But he'd brought her here. Was this his way of showing her who he really was?

Another portrait. An inordinately handsome man. Blond. Piercing ice blue eyes. Also dressed as if from a past century. Elizabethan, Karen guessed. A white ruff, garnet velvet doublet, puffy, gold-ribbed short pantaloons, embroidered hose, high-heeled shoes. His hair was long and curled at the bottom. He had a mustache and Vandyke beard, and a jeweled scabbard at his side. A court dandy.

There was something about his face, though, something that stirred discomfort in her. The face was so waxen, so arrogant, and danger sparked from the pale eyes despite his finery. "Who is this?" she asked, not getting very near the canvas.

"Ah, that gentleman," Miguel said very smoothly. "Merely someone I have known for a very long time."

"I don't think I'd like to meet him," she said.

Miguel gave a humorless laugh. "I daresay you would not."

She saw it on an easel in a corner then. A half-finished portrait. It was her.

"Well?" came his voice. "What do you think?"

Karen didn't know whether to laugh or be flattered beyond all expectations. The woman, her, was so angelic-looking with a Mona Lisa smile on her lips, blue gray eyes that were too pretty, too pure, and hair that framed the face in soft waves, catching gilded light. Pale rose in the cheeks, on the neck.

Embarrassed, she said, "This is not me. She's too... innocent. Too pretty."

But all he said was "It most definitely is you, Karen Freed."

The experience of seeing this hidden side of Miguel left Karen shaken when she sat in the library again, a cup of coffee clasped in her hands. It was as if he were trying to tell her something, trying to open her eyes to some mystery, and yet the more she knew of him, the less she could understand.

There were so many things about Miguel... For one, he'd claimed not to have a degree in history; nevertheless, his knowledge of the past was uncanny, as if he'd lived it. His eating habits were another enigma, and she couldn't really accept his excuses any longer.

Miguel was a night person. She was, too. But it occurred to Karen as she sipped on the coffee and watched him rebuild the fire that she'd never once seen the man in the light of day.

There was also that self-contemptuous side to Miguel. It was as if he'd seen too much in his life and had been made both harder and more vulnerable by what he'd seen, an exotic combination that fascinated her with a frightening intensity.

He put aside the iron poker and straightened, turning to her, his eyes fixing on her, giving Karen that now-familiar sense that he was probing the depths of her soul. She both suspected it and secretly craved it. She found herself wanting him with shameful desperation.

Stop looking at me that way, she wanted to cry out, but in the same space of time came the quickening in her, the deep, hidden ache. To have him touch her, those long fingers removing her clothes, his eyes drinking her in. His skin would be so soft, velvet over steel. . . . To have his lips on her mouth, neck, breasts.

Karen sucked in a ragged breath and prayed he couldn't read her mind. In time, of course, she'd know Miguel in that way, and it would be all the more beautiful for the agony of the wait. That was his plan. It had to be. She was the luckiest woman alive—Miguel wanted her, but he respected her, too.

The clock chimed in the entryway. Ten times. Karen held his stare and wondered if this would be the night. The torment of the notion was heady, delicious. Tonight. Maybe tonight.

Miguel smiled at her then, that half smile that was somehow sad, a quiet, beautiful curve of his lips. And then he got up, moving toward the fireplace, asking if she would like more coffee.

"Sure," Karen said, watching him, as always fascinated by his supple movements and imposing dignity, and that was when a part of her brain registered something, something that when recalled consciously would rock the foundations of her knowledge of the physical world. "More coffee would be fine," she said as he moved between her and the firelight.

CHAPTER SIX

IT WAS THANKSGIVING DAY, and Karen took the subway to Brooklyn, to the old familiar neighborhood where she'd grown up. The houses were pre-World War II but kept up nicely; on this day there was a watery sun that tried to melt the frost in the shadows.

She always visited her mother's house with a giddy mixture of foreboding and anticipation. Even though she only lived across a narrow strip of water from Brooklyn, it sometimes seemed light-years away, and she never went home except for holidays or special occasions, because the stress of dealing with her meddling family tore away at her hard-won independence.

And yet today was somewhat different. Karen wore her new coat, her new dark green shirtwaist dress, even the new pearl earrings. She felt a certain self-confidence that was new to her, akin to the competence she had when she worked in the ER, and it felt great. She would not let her mother browbeat her, she would not let her sister disparage her, she would give her father a big hug and draw him into the conversation.

Today, at her mother's heavily laden dining room table, she would not think of those tortured paintings, Miguel's strange habits, her own increasing uncertainty about this new relationship. She'd worry about those things later; her misgivings were no business of her family's. But she would tell them about Miguel—she would set the news down in the middle of the dinner conversation as if it were one of her mother's elaborate centerpieces, for everyone to ooh and aah over.

The house smelled of roasting turkey, and the familiarity, as always, shot through Karen with a bittersweet pang. There were the usual cries of greeting, kisses and hugs. Her sister, Lizzie, was there with her husband, Tom, and their two children, Paul and Cheryl. Karen loved the kids unreservedly, the adults more circumspectly.

"Let me see you," Karen's mother said, holding her daughter at arm's length. "A new coat, a new dress. Very nice. I only hope you didn't pay too much."

Lizzie and Karen looked at each other over their mother's head and rolled their eyes.

"I did just fine, Mom," Karen said.

"You should have called me. I would have taken you to that new store...."

Paul and Cheryl were hugging their Aunt Karen's knees, Tom and her father were completely engrossed in a football game on TV.

"Aunt Karen, can we play that game?" Paul cried. "Please, please?"

"Later, kids," Lizzie said.

It was the usual scene, warm and homey, but with certain tensions that never let anyone fully relax.

"So, what's new?" Karen's mother, Dorothy, asked. "Still on that awful night shift?"

"I like the night shift. You know that."

"Mother, leave her alone," Lizzie said. "You say the same thing every time she comes home."

"If Kenny lived here, he could talk some sense into her," Dorothy said. Kenny was the Freed's oldest, who lived in Atlanta with his wife and three kids.

"No, he couldn't, Mom," Karen said.

"He might come up here for Christmas break," Dorothy said. "Did I tell you?"

"That would be great."

"I haven't seen Kenny in at least a year," Lizzie said. "Will Mona and the kids come, too?"

"Naturally," Dorothy said.

Small talk, ordinary things. Dorothy's deft plump hands peeled and washed and cut and mixed. There would be far too much to eat.

"How's that apartment of yours?" Dorothy asked Karen. "Did the super fix that leak?"

"Yes, two months ago, in fact."

"What about that doctor, the one who complimented you? Do you see him still?"

"Mom, that was months ago, too. If you're fishing, I'll tell you, we're just acquaintances. He appreciates my work, that's all."

"A nice doctor like that..." Dorothy said wistfully.

"That's a pretty dress, Karen," Lizzie said to change the subject.

Karen smoothed the skirt with her hand. "I did get a few new things. Lord, I needed them. All that's hanging in my closet are white uniforms."

"Well, you should pay attention to your appearance, you know," her mother said.

"I know, Mom." She was dying to mention Miguel, to tell them all the places he'd taken her, the restaurants, the galleries, Carnegie Hall. But she wanted to drop the news casually when everyone was at the table.

Paul and Cheryl came racing into the kitchen. Cheryl was crying; Paul had punched her on the arm because she took his crayon.

"Okay, kids," Karen said, holding them, one in each arm, one crying, nose dripping, the other taut with indignation. And in a few moments she had them both giggling over one of her stories from her own childhood with Lizzie.

"God, I wish you wouldn't tell them those things," Lizzie said, but Karen only laughed.

When the kids were gone, Dorothy turned around and faced her daughter, hands on her hips.

"You should have some children of your own," she said bluntly.

"Mother," Lizzie said warningly.

"I need a husband first," Karen said lightly.

"Yes, that's right. So go out and get one."

"Mom, for goodness' sake," Karen said. "Lighten up."

"All right, I'll shut up." She shook a finger at Karen. "But I don't understand you, I don't understand you one bit."

Karen and Lizzie set the table. "God, she can drive you crazy, can't she?" Lizzie said, laying out the silver.

"I try to ignore it," Karen said.

"She's a hard one to ignore," Lizzie replied, and they both laughed.

There was turkey and stuffing, yams, mashed potatoes, cranberry sauce, pearl onions and peas, the works. Everyone ate, passed dishes, commented on the food. The kids lost interest quickly and were excused, but the adults sat around the table, gossiping idly.

"I ate too much," Tom said, patting his stomach.

"You always do," Lizzie chided.

Dorothy beamed. "It's good for him. Once in a while it's not such a bad thing."

"So, Karen," her father asked, "are you still on the night shift?"

Karen braced herself, but her mother answered for her. "Yes, she still is, honey. Can you believe it? She says she likes it." Dorothy shook her head, and her tight curls bounced.

"You know, Karen, I worry about you going home so late," her father said. "It's dangerous."

A scene flashed through Karen's mind, emotions shot through her, making her close her eyes for a moment. She forced a smile. "Don't worry, Dad. I'm careful. I stay on the well-lit streets and take the bus."

"Don't go down in the subway," he said.

"I won't, I promise."

"Tell me," Dorothy said, leaning forward, her large breasts perilously near the gravy and mashed potatoes left on her plate. "Tell me, how does a nice girl meet any men when she works all night and sleeps all day? It's unnatural."

Here was the opening, the perfect time. Karen let her mother's words hang in the air for a minute, and then she said casually, "Well, actually I have met someone."

All heads swiveled toward her. From the living room came Cheryl's high-pitched voice, punctuating the expectant pause, "Hey, it's my turn, Pauly!"

"Well, well," Dorothy said. "Thank you so much for letting us know."

"It hasn't been for long," Karen said. "I mean, I only met him a few weeks ago."

"Tell us his name, Karen," her mother said, as if talking to a child.

"Miguel Rivera."

"A Puerto Rican?" her father asked.

"He's from Spain originally."

"So, he has a good job, a nest egg?" Dorothy asked.

That stopped Karen for a moment. A job. Suddenly she didn't know how to explain Miguel; it was as if these people spoke a different language, and she wasn't able to translate. "Well, uh, Miguel has investments. He's retired, you see, and . . ."

"He's old?" Dorothy asked.

"No, he's not old. He's my age."

"Investments? Retired? What, is he in the Mafia or something?"

"Good Lord, no! He's just . . . he's quite wealthy."

"A rich man," her father said.

"How did you meet him?" Lizzie asked.

"Oh, well, in Central Park. I . . . ah, we were both walking, and we, well, we just sort of met."

"How romantic," Dorothy said.

The scene flashed through Karen's mind again and made her swallow. Romantic. "Yes," she replied.

"What's he like? What does he look like?" Dorothy pressed.

"Give her a chance," her father said, patting his wife's arm.

"He's very good-looking," Karen said. "A gentleman. He treats me very well."

"This is serious?" Dorothy asked.

"I don't know, Mom. It's too soon. We like each other a lot, that's all." And she thought of Miguel the night before, the suffering she'd seen, the hunger. *Miguel*, she cried inwardly, and she almost shuddered.

"Where does he live?" Lizzie asked.

"The Upper West Side. On Riverside Drive."

"Oh! One of those old brownstones?"

"Uh-huh."

"That's great, Karen," Lizzie said.

"Is he a nice man?" Dorothy asked.

"Nice. Yes, very nice. Well educated, very... uh...sophisticated."

"You bring him home to meet us, Karen," her father said.

Karen stifled nervous laughter. Miguel here, in this house, at this table? Enduring her father's questions, her mother's prying? *No!* her mind cried, *it's too preposterous.* "Oh, I think it's too soon for that, Dad."

"It's never too soon. We're your family. He takes you, he gets all of us," her father said. "And does he have family? Are they still in Spain?"

"He lost his family quite a while ago," Karen answered.

"That's a shame."

Dorothy looked at her youngest daughter. "He's not married? Karen, tell me..."

"No, Mom. He's divorced."

"Oh, God, he has children, visiting rights? Karen..."

She shook her head.

"Well," Dorothy said, and that was all she could come up with.

"Miguel...ah...took me to the opera the other night. At Carnegie Hall." Karen was embarrassed, but she wanted them all to know. She looked down and flushed a little. "And we saw *The Phantom of the Opera*. He's taken me to lots of places—restaurants, you know, and art galleries."

"Wow," Lizzie said, and her husband gave her a look.

"Well, I'm glad you're happy," Dorothy said. "That's what's important."

"Your mother's right," her father said, nodding.

Happy. Yes, she had been happy. Delirious, in fact, but that had changed somehow. Now she had doubts. Maybe it wouldn't, couldn't, work out. Miguel was so mysterious, so different. Just imagining him meeting her family brought it home. Oil and water, she thought. They can touch but they can never be united.

"Thanks," murmured Karen, and she picked at some crumbs on the tablecloth. She should never have told them about Miguel, never.

When it was time for her to leave, her mother took her arm and led her into the master bedroom.

"I want you to see something," Dorothy said, opening a drawer, carefully unlatching a jewelry box. She dug around in it and pulled a piece out. "Here," she said.

It was a bracelet of heavy gold links. "Mom, that's your bracelet."

"Oh, Karen, I never use it anymore. It should be worn." Her mother patted her arm. "You wear it to all those nice places your new boyfriend takes you."

"But it's yours. You should keep it."

"What, to wear to the supermarket, to your father's office?" She shrugged. "I want you to have it."

Karen took the heavy gold bracelet. It lay in her hand, warm from her mother's grasp. "Mom, you're sure?"

"Take it."

Karen put it on her wrist. It was beautiful. "Thanks, Mom."

Dorothy only smiled. She was a warm, generous woman who loved fiercely and protectively, Karen realized. It was just that she was too domineering for her youngest daughter to handle at times. Right now, though, they were close, and it made Karen feel good to be like this with her mother, to be accepted without criticism.

"I'll wear it all the time," she said.

Dorothy embraced her. "You show that boyfriend of yours that the Freeds are worth something, too. And when you're ready, you bring him home. I'll fix pot roast."

THE NIGHT AFTER Thanksgiving was a horror show at the ER. It was as if every kook in New York City had gone berserk. But then it was a long holiday weekend, and everyone knew the holidays brought out the worst in people.

There were suicide attempts—holiday depression— and knifings and shootings and drunken traffic accidents. Because it was a weekend, more babies than usual got sick. Why did babies always fall ill when the doctor's office was closed? There were cuts and poisonings and drug overdoses; the ER was a madhouse, as everyone employed there knew it would be.

Karen worked tirelessly, mostly assisting the doctor her mother had asked her about, Dick Freeman, who specialized in the treatment of trauma.

She liked Dick. He was cool under fire and yet caring, always aware of the family and friends who were wringing their hands and sobbing just on the other side of the partition from where he worked. Dick was thorough, too. At forty he'd learned to give it his all and not worry about soaring insurance rates from malpractice suits.

They worked side by side for most of that long night and lost only one patient, an old man, a street person, who'd been too frail to hold on after a bad bout with the bottle.

It quieted down after 2:00 a.m. and they were able to get a cup of coffee together in the cafeteria.

"What a night," she said. "I can hardly wait till Christmas."

"Yeah, well," he said, "summer's the worst. Heat spells. Drives 'em nuts on the streets."

"And full moons. Don't forget the full moons," she said, smiling.

They talked companionably for a time, trying to relax, trying to forget for a few minutes the frenzy down the hall. And then, taking Karen totally by surprise, Dick said, "You know, I like your hair. You get one of those hundred-dollar cuts or something?"

Instantly, in embarrassment, Karen reached up and touched her hair. "It's the same as it's always been, Dick. Good Lord."

He rolled his head to the side and studied her. "Well, you look different. Nice."

"Gee, thanks," Karen said lightly. "Guess I looked like hell before."

They both laughed, but in truth Karen knew that she did look different. She'd seen it herself in the mirror, a glow on her face, a happiness that had blossomed from her heart.

That night Dick offered her a ride home. Pulling up to her building, he said, "Hey, you wouldn't be off next Wednesday, would you? Maybe we could take in a movie, dinner. You know."

Karen felt heat crawl up her neck. "Wednesday," she said, opening the passenger door. "I, ah, I'm busy then. But thanks, really."

"A date?" he asked.

She nodded slowly.

"Should have known," he said. "It wasn't the hair at all."

KAREN AWAKENED at one that same afternoon and stretched, still a little sore from the long night. But, as always of late, the first thought that came to her was of Miguel, and she wondered what he was doing—a business meeting with his agent? An important luncheon at the Waldorf or some swank men's club?

Yes, she could see him as clearly as if he stood in her room—his fine clothes, the strong body, the infinitely knowledgeable look in his sapphire eyes. She'd bet he could wheel and deal with the best of them. Sure he'd told her he was retired, but how many times had he said he'd eaten too much at a meeting that day? Well, maybe managing his money was retirement to him.

Karen thought about that as she lay there snuggled under her warm blankets. All those meetings and yet he said he was retired. And when did he sleep? Maybe, like food, he didn't need sleep. No food, no sleep, no company—she'd never, ever seen another soul in that big, echoing house of his. It was as if he existed in a vacuum, a world of his very own, needing no one, and yet lonely. Oh, she knew he was somehow lonely, the ache positively oozed from him.

But he had her now. Not in the ordinary way, that was for sure, but he sought her out at every available opportunity. Last night when she'd gotten home there had been two messages from him on her recorder. Two. He had needs, all right, but in an uncommon way.

She showered and dressed and tried his number, knowing all the while he wouldn't answer. He'd never answered her calls during the day. Another meeting? Another meeting where he'd eat too much?

She left her apartment and went out into the cold to the corner grocery, picking up milk and coffee and fruit. She was on autopilot, though, her mind dwelling on Miguel, on all his "uncommon" habits, his strangeness, his secrets.

That night at work it was difficult for her to concentrate, a rarity for Karen. She kept going over and over in her mind those oddities that were in essence Miguel. She felt chilled all night, too, the hair rising on her arms every time he plunged into her thoughts. On a break she sat alone in the nurses' lounge and felt suddenly miserable—why hadn't she questioned these things about him before? What was she, a lovesick puppy?

On a later break Karen finally telephoned him. She knew he'd be up. Up and prowling that cavernous house or perhaps painting—no sun pouring through skylights for this artist—his brush reflecting the dark images of his mind.

He answered on the fourth ring.

"Look," Karen said, steeling herself, "would you like to go to the zoo tomorrow?"

He couldn't make it.

"How about the next afternoon?" she tried.

Not then, either.

"Wednesday?"

Silence.

"Thursday?"

More silence.

"Okay," Karen said, her heart beating a strong tattoo against her ribs, "when? Tell me when you can meet me during the day, Miguel."

There was a long, tense pause. And then he said, "I rarely venture out during the day, Karen."

"What about all your so-called meetings? When you overeat?"

"That's merely business," he said cautiously.

"But you're retired."

"Yes."

It was impossible. The more she questioned him the more convoluted the riddles became. A terrible, un-defined fear began to rise in her. And then, from out of nowhere, she recalled the newspaper article about the man drained of blood the same night she'd been attacked. Her mind turned away in horror. There couldn't be a connection.

"Karen," he was saying with that deep, hypnotic timbre.

But she couldn't let herself listen. "Miguel," she said, her voice shaking, "Miguel, I...I need some time. Time to think things out."

"No," he said, and she heard the pain in his voice.

But she hung up.

It was ten minutes later that another piece of the hideous puzzle suddenly fell into place, making her knees buckle. The other night, when he'd been going for more coffee, he'd passed in front of the fire-place.... She'd been staring at the Persian carpet on the floor, and when he'd come between her and the light from the flames, he'd cast no shadow. No shadow!

CHAPTER SEVEN

MIGUEL HUNG UP THE PHONE with exaggerated care and stared at it for a long time. The feelings that roiled inside him were so strange, so wildly implausible. He was set apart from those emotions that defined humanity, so how could it be that he was so affected by a few words from a mortal woman? Of course, Karen was right. It had been inevitable that she would recognize his unnatural qualities, and he couldn't imagine why he had thought otherwise.

Yes, Karen was absolutely correct. She needed time to think, and when she did she'd never again speak to him, never go out with him, never sit on that chair or make coffee in his empty kitchen.

Miguel moved away from the telephone and paced back and forth, feeling an urge, an overpoweringly strong desire, to be in motion, to run from something. He tested himself inwardly and realized, with a spurt of near shock, that he felt pain, visceral pain, an ache that was not physical but a part of him, a part of every one of his perverted cells.

Karen. He walked down the front hallway, toward the stairs, hands clasped behind his back, head down. Could he endure this new refinement of torture? After five hundred years he had come to a kind of bitter acceptance of his fate, but this was a new facet to his agony; this was unendurable.

He could pursue her, try to convince her that he wasn't . . . what he was. But if he did, she'd be in danger. Miguel whirled on his heel, a blur of darkness in the big tiled kitchen. He wanted her so badly—the thirst, the craving, it was unutterably powerful. Each time he was with her it gathered strength. He saw in his mind's eye her slimness, the purity of her smile, the long white column of her neck, the fluttering pulse at her throat, the fine blue veins under her fair skin.

Yes, the hunger was growing, but with it there were other, peculiar, feelings, equally strong, bizarre sensations that he could not put a name to, and they built inside him like lava in the seething caldron of a volcano.

The sweet pain of his need for her had been growing for weeks, an obsession he could not control. He was insane, totally possessed by this mortal woman whom he could never have in any way. How could this have happened?

He paced his huge, cold house that night and realized he'd been obsessed with Karen not just at night but during his daytime rest, a torpor that normally disallowed dreams, and yet she was there. When he awakened with the setting sun, he thought of her, feasting on his memories, his foul hunger as unbearable as his ceaseless loneliness.

A hundred times he had started out his door to hunt in the dark street, to use another body to assuage the need that was weakening him more every day, but he knew it would do no good. It was Karen he coveted with a single-minded lust, no one else. If only he could end his terrible existence. If only the threads that held him to his life were not so strong.

Miguel went up the stairs to the attic. Karen stared at him from the canvas. He groaned in anguish at her sweet gaze. What was the hold this one mortal woman had on him?

He lifted the painting from the easel and replaced it with a blank one, then he got out his palette, his tubes of paint, the deepest shades: crimson, purple, pure black. He swiped at the white canvas, a line of jewel-like red, then another, then faster and faster, slashing savagely at the canvas until it was a scene of carnage. He stepped back and cocked his head, examining it. "Yes," he whispered to the empty studio, "that is my soul."

The hours of the night crawled by. Miguel gave up his attempts at painting. He wandered around his house, restless, afraid to stop, the pain eating at him like a cancer.

What was Karen doing now? Holding a wounded person's hand, giving a sick child a drink of water, dispensing pills, drawing blood? Blood. His head jerked in an inadvertent spasm as he pictured the hollow needle, the rich, ruby-colored stuff that she handled so casually. His throat tightened spasmodically.

He prowled the library, the wainscoted parlor, the dining room with its crystal chandelier, long table and garland murals on the walls. Finally he put on some music—he'd almost forgotten about it in his desperation. Gregorian chants, yes, those ancient religious songs that reminded him of the monastery, of the peace that had been his. The men's strong voices, rising and falling, the Latin words that were like a balm, a cool cloth on his fevered brow.

He passed in front of the speakers, listening, mouthing some of the more familiar Latin phrases, and then at last he was able to sit, to remain still, to listen, to feel a small measure of calm.

His mind went back over the centuries, questioning, trying to remember. Had he ever been so agonized before? Had he ever yearned so, been so weak, so reluctant to assuage his needs? Had he ever felt about a mortal the way he did about Karen? No, his mind answered, and no and no again. Not in five hundred years.

Oh, there had been times of desperation, spells of hunger. In Paris during the revolution, a mere two hundred years ago. He'd tried to abstain, but the need had grown too strong, and he'd given in finally, searching the streets for the worst of the debauched murderers who took advantage of the turmoil. In the midst of that death and destruction, his small incursions had gone unnoticed.

Then, again, in Shanghai in 1875, down by the port. His urges had sent him there, into the midst of the lowest form of humanity and he drank, but only from the most derelict of men, the ones ruined by pox, gutted by the flux. He chose carefully.

He always picked his victims with care—when they were alone, in alleys and abandoned buildings, and he told himself that many of them would recover and live, none the worse for their experience. He told himself that, but he loathed himself, anyway, and his hunger for human blood would be suppressed for years at a time after one of those feasts.

Sometimes he thought he had his needs mastered, he almost convinced himself, but he always reverted to type after a time. But not like this, never like this.

He sat while the chanting of the choir swelled around him, and he reflected on his choices. He knew one thing with absolute clarity: he could never give in to his urges with Karen. She was too precious, too trusting. Whatever he felt, he could not touch her.

In any case, she'd all but told him she was done with him, hadn't she? His choice was obvious—give her up.

He put his smooth, pale face in his white hands while his inner voice cried no, never, and he knew he couldn't bear to do it.

His mind cleared with the simplicity of the decision he hadn't even known he'd made. He had to see her once more, just once. He had to tell her the truth.

He knew her schedule well, as she'd told him her hours. If he hurried he would reach the hospital when she was finished with her shift. He had to see her face-to-face—a telephone call would not do.

Miguel shrugged into his black cashmere coat, although he did not feel the cold in any true sense. He did it for the sake of normalcy, so that he might pass among humans and not be noticed. He felt calmer now, the terrible restlessness gone. His decision was made, and he would follow it through to the end, whatever that might be.

He passed among the night shadows swiftly, a dark blur almost undetectable by the human eye. As he went he thought of the remarkable pass he'd come to—telling a mortal not only who he was but what he was, throwing himself on her mercy. He had lost all his defenses, all his acceptance, all his dignity; he was an empty husk and could only race to his fate, knowing but unable to stop.

He passed through Central Park and turned north. A few souls were abroad at this hour, but they did not see Miguel as he dashed by. The hospital was ahead, close now. He knew what door she would emerge from, as he'd picked her up there once, an unobtrusive back door that led into a parking lot. He checked his watch. She would be out soon.

Miguel melted into the shadows and waited with absolute patience, preparing himself for this confrontation. It was cold, he registered, although he did not feel it as discomfort, but there was something else that disturbed his concentration. Ah, yes, he thought, his nostrils flaring, it was the scent of blood. He pulled back farther into the shadows, steeling himself against the coppery tang, and he waited.

She came out of the door with another nurse, talking, smiling, an ordinary human female, one with a job, friends, a family. For one stark second he envied Karen with such sickening intensity that he had to close his eyes. Then he watched her for a moment more from the shadows that embraced him, until she drew abreast of him. When he caught her scent—talc and sweet flesh and antiseptics—he stepped forward.

"Karen," he said.

She saw him instantly, halted and stared. Her body was as taut as stretched wire, her eyes wide.

"Karen," he said again and took a step forward. He saw her move, an involuntary jerk away from him.

"Karen, you coming?" the other nurse called out.

"Uh, go on ahead. Don't wait," Karen said, her eyes still on him, like a doe's in the headlights of an oncoming car.

"Karen, please," he said, and it was then that he saw the naked fear on her face. He recoiled with a pain so intense he nearly cried out, and he knew that this was the worst moment of his long, long life.

KAREN SAW HIM CRINGE as if she'd hit him. She saw as if she were inside him, the devastation, the wasteland of his heart. And she had done this to him without ever speaking a word. Her mind whirled, and she could think of nothing to say, yet as she stood there looking at him, the fear that had nagged her dissipated with the cold white puffs of her breath. They remained that way for an endless, tortured moment, and then Karen knew that whatever Miguel was, she could not leave him to his loneliness. She put out her hand, and he looked at it for a moment, then he reached out and grasped it, his fingers as cold as marble.

"Will you come with me, Karen?" he asked in that smooth low voice with its trace of an accent, and the pain in it scored her like a whip.

All she could do was nod.

His house on Riverside was full of shadows and disembodied voices crying in pain. He poured her a glass of red wine with care and handed it to her. His eyes had a gleam in them she had not seen before, and he regarded her in silence for a while.

"Don't be afraid," he finally said. "You are forever safe with me."

"Miguel. I...I'm sorry if I hurt you. I only meant..."

"I know," he said sadly. "I am not as other men. My ways frightened you."

"Yes," she whispered.

"You are not afraid now?" he asked, his gaze holding hers.

She shook her head.

"Good, good," he said, then a ripple of pain crossed his features.

"Miguel," she said breathlessly.

"Do you trust me?" he asked, standing by his desk, encased in a kind of waiting stillness.

"Yes," she whispered again.

"Karen, I have to tell you a story, and you must believe it. Then everything will be clear."

"Yes, Miguel," she said, but the truth was that she dreaded whatever he was going to tell her, dreaded it with every fiber of her being. She almost cried out, *No, don't tell me!* And she almost put her hands over her ears, but instead she sat there holding the wine-glass, gripping it so hard her knuckles were white.

Oh, God, don't tell me, Miguel!

He turned away from her for a moment, his head bowed, then he swiveled on his heel in a swift, fluid movement and fixed his eyes on her.

No, please . . .

"I am what you mortals call a vampire," he said, and Karen's hand jerked spasmodically. When she looked down all she could see was the wine spilled on her white uniform, a spreading red stain.

CHAPTER EIGHT

SILENCE HUNG IN the dusty room for an eternity, and then it was broken by the hollow sound of bare branches scraping at a window. Karen rose to her feet and shuddered, her heart pumping furiously, the blood rushing to her head, pounding in her ears.

A vampire.

Not possible, just not possible. Things like that—beings like that—did not exist.

No, her mind screamed, but even as she was awash in denial, a part of Karen knew it was true. Everything pointed to it. From the moment she'd opened her eyes in this high-ceilinged mausoleum, everything she'd seen and heard, even touched—his cold, cold hands and lips—told her that Miguel Rivera was a creature not of this space and time.

She stared at him, logic warning her to run, to run as far as she could from this thing that stood before her. Run, hide, don't ever let him find her.

Grotesque.

But still she stared at him, unable to tear her gaze from his eyes.

Grotesque, she thought again, but even as the word pulsed in her mind, she knew in her heart that was not the way she felt about Miguel.

"Oh, God," Karen breathed.

"Sit down," he was saying, his voice smooth, modulated, in complete control, but she shook her head warily. "Please, Karen," he repeated, and it seemed he'd closed the distance between them somehow, but he hadn't moved, surely he hadn't.

Her mind reeled, trying to fit what he'd told her around something familiar. And then, grasping at anything that would put his statement into perspective, she told herself that he was no different than someone—anyone—who'd staggered into the ER, sick, disfigured, and she realized suddenly that her shock was mixed with a strange sort of compassion for him.

She tried to swallow, but her throat was cotton-dry and her tongue felt swollen. And still he watched her, the way a patient watches the nurse coming at him with a sharp needle.

How had she not seen what he was?

It was written all over him. She'd been so blind; it was written all over that artfully carved face—in the flickering flame of his eyes, in the way he moved, in the way his expressions chased themselves across his face, materializing under his supple flesh, and in the flare of his nostrils. And then she remembered his many evasions.

Lust. He lusted so openly. Why hadn't she seen it before?

As they stood there facing each other, motionless, the scent of dust and old wood heavy in the air, Karen could feel it building involuntarily, that same, too-familiar ache deep in her belly. All he'd ever had to do was catch her eyes with his, and the response in her had been automatic. Had he only been biding his time, drawing out the moment until he'd fulfill his...what? His needs?

As if Miguel were reading her thoughts he moved even closer, and he spoke gently, calmly, his soothing voice penetrating her fear, carrying her along a dark, winding river of sound. "My Karen, my sweet, inno-cent Karen, do not shun me. This was destined, as was our first meeting. Don't you see...? There is no pain. Do you think I would hurt you? No pain, my sweet, gifted Karen..."

And then he was only inches from her, his eyes so beautiful, so full of bottomless desire that her belly crawled with the ache, and she knew he was not lying. No pain, no pain—she could submit. It would not be dark and terrifying. The submission, she knew sud-denly, would be unspeakably pleasurable, her life flowing into him, his to her, their senses on fire, their bodies pumping as one as he supported her weight, his lips on her.... She could almost feel it, the erotic sur-render, to be his, wholly his.

His head bowed toward her, so slowly, his eyes ablaze, fixed on the beat, beat of her pulse against the thin sheath of flesh. "I will take you to heights such as you cannot imagine," he whispered. "Karen, my Karen..."

He was so close. Oh, God, she thought, yes. And then something flared within her, an alarm, rocking her as she was closing her eyes. *No!* her mind screamed. *Not like this. No!*

Karen put her hands between them and pushed at his chest. She was aware of the tremor in her limbs, of the blood rushing through her, pounding. "No," she groaned. "No, Miguel, not like this."

She might as well have slapped him. Abruptly the fire died in his eyes and he staggered back, his shoulders hunching as he whirled and grabbed the back of the chair for support.

"My God, I almost..." he cried, and Karen felt tears rush to her eyes while compassion stabbed her heart.

"Leave me!" he said. "That I could have brought harm to you! Leave me!"

But she knew she wouldn't. Never in her life had anything been so clear. To turn her back on him was unthinkable.

"I won't go, Miguel," she whispered. "I won't leave you."

Suddenly he turned toward her and seemed to pull himself up, his body collecting strength from an unseen source. "You risk too much. I tell you, go, Karen Freed, escape while you can."

"You won't hurt me," she breathed. "Just now you could have, but you didn't."

"You are so sure of that," he snarled, and raked a hand through his hair. "Do not be too trusting, Karen. I warn you."

But somehow she knew she was right. Miguel would not have harmed her. If she hadn't stopped him, he would have found the strength to stop himself. She had to believe it. She simply had to. And what he'd said about their meeting having been destined . . . She had no idea how or why or what unearthly force was involved, but his words rang of truth.

"I'm staying," Karen said firmly. "No one's going to hurt anyone, Miguel. There's only going to be honesty between us now."

His eyes bored into hers, searching, probing, and again he warned her, but Karen was committed now, and all the demons of hell were not going to drag her out of there.

"I'm going into the kitchen," she told him, holding her ground. "I'm going to try to get this wine stain out of my uniform and make some coffee. And then I've got questions, Miguel, dozens of them. I'll be back in a few minutes." She left him there, her knees watery and weak as he watched her go, his face a mask of stone.

When she returned ten minutes later he'd built up the fire and was standing near the tall window, gazing out, his posture unyielding.

She sat on the sofa, stiff herself, and took a drink of the strong coffee. "So," she said after a moment, her eyes lifting warily to his back, "why me, Miguel? You could start by telling me that much."

A deep sigh came from him, although his body did not stir. "Why you, indeed," he said, and she could hear the pain and self-loathing in his voice.

"You said something about destiny," she prompted, wanting to hear it all and yet sensing she was treading on very thin ice.

"I have no answer for that," he said after a moment. "I know only that I felt a strong need for you from the first moment you opened your eyes in this very room."

"A need?"

He laughed bitterly. "A need in my soul, Karen, a need I have never known before. Impossibly, it seems I have been lonely for a very long time and have not known it."

She thought about that, his suffering, and then she asked a question that terrified her and yet had to be asked. "How long?"

Slowly, and in a tired voice, he told her.

"My God," she whispered.

"Yes," he said, still refusing to face her, "my birth was before the discovery of the New World."

Karen sat there with her coffee cup clasped in her hands and tried to digest his words. Five hundred years! Unthinkable.

"Have you nothing to say?" he asked, and she could see the curl of his lips.

"It's a little hard to swallow, Miguel. But I believe you," she said. "I think I've always sensed that, in fact. You . . . know too much."

"Quite so," he muttered.

So many questions battled in her head. Five hundred years . . . "How, how did you get like . . . this?"

"How did I first become a revenant?"

"Yes. I mean, who were you? You said you'd been married."

He laughed acidly. "And so I was, my dear—to the church, you see. I was a . . . priest."

Karen sat back as if pushed. A priest. Miguel a priest.

"Rather ironic, wouldn't you agree?" he said.

She swallowed. "It's . . . horrible. But how . . . how could it have happened?"

"The question is not how," he said, "but rather who." And he told her that, too, the whole terrible story—his sister, his mother, Miguel himself, and his return to the monastery, the confusion, pain and thirst. And then the remembering, the dawning of the knowledge in him of this Baltazar.

"I went on my first quest, if you will," he said, "to find the evil one. Of course, I did not find him, but I was on his heels for a very long time. Everywhere I went there had been fear and mayhem. Oh, I knew I was close."

"Baltazar," Karen whispered, trying the word on her tongue. "That painting upstairs, the portrait of the blond man..."

"Yes. It is he."

"And you've never once caught up to him?"

"Oh, we have indeed crossed paths."

"What happened?"

"We struggled. Sometimes we fought physically and sometimes we used politics or finances, trying to ruin each other. But it's very difficult to overcome men such as ourselves, so we have always come to a stalemate." He shrugged eloquently. "But the time will come...."

"Yes?"

He waved her off. "Let us just say the struggle will one day end in the vanquishing of either myself or my old nemesis. Perhaps both of us."

Fingers of ice ran along her spine, and she began to ask him more, but he skirted the subject, saying only, "The less you know of him the better."

He told her a lot that night, at least about the places he'd been and the sights he'd seen. Eventually he turned away from the window and went to stand by the fire, where he gazed into the red-hot embers, and he talked, opening up new vistas for Karen, but always, she realized, avoiding certain questions, questions about his true nature.

So she asked. "Miguel," she said after her third cup of coffee, "do you, I mean, well, how often does this... hunger come on?"

He turned and studied her and said only, "Periodically. I keep it at bay, but it is always there."

"I see," she said, dipping her head, recalling the many times she'd caught his eyes on her, the look in them. And tonight, earlier... But it hadn't happened. She would never let it happen. "The man in the park, the one drained of blood," she ventured. "What's going to become of him now?"

But Miguel shook his head. "He will recover."

"He won't be a...?"

"No, I assure you he will not become as I am."

"Then how did you, how did Baltazar do this to you?"

"I am not a scientist, Karen," he said. "Perhaps it has something to do with the amount one... drinks. The number of times. I only know when I must stop."

"God," she whispered, "it's so... terrible. And what if you never, you know...?"

"Never gave into my hunger?" he said for her, his tone biting. "I would grow weak. I *have* grown weak many a time. Forced abstinence," he said with his usual sardonic tone. "I have gone weeks, months, once I even went six years without... sustenance. It is difficult, but I can control it most of the time, that is, if I do not have to exert myself to any great extent. It is like being an alcoholic, craving, only worse, much worse. And yet, if I do abstain, even though I have grown weak, I do not die. I do not die!"

She took a breath. "Miguel, *can* you die? Are you really... immortal?"

"Ah, immortality," he said. "It sounds quite intoxicating on the surface, but in truth it is a living hell. And as for death, the old tales are accurate. I need only to walk out into the sun to end this cursed eternity."

"Don't," she said. "Don't torment yourself, Miguel. I can't stand to see you suffering, to hear you..."

"And I cannot abide your pity, Karen Freed."

"It's not pity I feel. It's—something else."

He looked at her for a long moment and then gracefully inclined his head. "You are indeed a woman of compassion. I have thought long and hard on this as I have come to know you. A gifted woman. A healer. I know you do not pity me. But as for understanding..."

"Miguel," she said, "are you alive?"

He laughed somberly. "I am flesh, as you can see, my dear Karen, and I am also blood."

"Stop it," she whispered, his bitterness unbearable.

"My apologies, that was crude, and I do not mean to be crude. To answer you," he said evenly, "I do live, yes, but it is not life as you know it. It is, rather, a dimension filled with shadows, a place of emotional detachment."

"But you have emotions," she said, "and don't try to tell me otherwise. I've seen them."

"Emotions. I suppose I do possess feelings of a sort, but they are always intermingled with the accursed need in me, the very hunger that is a lance in my soul.''

Karen stared blindly at the patterns in the rug. Of course what he'd just told her meant that his feelings for her were all a part of that hunger. He wanted her; he needed her, and she knew in exactly what way. Oh, God, she thought.

''You must know why you picked me,'' she whispered, her voice catching. Did he know how much she loved him—had loved him? Or did she still?

''You? It was surely your purity. You were a light in my dark world. You are still a light. I have never told any of these things of which we've spoken tonight to another soul. How could I? Karen,'' he said ardently, ''I was a priest. A man of God. You cannot imagine the guilt I suffered.''

''Suffered,'' she repeated.

''The guilt is always there, but I have come to a kind of acceptance. I try to…atone for what I do. And, you see, mortal man is also cruel. I cannot tell you the atrocities I have seen.''

''Yes,'' she breathed.

''So, I lost my faith, or rather, shall we say, I misplaced it. I know now the priesthood was not my true calling. I can never go back.'' He shrugged.

''Miguel…''

''There are men,'' he said in a low voice, ''far worse than I in this world.''

''Oh, Miguel…''

''We can only play the hand we are dealt,'' he said.

She nodded slowly, her eyes moistening, though she couldn't let him see, he'd take it for something else. She forced a mild smile. "So, are there many others like you, Miguel?"

"Yes," he said.

"And?"

"And what?"

"Well, where are they?"

"All around you. Most are reclusive, as am I. Some live apart from the bustling life in small groups. Their needs are individual, as are mine, I suppose."

"How long have there been . . . people like you?"

"Since the earliest of times. I know of one who saw the pyramids of Egypt being erected."

"Good grief," she said, trying to fit her mind around that—thousands of years. Inconceivable. It was like trying to grasp the concept of the boundaries of the universe.

"Miguel," she said, "do you . . . well, do you sleep in a, you know, a . . ."

He laughed brittlely. And then he shook his head at her. "You have seen too many Hollywood movies, but to answer you, Karen, I sleep in my bed."

Good, she almost started to say, but instead she said, "Oh, I see."

They talked on into the night, Miguel cautious still, as if wary of her, and yet she learned. Oh, did she learn! She discovered that he rarely went after humans, while others of his kind—vampires, she thought with a chill—preyed continuously on the weak and even looked forward to wars, all those battlefields strewn with bodies.

"Ghastly," she said. "Miguel, you never . . . ?"

"No. Never. That is Baltazar's territory. Wherever there is bedlam, hatred or disease, you can be sure he can be found." And then he looked at her strangely. "Does this make me seem better in your eyes, Karen? Does it relieve you to know that I curse my needs and run from them?" Again, the bitterness.

"Yes," she said, meeting his eyes.

"Well, don't elevate me so highly," he said. "How quickly you've forgotten earlier tonight. Did you think I would have stopped had you not stopped me yourself?"

"Yes," she said emphatically.

"Then you are naive."

She let out a breath. "I think it's you, Miguel, who's being naive now. You had all those weeks, all those times we've been alone in this house to . . . do that to me. But you didn't. In fact," she said, suddenly remembering, "it was you, not me, who broke us apart once before. Remember? I ran away. How do you explain that?"

"Perhaps I was prolonging the conquest."

"I don't believe that and neither do you," she said. "You never even touched me, for God's sake! It was driving me crazy. I thought . . ."

"And what did you think?"

"That you didn't want me in, you know, that way."

He shook his head. "You realize, do you not, that thing of which you speak between a man and a woman has never been . . . shall we say, mine to experience?"

It took her a moment, but then she understood. Miguel had been a priest. Of course. And with that realization came a sadness. He'd never been loved physically, never experienced that.

"I can read your thoughts," he said, "and you pity me. But please, do not. I was destined for a life that was rewarding. I was educated. There were compensations."

"Yes," she said quietly, "I can see you that way. I really can. No wonder at all you've chased Baltazar all these years. And your mother, your sister . . ."

"Yes," he said, "there is little wonder that I seek to destroy him."

"Can you?"

He hesitated a moment too long. "There are several ways. I could drag him into the sun, cut off his head, rip him apart . . ."

"Put a stake through his heart?"

"Superstition, mere superstition. It made people feel more secure. Alas, it does not work."

"So, is he stronger than you? I mean, if you haven't been able to destroy him . . ."

"We are very close in strength. Our confrontations require some rest afterward. Were I to succeed in destroying him, most likely I would have to destroy myself, too."

"Oh, God."

"As I told you once before, I am really a coward at heart. I have little now, but should I die, I would have nothing."

"But during the day you could find him...."

"During the day?" Miguel said, an eyebrow quirked.

"Of course..." she breathed. "You can't be outside in sunlight. I forgot. You would have destroyed him if you could. I know you would have."

"I am very glad you think so."

"I wish you wouldn't do that," Karen said, standing, stretching her legs, aware of his eyes following her.

"Do what?"

"Be so sarcastic. So bitter all the time. I liked you better when you were ... you know, taking me to dinner and the theater and art shows. At least then you seemed to be enjoying yourself."

"And now you are seeing my true nature," he said, "and it frightens you. Puts you off."

"No. That's not true."

"Oh? Can you stand there with the firelight catching in your hair, bathing you in red, for God's sake, and honestly tell me there is no fear in you?" He snorted in derision.

Karen turned to face him, ready to deny it all, but the second her eyes met and locked with his her resolve weakened. He was partially right, anyway. She could not lie to herself, or to him. The fear lurked, the tales of childhood, the ancient human fear of something different. But this was Miguel, and she knew him. She knew what he was, but then she'd always suspected, hadn't she?

"I'm not afraid. I'm wary of relationships," she said slowly. "You're the first man..."

"Man!" he said scornfully.

"Yes, you're a man," she said, "the first man I've even had a *real* relationship with, an...understanding. We like each other." She bit her lip. "More than like."

"Karen, do not tempt me. It could happen again," he said.

It was seductive, to be wanted so, to cause that kind of craving, suffering. Karen had never been desired like that before, and she felt the allure of it. And how could she deny that she wanted him in return? There he stood so handsome and wounded and God help her, she did want him; her belly coiled whenever she even thought about Miguel touching her, kissing her, their hands possessing each other. But did she, could she, conceivably want him in this way? The very notion terrified her, but not in the way he was thinking. She was scared to death that if he came close to her again, she'd be too weak to stop him. Maybe she didn't even want to stop him. Yes, she was frightened. Frightened of her own hidden desires.

"Well, Karen?" he was saying. "Tell me that is not fear I see in those eyes."

She took a breath and tried to tear her gaze from his. He was taunting her, trying to make her afraid; in his own misguided way he was showing her his naked lust, how powerless she would be to resist it. "I'm not so fragile, Miguel. Remember, I told you that before. My fears are my own and they have nothing to do with what you are."

He studied her for a very long time and then finally said, "If what I see is true, then so much the worse for us both."

For all Miguel's caution, Karen found out more about his life and his existence, how he managed to go unnoticed in this crowded world where it often seemed as if everyone was constantly, as Karen phrased it, "in one's face."

"In one's face?" Miguel said.

"You know, getting into your business, your private life."

"That is why I pay my agent so handsomely. He keeps my affairs quite private."

She thought a moment. "Does your agent ever notice that you don't grow older? I mean, surely..."

"Now, that is a good question. Were I to remain much longer in this city, he would certainly take notice."

"So you'll be leaving," Karen said, and she realized the idea sat heavily in her heart. And yet what could become of their... friendship? It was so unfair. For the first time in her life she'd met someone who truly meant something to her, with whom she could honestly spend a lifetime, and what was he? A vampire. A man who couldn't feel what she did, who could never share life with her. A priest. He'd been a priest, for goodness' sake!

"So sad," Miguel said. "Never have I seen you so unhappy. Tell me your thoughts, Karen."

She looked up sharply, tears threatening again. "Can you feel love, any love at all? Tell me, Miguel. You said you needed my company, that you'd experienced loneliness. But what about love?" She knew she'd exposed herself completely. She was desperate and didn't even care what he thought anymore. He'd done this to her, opened up his elegant world to her, wooed her relentlessly. What had he expected?

"Love," he said under his breath. "I do not know. As I told you, I have great needs, but they are one with my hunger." He was sitting in a tall wing chair now, his knees splayed, his hands clasped between them. He looked long and hard at her. "I can say truthfully that when I leave here I will miss you, Karen. I will forever miss the light you shed on the world of shadows that is my domain. It seems as if I have glimpsed the sun after a long abstinence. Yes, I will miss you greatly."

And then she did cry. She didn't care that he was a grotesque creature, that he'd hunted the night streets and alleys and forests for all those years. None of that mattered. The only thing she saw was goodness and pain, so much suffering. She'd been given a gift of healing, and still she couldn't do a damn thing to help him. It was so unfair. *Why?* she wanted to cry out.

"Do not waste your tears on me," Miguel said, and he rose and began to pace the echoing room. "All I can do now is apologize to you. Apologize for seeking out your company. It was wrong. I knew all along that it was wrong. I was just..."

"Just what?" Karen sniffled into a handkerchief. Tears were certainly not helping.

"Just that my sense of emptiness became mixed up with the pleasure of your company, and then, of course, there was the...need in me. I do not deny it. And that is why you should leave this house at dawn and never return. There is great danger for you here, Karen. The very notion that I could lose control and... But you understand that now. To think that I could rob you of your life, deny so many others the miracle of your gifted touch. This sickens me. And yet I know the time would come that my accursed need would overshadow all else. Do you see? The danger is too great."

But she really couldn't see. She didn't want to. How could he ask her to walk away and never look back? There had to be another way. What about the destiny he'd spoken of? This couldn't be all there was.

"Miguel," she said pensively, "there has to be another way. An answer. I mean, if only there were some sort of cure for you, a way you could reverse what was done to you."

He waved aside her words with a gruff gesture. "A cure, you say."

"Why not? In all the years your kind have been on earth, maybe there was one of you who somehow reversed his destiny. It's possible, isn't it, Miguel?"

He laughed, scoffing at her words, and yet when he stopped she saw something else in his expression, a hesitation, as if he were recalling something.

"What?" she pressed.

"It is nothing," he said, shaking himself free of the memory.

"There was something just now, Miguel, I saw it on your face. You just remembered something. Tell me."

He made an annoyed gesture. "Rumors, myths, that is all."

Karen shook her head. "What rumors? About a cure, a way to reverse..."

"I said they are nothing but fairy tales. Myths."

"You must tell me," she urged, her pulse beating a little more rapidly.

"Whisperings, Karen, that is all. Whisperings among us that there exists a cure."

"Where there's smoke," she said, "there's fire."

"I did once know of a being who... Ah, it is merely fantasy."

"So is your very existence," she retorted. "Tell me about this 'being', Miguel. What harm can it do just to tell me?"

He raised a dark brow at her. "Karen, Karen," he said. "You truly are an innocent."

"Humor me, then."

"If you must, then I will tell you. But I have never believed in these fairy tales, you need to understand that."

"Fine. Go on."

"His name was Yuri Karlov. I first met him in Russia two centuries ago. He was, perhaps, the only one of my kind that I ever had true communication with. Like myself, Yuri lived a wealthy and miserable existence. We met and we spoke of it and found that we both abhorred what we were, the deeds we had done. We talked till dawn each night for the better part of a year about these things and were able to keep our hunger at bay. I again met Yuri briefly in Madrid, and we renewed our relationship. This was, I believe, in the year 1849. I recall this because he spoke of traveling to the great American West, to see for himself this rush for gold in the hills of California. As well, he told me of Baltazar, who had apparently been in California at the time of the Donner Party disaster, that terrible winter of '46 when the immigrants had been stranded atop a mountain pass and resorted to cannibalism."

"You mean this Baltazar was there?"

"But of course, my dear. He is often at the very root of evil."

"But he couldn't cause all those snowstorms that trapped those poor souls."

"No. His powers are not that great. Yet. But he is perfectly capable of breaking an axle on a wagon or destroying food stores. And I believed it when Yuri said Baltazar had traveled along with the emigrating party and caused the many delays in their journey that ultimately brought them to the depth of human despair." A frown contorted Miguel's features, but he quickly masked it.

"At any rate," he said, "Yuri Karlov was off to the West. The next time we crossed paths was some fifty years ago in Finland. It was during the Winter War of 1939 to 1940, the one fought against Russia. I had heard that Baltazar had gone to . . . to take advantage of the carnage, and I went to find him. He was gone, but again I met Yuri. And of all things, he had met a woman."

Karen cocked her head.

"Oh," Miguel said, "do not ask me of their relationship, because I never asked myself. Suffice to say that Yuri was of the opinion that he could find this mythical cure and live out his life—his mortal life— with this woman, Hilkka."

"And?"

"And I have no idea as to the results of Yuri's dream. So you see, Karen, it is all still whisperings. I was not surprised that Yuri would seek a cure, because the man had been—or has been—roaming the earth since the days of Nebuchadrezzar. He was most weary."

"But what if he found a cure!"

"Karen, I knew I should not tell you of this."

"But what if he did?"

"If he did, Karen, that was fifty years ago. More. To think that, first, he found this mystic cure, and that, secondly, he would still be alive to tell of it . . . It is really quite out of the realm of possibility."

"Well," she said, "so are you."

"Come now, be realistic."

"Why? Why wouldn't you at least try to find out? What can it hurt?"

"Karen . . ."

"No," she said, getting to her feet, refusing to be cowed by his pessimism. "You said you're miserable. You told me you'd end your existence if you were not such a coward. Well, maybe you are at that."

"Karen," he said again.

But she was holding her ground. "It's worth a try," she said. "You talked about destiny. Maybe this is why we met."

He looked at her long and hard and then sighed deeply, suddenly tired. "You ask a lot, Karen Freed," he said finally. "And it is perhaps more than I am capable of."

CHAPTER NINE

BALTAZAR LIFTED HIS HEAD, and a few drops of garnet liquid flashed in the dim light and fell onto his clean white shirt. The heat penetrated him, relaxing him, and he felt the warm girl in his arms, her heaviness, her juiciness. Sweet was the smell of her blood, the succulence and thickness of it. He lowered his head again to the paleness of her throat and slowly drank, feeling the last quiver of consciousness pulse out of her and into him. The phosphorescent cat glow in his eyes faded to a mere ember, a pinpoint of light in each pupil, and he sat back on his haunches, satisfied.

He looked down at his victim, a plump, dark-haired girl, very young. He'd picked her up in Greenwich Village a few hours ago, weaving a seductive web of charm, using his magic, his physical beauty, to lure her up to the place he called home in New York, the wrecked apartment in an empty tenement. He liked the location of the Lower East Side, because few people dared to enter the condemned building, and those who did he'd frightened away with swift brutality. Word had spread to the homeless, the addicts, the dealers, and now no one came near the abandoned tenement.

He could easily have afforded a suite at the Ritz, an elegant brownstone like his old friend Miguel's, a penthouse apartment on Fifth Avenue, but he preferred this derelict place; it suited his sense of irony.

The girl was still alive, though barely. She'd be sufficient for perhaps one more feeding. He put out a finger of polished ivory and touched her cheek. It was so pale now, when only minutes ago it had been pink with the rich blood of her life. She was cooling as he watched her, poor thing. Baltazar chided himself for being such a glutton.

After a time he stood and looked down at her, then pulled a blanket over her to preserve what little life essence still whispered through her. How unfortunate, and she'd been so delectable.

Well, there were hours left in the night, and things to be done. He glided down the filthy stairs to the ground floor. He could still lure another young thing to his place tonight after the first one was used up. He could kill in a dark alley, he could exact whatever he wanted from whomever he wanted. The city was his at night. No one was his equal, not after the millennium he'd had to nurture his powers.

He didn't always kill; when he did, it was usually on a whim. But sometimes, when he appreciated the physical aspect of particular humans, he wished to preserve them for eternity. At other times he transformed them into creatures of the night for no other reason than a perversity of spirit. He always chose his victims deliberately for their virtue.

All those fledglings, those offspring of his, spread around the world. Most worshipped his memory, some he saw from time to time, and they respected him as they would their father. All except Miguel, the innocent, the naive, the good.

Baltazar sped through the streets, grinning, watching for a drama that might attract him. There—his eyes lit on a prostitute picking up a man, and there— a scrawny kid shooting up. There—lovers quarreling—that could be interesting.

He moved through Washington Square Park and saw a group of students, unkempt, stinking of marijuana—what a rush, man!—and he stopped, drawing back, a shadow converging into itself, to watch them. A drug dealer peddled his wares right under the arch of Washington Square Park, and over there were three women, students, too, probably, walking together, giggling, yattering. Luscious-looking. Perhaps he should dispose of the half-dead one in his room and take a fresh young thing to replace her.

He reveled in his own power. He could do absolutely anything he wanted. But he did practice a kind of discretion; not too many dead in one area on the same night.

It was really so easy.

Baltazar had nothing but scorn for those of his calling who did not exercise their powers to the fullest. He himself honed his like a swordsman did his blade, like an athlete his muscles and skill. For most of Baltazar's existence, mankind had been involved in survival, and it was only recently that humans had the leisure to perfect their bodies, their talents, their aesthetic senses. Of course, Baltazar had been doing it for centuries. His strength, his mental powers, his eyesight and hearing and sense of smell, all were brought to an exquisite height of power, tuned like fine instruments.

His eyes were fixed on a whore standing near the archway. She was young, with café-au-lait skin, very lovely. Ripe. Despite the cold she wore a short skirt that showed dimpled brown knees and high black boots. Truly an exciting woman. He watched her for a time and weighed his choices. But, really, he was so full, every vein running hot, engorged. He'd wait.

In any case there was something he'd been going to do. He'd been in New York for some time now. It was such an easy place to kill without raising suspicions. People died of so many things every day that it never occurred to the authorities to investigate. He'd been enjoying himself here, doing outrageous things, leaving signs of his work all over, blatantly, yet no one noticed. *New York, New York, it's a hell of a town,* he sang inside his head.

Ah, yes, he did have an errand this night. How remiss of him to have remained in this city for so long without calling on his dear old friend.

He knew where Miguel had his lair; he'd scented him from miles away. An ostentatious old hulk of a house in an upper-class neighborhood. Typical of

Miguel, who craved the semblance of humanity. Yes, time to pay a visit.

Baltazar passed through the night like a particularly sleek, graceful feline, his presence unnoticed save for a few who felt only a disquieting sense of something evil in their midst. No one ever really saw Baltazar, unless he wanted them to.

He crept around the side of the brownstone that belonged to Miguel and into the overgrown garden at the back. It was a thick tangle of bushes and trees, their branches bare and black. A little snow remained at the base of some and also along the brick wall that enclosed the backyard. Baltazar smiled to himself: apparently Miguel the meek had not taken up gardening. Perhaps he'd had his fill of tilling the soil as a priest.

Oh, yes, he could feel Miguel now. He could feel the anguish that always surrounded the man. He was just inside that tall, heavily draped window from which light leaked around the edges. And—the devil!—there were the shadows of flames leaping behind the drapes. A fire. Was that damn fool Miguel trying to be human again? How revolting.

Baltazar stood motionless, waiting. Another scent tickled his nostrils, a hot, heady scent—a human female. In there with Miguel. Well, perhaps he wasn't such a weakling, after all. He had his prey this night.

Baltazar decided to linger in the garden for a time. After all, dawn was still an hour or so away. Of course he could enter Miguel's lair, but that would mean one of those ugly, draining confrontations the priest always insisted upon. They were so dull. Such a waste of energy that was best spent elsewhere, namely on the hunt. And, oh, it was so much more enjoyable to merely leave his scent—perhaps near the front entrance to this stately house—it did so torment Miguel.

He stared at the light visible in the crack in the drapery. And he drew in the two aromas, male and female. What a pleasant night, he thought, he should have visited sooner, really. But in truth time had no meaning for him; only the inevitable rising and setting of the sun had significance, and there was always and forever a tomorrow.

So he lingered, hunkering in the shadows, his mind rolling idly like a reel of film as he entertained himself. Finally, there was movement, a sound. The door. Swiftly Baltazar glided to the side of the front steps, his form a mere shimmer in the night. Yes, someone was coming out. Miguel? Ah, no, the woman, the one he'd scented. There was a taxi waiting at the curb. For her, no doubt, as Miguel certainly didn't need one.

He heard Miguel's voice. "I will phone you before you go to work. Sleep well, Karen."

Then the woman replied, "Will you think about it, Miguel? Please, at least consider it."

"For your sake, my dear?"

"No, Miguel, for yours. Please."

"Good night, Karen."

"Please, Miguel . . ."

And then the female was walking down the steps, along the dark path toward the taxi, and Baltazar could see her. A skinny wench, hugging herself, turning back one last time, giving Miguel an anguished look, waving to him.

Baltazar took in every detail of this female. She was sweet, yes, and innocent. He drew in a quick, rasping breath, and his eyes glowed like coals. Was it possible Miguel had made her one of them? Miguel? But no, Baltazar would have sensed it instantly. This one was very much mortal, still pulsing with lifeblood.

Then why, why, was Miguel letting her go? And that ridiculous, sentimental claptrap he'd spoken to her. What kind of a fool had Miguel become? Talking like a mortal to this woman!

Who was she to him? Who was she? He would certainly find out. Perhaps a new game was at hand.

A growl, a low rumble, escaped Baltazar's throat and a terrible, beautiful hunger filled him as he watched the female, Miguel's female, step into the bright yellow taxi and disappear.

KAREN WAS STILL NUMB the next night when she went to work. She had not heard from Miguel, nor had she tried to call him. She'd barely slept, only dozing a little, her mind so caught up in what had happened that she felt feverish. She'd thought of calling in sick to the hospital, but then she knew she couldn't bear to stay home alone, thinking and thinking and thinking, until she really might go mad.

Miguel, her kind, witty, urbane friend, the first man she'd ever really had a relationship with, the man she'd bragged about to her family—a vampire.

It couldn't be, and yet it was. Somehow Karen's mind accepted it, doing a delicate, internal balancing act, her mental wheels spinning in neutral, unattached to the demands of reality. She put aside the impossibility of Miguel's existence and tried to concentrate only on the practical matter at hand: how could she and Miguel have a relationship now? A real relationship.

She pondered the question on the bus, in the nurse's lounge, in the ER. She thought back on what Miguel had said, examining every word, his tone of voice, his expression. Her hands did their work, soothing, holding, sterilizing, giving injections, taking temperatures, inserting IV needles. Once, around two in the morning, a critical case was brought in, a car accident victim, trauma to the head and neck, and she snapped out of her reverie. But when the patient was stabilized, she went right back on to autopilot, speculating, considering every angle of Miguel's story.

How could she love him if he was a vampire? She did, though. She loved him, and that was the bottom line. She couldn't, she wouldn't, give him up. There had to be a way out.

"Karen, could you get that patient some pain pills," one of the doctors said to her in passing, "the Percodan. I'll sign the order later. And then get a history from the lady in that cubicle. Asthma attack."

"Yes, doctor," she said, but after her tasks were completed, her mind immediately turned back to her problem.

In life there were always choices. She could live with him the way he was. There was a fatal downside to that, though, because she'd grow old and ugly and sick and Miguel would stay as he was now, as he'd been for five hundred years. Eventually she'd die, and he'd be alone again. She shuddered. Awful, awful.

She could...join him in his unnatural life. She frowned. No, he wouldn't do it, he'd refuse. He hated himself too much already, and he'd suffered so because of what had been done to him. She knew, without further reflection, that Miguel would consider that choice abhorrent. It was not an option.

Her mind came around full circle, back to the possibility of the rumors, the whispers. This Yuri, the one who'd met a woman in Finland. Maybe he'd found a way to reverse his condition, to alleviate it somewhat. Maybe he was very old now, living with his wife, Hilkka, and maybe...

Romantic ravings, Miguel would say.

"Karen, please, could you go talk to that Mr. Wexler? His wife's the woman who had a mild infarction, and he's very upset," one of the other nurses said. "I can't do it because I'm helping Dr. Freeman with a broken leg."

"Sure," Karen said, and she saw the elderly man, sitting on a chair in the waiting room, wringing his hands. She went to him, cool and professional. She took his hand, felt his desperate fear, and let her calmness engulf him. "Your wife had a slight heart attack, but she's comfortable now, and you can see her in a few minutes. She'll be fine, Mr. Wexler."

The couple must have been married fifty years, Karen thought as she went about her duties. Her heart was full, noting how much Mr. Wexler had worried, as if his wife were part of him, and knowing that if something, God forbid, happened to Mrs. Wexler, then Mr. Wexler would not be far behind.

Like Yuri Karlov and his Hilkka?

Finland, that was the last place Miguel had seen Yuri. Fifty years ago. If there had been—if there was—a Yuri Karlov in Finland, there would be records of his existence somewhere. It was a chance, worth a try.

Karen looked up from holding a pan for a very sick young boy suffering from alcohol poisoning, and smiled to herself. Yes, it was worth a try.

Convincing Miguel would be hard, though. She would have to be firm, strong, patient, compassionate, all those things that she was trained to be as a nurse. And she would convince him.

A certainty came over Karen then, a knowledge of what she had to do. She was filled with sudden strength and an enormous relief that she could at last do something. Her tiredness, the burden of dread, the numbing doubts, all lifted from her shoulders. And when Karen's shift was over she went directly into the office of the doctor who headed the ER team.

"Dr. Conti, I'd like some time off," she said.

"Sure, Karen, but can it wait till after New Year's? You know how..."

"I'm afraid not. I have to take it now."

He cocked his head. "A few days? I guess we can cover you."

"No, Dr. Conti, I need a month, maybe more. It's...it's important."

"A month? That's asking a lot, Karen."

"I know, but it's a matter of life and death, it really is. You know I wouldn't ask otherwise."

"This is awfully sudden. You in trouble, Karen?"

"No, of course not, Dr. Conti."

"You angling for a raise? You know we always review salaries in January."

"I'll take it off without pay if I have to," she said firmly, "but I'm due a lot of vacation time."

He sighed tiredly, and leaned back in his chair. "Hell of a time, Karen."

"I know. I'm sorry."

"Okay, I'll take it up with Personnel."

"Thank you very much, Doctor."

Karen went home that cold November morning and slept for a few hours. She rose in the afternoon and ate, watching the news on television, reexamining her decision. Yes, it was the only way. She took a shower and washed her hair, drying it, curling it with hot rollers.

She dressed carefully in her new plaid skirt and a brown sweater, and put mascara on her pale lashes.

She wanted the added security of looking as attractive as possible when she confronted Miguel. An irrational idea, perhaps, but it wouldn't hurt.

She waited until twilight was falling over the city, until the weak beams of sunlight that reached into her kitchen window from her building's central square had faded, and then she went out.

It took her an hour to walk to Miguel's house, but she needed the time to prepare herself. Her cheeks stung with cold, and her hair had blown straight by the time she got there. It was full dark, close to the shortest day of the year, and she saw the light spilling from behind the heavy drapes in the study windows.

Miguel was home.

When he opened the shiny black front door and saw her, his shoulders straightened, but his expression stayed somber and, uncharacteristically, a bit uncertain. "Karen," he said softly. "Please come in."

He took her coat in his formal, courteous manner, and Karen knew better than to rush things. She followed him wordlessly into the library, where there was dark, swelling organ music playing on the tape deck. He switched it off, and turned to her amid the sudden, crashing silence.

"Miguel," she said, and then could not quite frame the right words. Tongue-tied, just as she'd been that first night.

"My dear Karen, I did not expect you would come..."

"I've been thinking," she blurted out, cutting him off.

"Yes," he said, his body very still.

"Miguel, you have to listen to me." She met his gaze, and it was not so much tortured now as resigned. Oh, God.

"I've taken a leave from my job," she said, "and we're going, we're both going together, to search for Yuri Karlov."

Suddenly it seemed as if there was no air in the room. Karen's throat constricted, and her tongue was dry.

"My poor Karen," Miguel said gently. "You would give so much up for me?"

"Yes," she said firmly, "and you can't change my mind."

He shook his head sadly. "You would chase a fantasy? It is no use, do you not see? You have only latched on to this idea out of hope. False hope."

"It's worth a try."

"It is simply a waste of your time, and your life is very precious."

"Miguel, my life is worth nothing without you."

He put a hand on his forehead and bent his head. Without looking up, he said, "You cause me pain, Karen. I beg you..."

"What? You beg me to leave you, just go away?" She hugged her elbows and walked to the tall window, then pivoted to face him. "No, I won't. Do you hear me, Miguel?"

"Te escucho," he breathed.

"What?"

"I hear. Excuse me, at times I lapse into my native tongue, those times I am...distracted."

"Listen to me. Go to Finland. I'll help you. What have you got to lose, Miguel?"

"Coward that I am I could lose my paltry existence, such as it is. It is still all I have. No," he groaned, "I could lose *you.*"

"Miguel, try, please. For my sake, try!" she cried.

He moved toward her, put a hand out to touch her hair. "You are so good, so pure. This is not your problem, not your burden."

"Yes, it is," she whispered.

He stood there facing her, and she finally recognized with a jolt the stillness in Miguel—his chest did not rise and fall with breathing. His fingers slid down to her cheek, so smooth and cool. She inclined her head, leaning into his hand, and she saw the light kindle in his eyes, saw him swell with a kind of potency that sent a fierce heat rocketing through her veins.

"Karen," he murmured, and she knew somewhere in her mind that she should be afraid. She wasn't afraid, though; she was weak with wanting what he could give her. She could let him, she could expose her throat to his lips, her body to his needs. A small voice deep inside her head whispered that it would be unending pleasure, a special pleasure reserved only for the select. Yes...

She was hypnotized by his eyes, by the keen blue flame in them as his head bent toward her, as his hand moved, snaking around to the back of her neck. They could possess each other, they could. And then adrenaline shot through her in an icy-hot flame.

"No," she whispered brokenly, and the spell was shattered, the light dying in his eyes, his expression turning into one of horror.

Karen's pulse was galloping, her head faint. A fine perspiration dotted her upper lip. She drew in a deep breath, her body still shuddering. "Miguel," she said quietly, "I'm going to leave you now. Not because I'm afraid. I'm leaving because you won't even try... you won't even make an attempt to find a solution for us." She put her face in her shaking hands. "I've done everything I could, and now it's up to you, Miguel. I can't see you again unless you try to find that cure and give us both a chance, yes, only a chance, at happiness."

"Go, Karen," he said in a thin voice. "Please, *por favor, mi alma, mi corazón.* Go."

She went. She gathered her coat and left his house, left him standing in the library, his face blank, his body rigid with torment. She rushed away from his wide black door, down the marble steps, along the walk to the street. Her mind was a broken record, going around and around with the same hopeless line: Miguel, please, try. Her heart was hollow, yet brimming with pain.

The night sky was black, but with the glare of the city lights, she could see quite well. Something shadowy moved in her peripheral vision, and she turned around quickly—Miguel had changed his mind, he was coming. But no, he wasn't there. Nothing was there but the deep shadows of his garden beyond the wrought-iron fence.

She tried to put aside fanciful thoughts, but still she stood and stared, filled with a terrible, cold feeling that something was in that tangled black mass of trees and overgrown bushes.

For a very long time she searched the shadows, and then finally she shrugged, chiding herself for her foolishness. Then slowly, tiredly, she walked on down the street, leaving Miguel and his big empty house behind.

CHAPTER TEN

OUTSIDE THE BROWNSTONE a watery sun bathed the city in a hazy white light as it made its slow arc across the sky. But behind Miguel's heavy draperies it was very dark, cool and damp.

To an onlooker it might have appeared that he was dead, laid out in his elegant master bedroom as if prepared by skillful hands, waiting to be placed in his coffin. In the dimness his face was waxen, polished, devoid of life. Even his hands, clasped over his black sweater, looked unreal, too white, too smooth. And if his chest actually moved as he breathed it was not visible to the human eye. A sense of unnatural stillness pervaded the room.

Of course Miguel was not dead, not in the ordinary sense of the word. Rather, he lay in a trance, a coma peculiar to this shadow-world in which he dwelled. He was neither conscious nor wholly unconscious. It would have been nearly impossible for him to rouse himself, however. Certainly not before the setting of the sun.

Miguel did not dream, but his mind filtered the impressions of his surroundings, and something close to thought was possible.

It was the fourth day since Karen had left him. Four sunlit days and four endless black nights. Usually his rest was unbroken by these thoughtlike processes, but for the past few days he'd been tormented in his trance, with ghostly images of Karen pressing at the edges of his consciousness. Karen and her soft innocence. Karen on fire with her hopeless quest. Karen. Karen. Her slim white neck bathed in red after he... He could almost taste the sweetness of her, and there was no rest.

On the fourth evening, Miguel left his trance and rose, his brain assailed with memories of this mortal female who now seemed so beautiful to him. Oh, how vividly he could conjure up her image, at the theater, across a table, the candlelight dancing in those blue gray eyes, leaping on her pale skin. In his own home, curled up on the Victorian sofa, firelight playing on her silken hair, her cheeks brushed by pink from the warmth of the hearth. He paced his empty house that evening in an agony of remembrances, and his craving grew stronger, unbearable, the urge to catch a mere glimpse of her overwhelming. There were the darker images, too. To feel her life force flowing into him, to taste at last the sweetness of her would be pure ecstasy. Surely no mortal man would extract such pleasure from this woman!

He attempted to paint. Usually the act of creating the images that swam in his head diverted his attention from the thirst in his body. Perhaps if he worked on Karen's portrait, concentrated on the feel of it, his need would abate. But that didn't help at all. Quite the contrary. And he found himself throwing the palette across the room, an animal groan welling up from his chest as he stalked out of the attic.

After a time Miguel put on his heavy black overcoat and went out into the city. His torment was such that he passed straight through his yard and never picked up the scent that Baltazar had left there. For Miguel there was only that strange ache inside him, human yet so inhuman. All the urges in him seemed more powerful than usual, controlling him, the fire in his eyes visible were anyone to look. He roamed the nearby streets and alleys, the night bitter cold, a light, dry snow drifting out of the starless sky.

He wandered through Central Park, thinking desperately that if he were to come across a mortal here, he would pounce on the poor soul, assuage this hideous thirst. His need was ferocious.

But there were no mortals in the park this terribly cold December night.

He left and moved silently, unseen, down an avenue, but Christmas lights adorned the shops and stores and hotels and cast too much light, making him seethe with anger and frustration. There was no way he could feed in peace here!

Christmas. For five hundred years he'd suffered the bittersweet memories of Christmas. And with stark clarity he recalled his first Christmas at the monastery, the solemnity, the stillness, the soothing hymns of the monks.

He moved toward the river now, across town, away from the twinkling holiday lights that held too many reminders of a time lost. There was barely a soul around, and his frustration grew. A part of him tried to rejoice, for ironically the bitterness of the air that he could not feel was keeping him from feeding, and yet another part of him cursed his bad luck. But still, with every stride he took, every burning glance into the shadows, he was aware of only one destination that would truly ease his pain—the building that housed Karen. As for her door, no lock, no iron bar, had ever stopped one of his kind. And then there she would be. He knew this was not a work night for her. Yes, she'd be there. If he waited till almost dawn she'd most likely be asleep. He would stand over her bed and savor the sight of her, let it fill him, let the need grow, engorging itself, and then gently he'd sink down beside her, position her head, and his lips would taste the warm flesh of his Karen before he would possess her, and she him.

Miguel stopped and tore himself free from the thought. He could not do that to her, not Karen, not the only female who had ever touched his soul. No. Never would he take her; no matter how strong the lust, he could not do it.

A subway entrance. Yes, just over there. If he waited, surely some fool would go down those steps, even at this hour. Some complete fool...

It wasn't a minute later that first one man appeared and went down into those stinking depths and then another, a mere child by the looks of him. The second one, the child, stopped at the entrance and glanced furtively behind him. Miguel sank soundlessly into the shadows, watching, surmising that the boy was going to rendezvous with the older one. A drug purchase? And then the boy went down into the subway, too, and Miguel followed them into that hell.

KAREN AWAKENED with a start and a terrible sense of foreboding.

She was in her apartment. Of course. She glanced at the door. It was closed. And yet she knew she was not alone, and a chill walked along her spine.

"Who...who's there?" she whispered, her throat closing.

No answer. It was too still, though, as if someone were trying very hard not to make a noise.

She peered into the darkness, and it was there, next to the curtains. She tried her voice as the shadows materialized into a vague shape. "It's you, isn't it, Miguel. Answer me."

And then finally she heard her name, a whisper, a breath of sound, "Karen."

Her heartbeat drummed in her ears. The figure coalesced in her vision as her eyes grew accustomed to the dark, and relief washed over her, tinged with a slight frisson of fear.

"Karen," she heard again, and he approached, his face terribly pale against the black of his clothing, the eyes... They held hers, two glowing embers piercing the night. And then he was standing over her, his face all beautiful angles and planes and yet ravaged. Was there . . . could that have been a drop of . . . of blood at the corner of his mouth? Oh, dear God!

"Miguel," she said, staring up at him, at the need she saw there, and she marveled at how unafraid she was. "No."

He stood there above her, and she knew, even though he stared at her, that he did not really know her. But he wanted her, and she became abruptly aware of her own involuntary response, the hot rush of blood through her veins.

The moments stretched out, each one a separate, tumescent entity, and Karen waited breathlessly, waited for him to awaken from whatever spell held him.

She saw the flare of his nostrils, the way in which he drew in her scent. This was who he was, *what* he was, at the very pinnacle of his power, and yet it was also the bottom of an abyss, Miguel's singular brand of hell.

Karen groped for the lamp, touched the switch, twisted it. Suddenly light filled the room, and Miguel took a step back, the blaze in his eyes dying. She watched, speechless, fascinated, gathering her own strength as his seemed to fail, ebbing from him, his face twisting as torment replaced desire. "I am so very sorry," he finally said, his voice gravelly, thick. "I don't know how I . . . How I even got here."

"Oh, Miguel," she said, and she swung her legs over the side of the bed as he moved, almost staggering to the far wall, putting his fists against the old flowered wallpaper, leaning into it. "What happened tonight? There's... blood, Miguel."

A groan escaped him. "Ah, yes," he said, so bitter.

"What did you do?" Carefully, still watching his back, Karen pulled on her jeans and a sweater, tossing her nightgown aside. "Tell me. What did you do?"

"I fed!" he growled.

She licked suddenly dry lips. "Who? How did...?"

"Does it matter? A lowlife. Someone who deserved everything he got. Rest assured, he will do no harm again."

"Judge and jury," she breathed, not certain at all what she thought about this revelation.

And then he spun around. "Yes! That is what I am! Judge and jury, if you will. Do you think I enjoy this role?"

"Miguel," she said softly, knowing she had to reach him, help him. "You're not alone any longer. I'm here now, and together we can work this out. Please, Miguel."

Pivoting his head, he bared his teeth in a mirthless grin. "You are so innocent. You really think there is a happy ending to this story?"

She met his eyes without flinching. "Yes, there will be. I know it."

"You are hopeless, Karen. Hopeless and wonderful." He passed a hand across his brow. "Too wonderful to risk . . . being near me."

"I'm not running away," she said.

Lines deepened in his face. "I tell you I cannot even recall coming here! I have so little control where you are concerned, Karen. Tonight, after I . . . fed, I was aware only of the hunger that still pierced me. Even after what I had done I could think only of you! You must listen. If you stay here, the day . . . the night will come . . ."

"It will not," she said quietly. "I'm not the least bit afraid. I trust you, Miguel."

"Foolish," he muttered.

"No, I'm not foolish, but I sure am stubborn. Miguel, have you been thinking? About going to Finland, I mean? You have to go. *We* have to go."

"Karen," he began.

"Miguel, you have to . . ." But whatever she was going to say died on her lips as she gasped, pointing at the window. "It's dawn, Miguel," she whispered.

And he spun around. A curse escaped him. "I must go," he said quickly.

"Could you stay here?" she asked.

"No, no." He looked around desperately. "This place is unsafe for someone like me. I must get home."

"All right," she said, "I'll call a taxi. Should I call a taxi, Miguel?"

"Yes, yes, and hurry."

Her hands shaking, Karen dialed the telephone. While it rang, she said, "I'm sure we can get one right away. At this hour..."

Indeed, the cab pulled up in front of her building within minutes. She stood waiting alongside him, her shoes and coat hastily thrown on, her eyes trained on the sky. "I'm coming with you," she said abruptly.

"No," he said. "It is pointless. You do not understand."

But she slid in beside him, determined.

"Karen, Karen," he said as the taxi sped away, "what have I done to us?"

"You haven't done anything," she replied, staring at his profile. "You know, Miguel, I'm in this with you."

He looked out the window. "Damn it, man, hurry!" he said to the driver, and then turned back to Karen. "I would give up everything," he said to her, "my wealth, my power, even eternal life, if I could convince you to leave this city."

"I won't. I have a free will, Miguel, and I'm not leaving, no matter what you say or do. Don't you see? Tonight was proof that you've got to try to find your friend Yuri. You have to. You even said yourself that if I stay you'll eventually... do that to me. You admit you can't control it. And I'm not running away. So there's only one choice."

"Blackmail," he snorted.

"Sure, yes, why not? I'll do whatever it takes. We are going to Finland, Miguel. Do you hear me?"

But he didn't. It was clear that at any minute the first rays of sun were going to spill over the city, and Karen could see his anxiety. She even leaned forward herself and told the driver to hurry, that there would be a good tip in it for him.

The cab sped up the avenue, missing a light, making the next three. Almost there, Karen thought. Hurry. What if they didn't make it?

His street. She looked desperately out of the window. It was so bright in the east. Any second now the sun . . . "Give me the money for the cab," she said to Miguel. "Miguel. Let me have your wallet. I'll pay. You can hurry inside. *Miguel!*"

Somehow she got his wallet, half pulling it out of his trouser pocket herself. She threw a twenty at the driver and then grabbed Miguel's arm, tugging him as she pushed open her door.

"Come on!" she whispered desperately, and it was then that the first pale ray of sun struck the top of the filigreed iron fence.

She tugged fiercely on him now, dragging at his heavy black coat. But he was slumping, as if all the strength had been drained from his muscles, and then, as they headed up his walk, the sun caught the side of his face.

He buckled with a cry of agony, grabbed the lapel of his coat and pulled it up to shield himself. Karen could have sworn she saw a curl of smoke rise from his flesh. "Hurry, Miguel!" she cried. "We're almost there!"

She was bearing his full weight now—a few more steps, that was all. But the moan of pain that escaped him seemed unending, as if his soul was being ripped to shreds.

The key! She got him to the door and frantically searched his pockets, still bearing his weight, the sun relentlessly moving toward them.

"Miguel, oh God, where's the key?" she wept.

"Right . . . pocket," he breathed, gasping.

She got it, and with fumbling fingers inserted it in the lock, twisting it, shoving open the heavy door, and they both stumbled inside.

Somehow she got him up the long flight of stairs and to his room, the bed. He fell on it, writhed, his pain obviously excruciating. What could she do? Was he burned?

She thought desperately as the vitality seemed to leak out of him. Was he dying? But after a few more moments it was as if the tension and pain subsided. His face relaxed, his limbs straightened, and he appeared to have slipped into a kind of coma.

She held her breath and stared down at him, frightened and yet fascinated. For a very long time she stayed like that, unmoving, her eyes fixed on his face, the eerie stillness of it, the pallor and marble smoothness. She thought she saw a burn there, too, but the room was so dim and she couldn't be sure. Should she treat it? Find something to put on it? How did you treat a wound on an immortal being? She was afraid to touch him, and yet she knew somehow that whatever she did or said could not reach him now. She wondered where he was, where his mind traveled to.

She saw it then, that smear of dried blood still at the corner of his mouth. And she couldn't bear the sight of it. All the bleeding she was witness to every night, the pain and suffering, somehow that was different. This single drop on Miguel touched a profound place in her heart. The torment he endured, the terrible need in him. It wasn't fair!

Karen spun around and looked at the room. Austere, elegantly understated, with striped wallpaper, a marble-topped dresser, a lovely tall wardrobe, an upholstered chair. All dusty. Dull. The bathroom. She went in and wet a washcloth, returned to his side, leaned over and gently removed the smear. Just touching him like that, without his knowledge, gave her a spurt of pleasure, a sense of control over Miguel Rivera. He was so vulnerable lying there in this state of unawareness. She dabbed gently at what she thought might be the burn.

Karen straightened and stared at him, the washcloth dangling from her fingers. She took in every detail, every beautiful feature, the way his dark mustache followed the line of his lips, the generous, imperious arc of his nose, the long dark lashes lying against the pale skin, the straight brows, the wave of his thick hair. How could he be anything but totally human, totally male? Yet he was different, a being she could barely comprehend, a man who'd lived for five hundred years! Who'd live forever.

After a long time Karen went downstairs and built a fire in his hearth. She fixed coffee and looked at the clock. It was only ten in the morning. The sun wouldn't set for hours and hours. She curled up on the couch and tried to read one of his old books, but the story didn't hold her interest, and after a while she went back upstairs to his room where she sat in the cushioned chair near the heavy drapes and simply stared at him.

"KAREN," SHE HEARD as if from a great distance. "Wake up, Karen," the voice persisted, and she had to force herself awake, uncertain of where she was, how she'd gotten there. With a start she sat up straight and looked around.

His bedroom. A lamp turned on. It was dark out. And there Miguel was, near the door, his clothes changed.

"I must have fallen asleep," she said.

He only nodded.

"How long have you been . . . up?"

"Awhile."

She stretched, stiff from sleeping in the chair. "You should have woken me earlier."

"I would have," he said, moving toward her now, "but I had a task to accomplish." And then he was standing over her, his expression hidden in shadow.

As always, Karen's heart began a heavier rhythm. "And what was that?" she managed to ask.

"I needed to book passage to Europe," he said very slowly, deliberately. "We sail in a few days' time."

"We're... taking a ship to Europe?" she breathed, confused.

"Yes. Two cabins, of course. I believe you'll enjoy it."

Europe. Finland... "We're going to find Yuri! Miguel, you mean we really are..."

"Yes," he said. "I do not know what destiny lies across that ocean, but I can no longer do this to either of us."

And then he reached down and took her warm hands in his cool ones and brought her to her feet. "Does this please you?" he asked.

"Oh, yes!" she said. "Yes!"

"And what if we cannot find him?"

"We'll cross that bridge when we come to it," Karen said, and she dared to look deep into his eyes, so close to him that she could see the very texture of his ivory-smooth skin, the thickness of his mustache and length of his eyelashes. The mark where the sun had burned his cheek was gone, vanished as if it had never been. Then she sighed and laid her head against his chest, which was hard and manly but absolutely, unquestionably, still.

CHAPTER ELEVEN

THERE WERE FEW WINTER crossings of the Atlantic, but Miguel's agent had found them a stateroom suite on the *Fjord Nymph,* a Norwegian luxury liner that made an annual Christmas voyage to England. When Karen arrived outside the covered pier and stepped out of the limo with Miguel, she was awed by the size, the height, the sleek whiteness of the liner. Streamers flowed from the many decks and music filled the air.

She didn't want to gawk like a country cousin, but it was hard to act blasé about this incredible adventure she was undertaking.

It was six o'clock on a chill December evening, and the pier was a seething frenzy of people and luggage and cars. Women in fur coats, men in elegant topcoats, piles of Louis Vuitton butter-soft leather bags filled the warehouse-size area. Porters shouted and waved and pushed dollies, taxis disgorged friends loaded with champagne bottles to see travelers off. Parties would go on until the revelers were ushered off and the big ship sailed on the dark tide.

"This way, Karen," Miguel said.

"Wait, Miguel, my bags..."

"They will be taken care of," he said, and she gave one backward glance at the limo driver, who was unloading Miguel's matching black leather bags and her own canvas ones.

They were going first class, of course, and Karen had packed her few decent things, knowing they were hopelessly inadequate. She'd spoken to Miguel about it reluctantly.

"I won't look right," she'd said. "I'll embarrass you. And we're sitting at the captain's table the first night."

"Karen, have no fear of your appearance. There are places on the ship you can purchase whatever you need."

"But—" Karen had looked away from him, uncomfortable with her confession "—I really can't afford things like that."

"It will be my pleasure to take care of everything. You are not to worry."

"I can't expect you to do that. It isn't right."

"Karen, please. You've given up your work for me. It is the least I can do. Accept my gifts in the spirit in which they are given," he'd said.

She'd backed down simply because she had to be with him and she wanted so badly not to shame him in the exalted circles he traveled with such aplomb.

They were whisked through the routine of boarding and shown up one of the gangplanks that connected the *Fjord Nymph* to the pier. Christmas decorations were everywhere, garlands of pine, can-

dles, ornaments. The main lobby had a huge decorated tree in its center. They were ushered across this
vast space, so that Karen only had time for an impression of art deco styling, thick carpets, a huge
chandelier and two grand, sweeping staircases rising
from the floor. Liner personnel in crisp, immaculate
uniforms greeted them and sent them on and on into
the bowels of the ship, until they reached two stateroom doors.

"Madame," Karen's steward said, handing her a
key, then striding across her stateroom and dramatically pulling open drapes, uncovering sliding glass
doors and a veranda that abutted the ship's rail.

Her bags had miraculously appeared, one already
on a rack, the other nearby in the bedroom. There was
a raised sitting room with pastel furnishings, poinsettias in a basket, and wine cooling in a silver bucket.
She gaped, standing in the center of the suite, turning
slowly, taking it all in.

"Will that be all, *madame?*"

"Oh, yes, that's all," she said, and Miguel appeared as if by magic through a connecting door as the
steward left.

"Miguel," she breathed. "Look."

"My suite is similar," he said. "Will you be comfortable?"

"Comfortable?" She laughed. "It's like a fairy
tale!" She walked over to the couch and smoothed the
rose velvet.

"I am glad you like it. I must say that if one must travel, this is the most convenient way."

"Convenient? It's wonderful."

"I came to tell you that dinner will be served at ten, after we set sail. Tonight the custom is to dress informally."

"Oh, thank goodness." Karen smiled. "Do you think we can explore a little? I mean, walk around? I'm afraid I'll get lost, Miguel."

"You're not tired?"

"Lord, no, I'm as high as a kite. And I wouldn't miss watching us leave the harbor for anything."

"Such enthusiasm," Miguel said as if to himself.

"Come on," she said. "We'll unpack later."

It was an adventure. They moved down endless, slightly curved companionways that opened up into public rooms, banks of elevators, shallow flights of stairs, endless numbered stateroom doors. There were diagrams on the walls, but Karen was still disoriented. Lounges appeared, restaurants, bars with dance floors, a darkened casino that opened only when the ship left port. There was a hospital, a state-of-the-art spa and glass-walled fitness center, beauty salons, one for men, one for women, a travel desk.

The other passengers they met as they strolled were generally older couples, for who else could afford a crossing like this?

There was a theater and a promenade lined with boutiques. Karen stopped and studied the window displays.

"They're so expensive," she whispered to Miguel.

"Do not consider cost," he said. "Purchase what pleases you. I insist."

Miguel's manner was rigidly contained lately. Karen knew that he was keeping himself tightly in control after that morning he'd come to her apartment. He had not touched her since he'd made the decision to go to Finland. He did not even allow himself to get too close. They'd seen each other seldom in the previous days, Miguel's excuse being that he had business matters to attend to, but she knew he was only being cautious. She'd decided not to add to his burden, so she tried to be unemotional herself. And yet there were times when his gaze rested on her, hot and heavy, just for a moment before he turned away. And then the ache would build inside her and her heart would beat too quickly.

It was exquisite agony for both of them.

They went on, down more companionways, past a small library and a windowless computer room, more stairs.

"Can you find our way back?" Karen asked. "I can't."

"Yes," he replied, "but then, you see, I have been on this ship before."

"Of course you have," Karen said. "You've done everything."

"Alas, not quite."

And then it was time to sail. All the passengers came out on the decks for the event, champagne bottles were passed around and everyone cheered and waved to friends and relatives who still stood on the dock.

It was quite a spectacle, streamers breaking loose as the mighty ship slipped from her berth. Karen could feel the entire vessel vibrate, a hum beneath her feet as the tiny tugboats and their own engines carried them out into the harbor.

And there was the Statue of Liberty! "Oh, Miguel," she said, turning to him. "Isn't it beautiful?"

"Yes. New York is perhaps one of the more exciting cities from which to embark." He pointed at the brilliantly lit skyscrapers as the big ship was led out to sea, and Karen drank champagne, feeling the vibration deep inside her as they gained momentum, the waves slapping the great hull.

"Cold?" he asked her when almost everyone else had gone back to their cabins.

"Cold?" she said. "How could heaven be cold?" And she thought to herself that she was changing, and never again would she be just plain old Karen Freed. She glanced up at Miguel as the lights of New York fell away, and he was staring at her. "What?" she said, cocking her head as the stiff salt breeze caught in her hair.

"Nothing," he said. "I was only thinking how much I would like to see the world through your eyes, Karen, through eyes not so very old and jaded."

"Soon," she murmured. "I know that you will soon."

Back in her stateroom Karen showered in the bathroom, using the perfumed soaps and shampoo and lotions provided. She wrapped herself in the soft terrycloth robe that hung on a hook, and then she went to sit in a chair in her sitting room, pour herself a glass of wine and glory in the absolute opulence of this floating palace.

This is how Miguel had lived for hundreds of years, she thought. He took it for granted. He hated his existence, but it had its compensations. And to think she was sharing it with him. What would her mother say if she saw her now? Karen laughed softly to herself, twirling the wineglass.

Well, her mom and dad knew she was taking a vacation, going to Europe with Miguel. She'd informed them in a brief phone call and ignored their shock and their questions. It had been easier than she'd thought. Maybe she was developing some courage after all.

He knocked on her door at a quarter to ten. She'd put on her green shirtwaist and new heels, pearl earrings, her mother's gold bracelet. She hoped it was okay, because that's all she had that was informal.

"You are ready," he said, so handsome in a tweed jacket over a black cashmere turtleneck.

"Yes, and I'm starved, too," she said, then she gave him a startled look.

He smiled. "No one will notice, my dear. They'll be too busy with their own food."

The first-class dining room was decorated with white upholstery and black lacquer; a warm blaze of lighting and a holiday centerpiece on every table lent it a comfortable yet festive atmosphere.

They were escorted to the captain's table, introduced to the plump, bald Captain Warner, a novelist, an actress, an elderly couple, a French diplomat and a racehorse owner. Karen smiled nervously, shook hands and nodded but spoke very little. She wished she'd done something more with her hair, and her dress was so plain.... But Miguel fit right in, easily conversing about hotels in London, restaurants, business trends, art galleries, a new play.

Should she admit she was a nurse? Maybe she'd avoid any mention of what she did. Maybe they'd take her for a rich woman and assume she didn't work for a living at all.

Karen was thrilled when the novelist said something about Carnegie Hall, and she could agree that *The Magic Flute* had been a wondrous production. Maybe this wouldn't be so difficult after all. And Miguel had been right. No one noticed that he only moved his food around his plate, raised his glass to closed lips. He met her eyes across the table often and smiled. Did he know how awkward she felt? How happy yet full of trepidation?

"And what does your husband do?" the elderly lady beside her asked, her diamonds twinkling.

Karen swallowed and gave a nervous laugh. "Miguel and I... we're not married."

"Oh, pardon me. I'm so dense sometimes. Of course not, dear. Well, never mind, I'm sure you will be soon."

Karen looked at Miguel helplessly. He smiled and nodded. She wished suddenly that they were alone, that she could let her hair down and be herself. But she had to do this for Miguel, she had to be strong for him.

After dinner they went into one of the bars and watched people dance. "Do you know how to dance, Miguel?" she asked.

"I learned the minuet once," he said, "but I fear that it is not done anymore."

"I can't dance either," she said. "Never had much chance to. Maybe we could . . . learn."

He looked at her, that mixture of yearning and self-contempt. "I do not think it a good idea, Karen." Nevertheless, they stayed up very late, always with other people around. Miguel gave her rolls and rolls of silver dollars for the slot machines in the casino, saying he enjoyed watching her play.

When she'd lost about fifty dollars, she turned to him, upset. "I'm losing all your money," she said.

"Let me," he replied, taking a coin from her and rubbing it between his fingers. "I will give it luck."

"I'm not the least bit superstitious," she said. "You know that won't do any good. It's a game of chance."

"Try again," he urged, giving her back the silver dollar.

She won the jackpot that time, lights flashing, bells clanging, and coins spilling out through her fingers. She stared at him, eyes wide, and he shrugged, smiling. "A game of chance, as you said."

"Miguel!"

"Now, my dear, you can afford one of those new frocks you were admiring earlier," he said smoothly. "What luck."

It was near dawn when they retired to their staterooms.

"Lock the connecting door," Miguel said gravely.

"Is it really necessary?" Karen asked.

"I will rest easier."

"But, really, you could open it if you wanted, anyway."

"It is a symbol, a reminder. We should never make it easy for ourselves to give in to temptation."

"Have it your way," she said softly.

"Then I will bid you good-night. Until tomorrow at sunset."

"Good night, Miguel. I wish..."

He stood there looking at her, an eyebrow raised inquiringly.

"Nothing," she said. "See you tomorrow."

Karen awoke just after three the next afternoon. She ordered a huge lunch and ate most of it, showered and dressed and set out to find her way to the shops she'd seen last night. She had to ask directions to the promenade several times, but the stewards all seemed used to that, and they were very helpful.

She was timid at first, fingering the gowns, afraid to try them on or look at the price tags. She needed three formal dresses, she knew, one for each night except for the last, which was, like the first, informal, since the passengers were expected to be packed and ready to disembark the following day.

"May I help you?"

Karen almost jumped. The saleslady. "Well, yes, I, uh... I don't have anything to wear for dinner, and..."

The lady was sizing her up. "Size six, pastels. Yes, I have a few things you might be interested in."

Karen couldn't believe how she looked in the gowns the lady brought her. Pale yellow chiffon, backless, slinky pearl gray silk knit, blue sequins with a slit to the knee and a bare shoulder.

"Very nice," the saleslady said. "You'll need shoes, of course, and I might recommend Darcy at the hair salon. She can do wonders. Now, who shall I charge this to?"

"Oh, wait," Karen said. "How much are these dresses? I mean, what's the total?"

"Three thousand fifty-six," the lady said, "and no tax now that we're offshore."

Karen felt faint. "I'm not sure," she stammered. "Maybe I should..." Then she straightened her shoulders. Miguel had told her not to worry. She could always return them, after all. "Please charge them to Miguel Rivera, suite 103."

"Yes, *madame.*" And that was that.

She bought an evening clutch purse and one pair of shoes, silver ones, that would have to do for all three dresses, and then she went into the beauty salon and asked for Darcy. When she left two hours later, her dull brown hair had been frosted and blunt cut to her jawline, so that it hung straight and silky.

She got back to her room, to which all the purchases had been delivered, and stared at herself in the mirror. My Lord, she wasn't plain anymore! She wasn't gorgeous or anything like that, but she looked nice, her face piquant and heart-shaped, her hair simple but much more flattering. Why hadn't she done this years ago?

Miguel's knock brought her out of her musing, and abruptly she was nervous—what if he hated the way she looked?—and proud at the same time. She pulled the door open. "Miguel," she said breathlessly.

He glanced around her stateroom. "You have been busy, I see."

"I'm terrified at what you're going to say when you get the bills," she said in a rush. "Over three thousand dollars, Miguel, and my winnings didn't even come close."

He waved his slender, pale hand. "It is nothing."

"It's more than a month's salary," she said.

He laughed lightly. "I only hope you enjoyed yourself, my dear."

"Did I ever!"

"I see your hair is different."

Her hand flew up. "Do you like it, Miguel? I think it's better, I really do."

"Very becoming, very becoming indeed."

She wanted to hug him, to kiss him, to show him in every way how much she felt for him. She wanted to hook her arm through his and stroll proudly into the dining room. Instead she could only smile and mouth words that held barely a fraction of her love, and hope that he would read in her eyes what he truly meant to her. "You've given me so much, Miguel," she said in as even a tone as she could manage. "I can never pay you back, you know."

His dark blue eyes gleamed like sapphires as he held her gaze. "You will never know what you have given me, Karen. It is worth far more than material objects. I could never purchase it, not anywhere or anytime."

"I haven't done much at all."

"You are too modest. You have given me back a small measure of my humanity, and you have given me hope."

"Then I'm glad, Miguel." They should have embraced then, touched lips, given each other the sweet closeness they craved so desperately. Instead they could only lock hungry gazes across the width of the elegant stateroom. Karen wanted to cry.

She wore the silver gray clinging dress that night. It was remarkable, she thought, how different she looked: sophisticated, slender rather than thin, her fair, shining hair swinging against her cheek. She put on a little makeup, some pale lipstick. She looked in her mirror, mesmerized. And with the change in her appearance, she felt a new confidence, a developing sense that she was attractive, that she was intelligent and worthy, even interesting. Miguel, at least, seemed to think so.

Miguel. He was so splendidly handsome in his formal attire, Karen was sure she heard a collective gasp when they entered the Grande Dining Room. Heads swiveled toward them, and she almost burst with pride. The maître d' seated them at a private table in the center of the huge room. A complimentary bottle of champagne awaited them, cooling in a silver bucket that wept tears of condensation.

The menu was extensive, with many holiday favorites—turkey, goose, incredible salads and vegetables, delectable desserts. Karen had barely tasted her food the previous night because she'd been so nervous, but tonight . . . tonight she felt infused with glamour and self-confidence. She ate with unabashed pleasure, enjoying every morsel. Miguel held out a forkful of his plum-and-apple-stuffed pork roast for her to taste. He played with his food, as usual, but mostly he watched her delight in hers.

Karen's cheeks were flushed both with the champagne Miguel poured for her and with this heady experience; she knew people were casting admiring glances in her direction, and she absolutely glowed.

"Are you enjoying yourself?" Miguel inquired over coffee.

"Do you need to ask?"

"I was afraid you would be bored." He waved a hand negligently. "All these old people, nothing to do. I have always had to make long voyages by ship, but you do not."

"I've never traveled anywhere," Karen said. "Well, I did go to Bermuda once, and Disney World in Florida."

"You went by plane?"

"Yes."

"I am only able to do short journeys by air, those flights that are at night."

"Of course."

"We are booked on one from London to Helsinki."

"London," Karen said dreamily.

"An interesting city, but I am afraid our stay there will be too short to see very much. And the weather can be quite dreadful at this time of year," he said.

"It will be exciting just to be there."

He smiled. "I do adore your enthusiasm."

Karen sipped at the champagne, emptying her glass. "It isn't enthusiasm, Miguel, it's ignorance."

"I adore your ignorance."

"No, don't do that. I want to be worldly and sophisticated like you," she said earnestly.

"That would be a shame. Do not change, Karen, please. Stay as you are."

"Miguel—" Karen met his gaze with absolute frankness "—I'm afraid...no, I'm glad...but I am changing, I *have* changed. I feel, well, different inside." She took a breath and closed her eyes. "Better. I feel better, about me, I mean." She stared at him again, her wide, blue gray eyes glistening. "It's you. You've done it. You make me feel . . ." She wanted to say loved, but didn't. "You make me feel appreciated."

And then, as their gazes met, clashed, clung together across the table, Miguel reached a hand over the pure white linen, and Karen met it with hers. They sat there for a very long time, their hands clasped, their heads bowed close together.

Another night passed on the wondrous ship, a night full of entertainment—a stage play, gambling, exploring the ship together. At dawn Miguel wished her good-night and saw to it that she locked the connecting door. Karen lay in her king-size bed, felt the great ship roll beneath her, felt its enormous engines purr like a giant tiger, and thought about Miguel.

To anyone else they must have appeared to be carefree lovers, drinking each other in, exchanging knowing glances. They weren't. Miguel was with her, yes, but there was always a distance between them—one enforced by his caution and one that arose from his condition.

He'd tried to explain it to her as they walked the enclosed decks of the ship after dinner.

"I am not quite here," he'd said. "Not all of me. There is a part that . . . um, lies elsewhere. I cannot explain it very well. Everything is clear and sharp to me, but it is as if I am watching a very realistic film. I am . . . removed.''

There were those times, too, when she caught the flame in his eyes, fixed on her, probing, waiting, wanting, and then she sensed his subsequent self-disgust, his swift turning away.

Oh, God, she wished she could help him, relieve the need that tortured him. Maybe she shouldn't have come on this trip—proximity only made things worse. Yet she knew he needed her; she didn't question that.

She lay there, bathed in luxury, surrounded by un-imaginable opulence, and felt her belly throb in need. What if . . . ? What if she let him . . . ? He'd told her it took several times before she would become . . .

Karen rolled onto her side, curling into a fetal po-sition, her hands between her thighs. No, that was not the way. Yet heat filled her, dotting her skin with a faint dew, and she tossed off the rose satin quilt.

The next afternoon when Karen finally awoke she bought a few more things, a good wool suit to travel in, a simple blue gabardine shirtwaist dress. It was dark by the time she stopped at the post office to send a postcard to her parents, sister and brother, hurrying because she knew Miguel would be up by then. One of the postcards fell to the floor, and an attractive blond man picked it up for her.

"This is yours, I believe," he said.

"Oh, thank you," she replied, taking it from him, barely giving him a glance. But she thought as she walked back to her stateroom how unusual it was to see such a young man in first class. Must be quite rich, Karen mused, and then put him from her mind.

She wore the yellow chiffon that night. It swirled around her ankles and whispered when she moved. It was Christmas Eve, and everyone was merry. The waiters were dressed like medieval pages; they carried a whole boar on their shoulders while a trio played Christmas carols.

Miguel was a little withdrawn.

"Is something wrong?" Karen asked.

"Nothing more than usual," he said dryly. "Sometimes Christmas arouses memories." Then he smiled. "But forget that. You are radiant tonight, Karen. I may have to fend off your admirers at this rate."

She blushed. "You'll never have to do that. Men don't notice me."

"Oh, really?" was all he said.

After dinner Karen asked if they could take a walk. "I'd love some fresh air. It seems as if we haven't been outside in days. There's a lounge in the rear that's open-air, Miguel. I saw it on a diagram of the ship."

"It is very cold and windy," he said, but Karen was not to be deterred. It was a mistake.

They fetched their coats. And when they walked along the companionways Karen felt curiously light-headed, as if she'd been dreaming a wonderful dream and then woken to find that it wasn't a dream at all.

How could a person feel so... special, so blessed? Oh, she knew it was the ocean crossing and this beautiful ship, Christmas, and, of course, Miguel. It didn't matter who he was, what he was, it was still magic. *He* was magic.

She told him that.

He pushed open the door to the open-air lounge and laughed a little with her. And they talked about how Karen saw everything as if for the first time, as if everything and everybody were inherently good. "No wonder you are a fine nurse," he said as they crossed the lounge. "You have a way of making a person feel ... alive."

"Well, I suppose that is a quality a nurse should have," she said and laughed again.

It was damp and cold on deck, with a brisk wind that caught at her hair and tugged at her coat. It seemed not to touch Miguel, not to muss his hair or flap his coat. He stood at the rail, straight and immaculate, his face a glimmer of white, his eyes hollow pits of blackness. There wasn't another soul there.

"I guess I'm nuts," Karen said, leaning her elbows on the rail, "but I love this." She drew in a deep breath. "Sea air."

"You are warm enough?"

"I'm fine." She turned to rest her back against the rail, then held a hand up to keep her hair from blowing into her eyes. "And you?"

"I do not feel the cold."

"Um," she said, sighing, absorbed in the hissing swell of the sea beneath them, the air stinging her face. She had everything she'd ever dreamed of—except for one thing.

And yet, a secret part of Karen still wondered about that one thing and just the image of Miguel's hungry lips against her made her flush all over.

"Tell me about London," she said, trying to shake off her thoughts. "Does it snow there?"

"Rarely," he said, watching her. "Mostly it is raw and chilly. Or so they tell me." His lips twisted in irony.

But Karen ignored his sarcasm. "I know I'm going to love it. London," she said.

"You must be cold by now," Miguel said. "We should go in."

But she didn't want to. They were the only two people on earth, on this black ocean that went on forever.

"Karen, I really do think we..."

It was as if she couldn't hear him. Or didn't want to. She could stay out here all night, for eternity, as long as Miguel was with her. God, how she wanted him. How desperately she wanted to be a part of him, to know him, really know him. If only they could... She dared to raise her eyes up to his. Yes, he was thinking the same forbidden thoughts, she knew that, seeing the barely suppressed fire that kindled so deeply in his eyes.

"Karen," he said, a whisper that was carried away on the wind. "No."

She closed her eyes then, fighting for control. And strangely, in an isolated moment of time, she thought of Adam and Eve, and she knew why they'd tasted the forbidden fruit.

The minutes stretched out, and Karen's senses sharpened while she was buffeted with a million sensations. Everything began to feel new, different, as she stayed there unmoving. The rail at her back was cool and smooth, the wind stinging, and the hiss and suck of the bottomless water below mirrored the feelings inside her.

She swayed toward him, Eve, offering the fruit. And when he neither moved away nor moved toward her, she reached up and touched his face, opening her eyes, saying yes with her body, her mind, her soul. *Yes*.

Miguel said something, but Karen scarcely heard or cared, she knew only that he'd reached out, too, one cool, smooth hand tilting her face up to his, his other hand at the small of her back.

He kissed her then, but it was only a brush of his lips on hers before his head lowered, his mouth grazing her cheek, her jawline, her throat.

"I...cannot," he groaned, tensing, pausing, but she let her head fall back and felt the sudden, strong pressure of his arm around her, forcing her against him as his lips moved to the place on her neck where her pulse leaped.

White-hot fire burned through her veins, and she moaned, "Yes, do it," and suddenly she couldn't tell if the wind or Miguel was colder, fiercer, more desperate. For only a fleeting moment he raised his head, his eyes dark jewels flashing with internal illumination, and then he came down on her swiftly.

A sudden sting, a puncturing of flesh and then the flow of her lifeblood. Karen gripped his shoulders, feeling as if she were drowning, her knees buckling as her body gave itself to him, and something inside her swelled as his lips possessed her, as she gave him life.

The sensations in her grew, promising, and her throat closed on an involuntary cry as they seemed to meld together, the very essence of them, their minds, their souls. Never had she known raw desire, such sweet, hot . . .

"No!" she heard at the same instant he tore himself away. And then he was staggering back, and Karen felt as if a lifeline had just been severed and she was floundering, catching the rail with a hand, the desire still burning inside, her head reeling.

"Dios, perdóname," he whispered, moving away.

"Miguel," she said faintly, but then there was an unearthly wail, a dark flash that displaced the air where he stood, and he was gone.

CHAPTER TWELVE

DRESSED IN A TUXEDO, Miguel lay on the satin coverlet of the king-size bed in the elegant stateroom. He appeared, by some trick of the light, to be a statue, with none of the tiny movements that imply life. Outside the drawn draperies the last bleak ray of sun slid below the watery horizon, and the room was bathed in twilight.

Miguel's eyes opened suddenly, and there was a fully sentient gleam of deep sapphire between dark lashes. He was awake.

Then memory struck, and he shut his eyes again as a rictus of pain pulled at the smooth skin of his face.

What had he done?

He rose to a sitting position as if pulled by invisible strings. Karen, he thought in his first second of cognizance. Then his head jerked to one side, and he sat there for a moment as the cold hand of knowledge gripped him, but this sense of dread, this internal discovery, had nothing whatsoever to do with her.

"Baltazar," he whispered into the bleakness of his stateroom. He was here, on the ship.

He rose to his feet, propelled by an unseen force, and paced the width of the room. He should have known! He would have sensed Baltazar sooner had he not been so wrapped up in Karen and his own damnable needs!

For himself it did not matter, but for her... This was new, this fear he felt, because it was for her, for a mortal he had put in dire peril—and not only from Baltazar!

Where was she? A momentary panic wrapped coldly around his innards, and everything he had felt the night before came crashing back into his brain.

Karen at the rail, her slender body pressed to him, the salt air stirring her hair, the searing warmth of her lips on his, the scent of her, the quick laboring of her heart against his hands the moment before he'd taken her. And the release. Oh, God, the blessed, slow release of his need as her lifeblood had flowed into him, a hot, velvet liquid. And he'd floated in that ecstasy, in that warm, dark place of raw sensation.

He went to her door and knocked. "Karen?" A moment, an eternity, and then she replied, "I'm getting dressed, Miguel."

Relief flooded him. He would not let her out of his sight again, not for a moment. He'd have to tell her, have to explain that Baltazar was here. And how on earth was he to talk to her, be with her, after what he had done last night?

Five minutes later she knocked on his door and came in, and he could see that she had made some sort of decision. She'd steeled herself to face him. For the moment, though, all he could do was stare. It was as if with each passing hour on this voyage she grew more beautiful. Tonight she wore a fitted blue sequined gown, a shimmering thing that danced with light and was split to the knee. It left one white shoulder naked, and he could see the delicate bones and the faint tracing of veins under her pale skin. And she was paler, he thought, or was that merely his imagination?

"Merry Christmas, Miguel," she said, and there was a new authority in her voice, in her manner. A new awareness and two tiny new marks on her fair neck. He could not answer her at first, the irony of this day, this time, Karen, Baltazar.... It smote him with a kind of desperation that he knew he had to control.

"Miguel, please don't blame yourself for last night," she said. "It was my fault. Last night you... you left me so quickly, I... Miguel, I cried myself to sleep."

"My behavior was inexcusable," he said faintly. "It will not happen again." But even as he spoke, he was besieged once more by the knowledge of that beast's presence on the ship. He was a fool to have let his guard down!

He looked at Karen, trying to concentrate on what she was saying. A wave of shame swept him anew; it was like drowning. He bowed his head. "It will not happen again," he repeated.

"Are you angry with me?"

"Never."

"But it's... it's different between us, isn't it?"

He met her gaze and saw moisture in her eyes. "Perhaps so. I may have been misguided in bringing you on this voyage."

"No!" she said. "Let's not go into that again. It's too late, anyway. I'm here."

He wanted to reassure her, hold her close as he had done before, protect her from all harm, all pain, all unhappiness. It was not to be. "We will try, Karen."

"Yes," she said.

"We will try to enjoy the rest of the voyage."

"Yes, Miguel." She was smiling now, relieved. He could do that much for her. Until he had to tell her about Baltazar, of course. But he would undertake that task later. And when he did tell her, how would she react? To frighten her unnecessarily would be unconscionable. And yet to let her believe she was safe was dangerous.

They walked together down the companionway to the dining room. Silently, carefully not touching.

They were seated at their table, where small wrapped Christmas gifts awaited them.

Perfume for her, a gold key chain engraved with the ship's name for him.

"How nice," Karen said, childlike in her delight.

Yet she ate very little, an ironic mirror image of his own dining habits. Miguel tried very hard to put from his thoughts the incident at the rail that lay between them. And yet he could not do it. He kept staring instead at the nearly invisible marks on her throat. She'd tried to cover them with makeup, he could tell, but he saw them—two points of red, a brand, his brand. And his physical being remembered, too, the deep, shimmering relief she'd given him. Never in all these centuries had he gleaned pleasure from the act. It had never been something other than to ease the need in him. But with Karen it had been something entirely new. And despite its wrongness, there had been beauty.

No, he thought abruptly. He could not allow himself to think of their joining as anything but forbidden. All they had accomplished last night—all he had accomplished—was to feed the monster within him.

The room was crowded, loud, tongues loosened by fine wine and holiday cheer. Karen gave him a tentative smile, then went back to gazing at the diners, the steady flow of waiters carrying trays of the most succulent foods. In the center of this particular dining room was a bubbling fountain surrounded by dozens of scarlet poinsettias. She stared at the plants for a very long time, her fork poised in midair.

He wondered what she was thinking. Was it about last night? Did she know how close she'd come to the unthinkable?

And yet he knew that something had awakened in Karen in the cold, salty air, something so primitive he dared not think about it. She had come alive in his arms. She'd shared those fleeting moments of ecstasy with him, and neither of them could deny it.

Was this what mortal men endured, this craving? Was this the true nature of desire, the longing and ache of which the poets wrote? Certainly Miguel did not suffer those same physical sensations, but was this pain in his soul so very different?

As if she read his thoughts, Karen said, "You're still the best thing that ever happened to me in my life, Miguel. I'll never regret a moment of it." She smiled tremulously, glimmering with her rare new beauty. "Not one moment."

"You speak from vast inexperience, I am afraid, Karen."

"Not as inexperienced now, Miguel. Maybe I'm catching up." And she gave him a grave, knowing look, one that she never could have conjured up days before. His Karen, losing her innocence, and yet her inner beauty shone as brightly, and he was still utterly captivated by it.

"Miguel," she said, leaning across the table, "can anything between us be so wrong? I know we can't, we shouldn't, ever let that happen again, but I . . . It's the first time I've ever really touched you, been a part of you. . . ."

"Enough," he said, and he rose to his feet swiftly. He could see the unshed tears in her beautiful eyes, and the sight tore at him, but she did not understand. She could not know the fire she was playing with. God help them, he thought, they had to find the cure! And now there was Baltazar's presence to be dealt with, as well.

It was Karen who wanted to stop in the ballroom. Music flowed from it, dance music, and dancers filled the floor, all bejeweled and brightly dressed, hair stylishly coiffed. He couldn't blame Karen for wanting to be among these vibrant people, for wanting to see and be seen. She did look so lovely tonight, and Miguel was aware of the appreciative glances in her direction as they entered. Twinkling Christmas lights were strung everywhere, and a mirrored ball hung from the ceiling, turning, throwing tiny patches of light on her hair and the sequins of her gown. Indeed, Miguel thought, she was the most beautiful creature on earth. How could he have plucked her from her life, expected her to flourish in his company? How could he have touched her as he had last night? She deserved so very much more than the dark existence that was his. And what was going to become of them when they discovered that there was no cure? Hadn't he and his kind always known that the rumors were pure myth? This entire journey was a flight from reality, and Karen's disappointment would be more than he could bear.

They stood together at the edge of the throng and watched the dancers. Miguel scanned the room, alert for that familiar presence. He hadn't been in the dining room, of course not, but he was close now. Yes, Baltazar. This would be a playground for him, and indeed, who would note that deaths were more frequent than usual on this ship full of elderly people?

"It's so beautiful here," Karen said. "The people, the lights, the music. Isn't it lovely, Miguel?"

"Yes, lovely," he replied, distracted. *Close, he was close.* "Perhaps we should go, Karen," Miguel said after a moment, his senses sharpening. "There's something I have to tell you. Something you must be made aware of..." But before Miguel could finish, he was there.

It all happened very quickly. Somehow Baltazar was in front of them, and he was smiling, introducing himself as an acquaintance of Miguel's. "Business, you understand." And he'd taken one of her hands, brought it to his lips, his piercing ice blue eyes boring into hers.

"What a lovely creature," Baltazar said. "And keeping her all to yourself on this voyage. For shame, Miguel."

But Karen caught none of the nuances in his words. Her eyes held by Baltazar's, she said, "Haven't we met before? Weren't you the one who..."

A slow, insolent smile stretched across Baltazar's sculpted lips. "If we have not met it is most assuredly my loss."

Miguel stood there with rage coiling like a serpent inside him, his eyes fixed on his enemy of five hundred years, his creator. And as much as he loathed the vicious killer, he could see the attraction Baltazar held for women.

He had been in New York, of course. Miguel had sensed his presence. What better place to prey on the sick and homeless? But Miguel had not anticipated his enemy's next move, and that was another matter altogether.

"I'm so sure we've met somewhere," Karen was saying. "You were never in the emergency room where I work?"

"Emergency room? What an interesting idea. I imagine it would be most fascinating," Baltazar replied smoothly. And then he turned to Miguel, oozing charm. "You wouldn't allow me to borrow her for a dance, would you?"

And before Miguel could do a thing, Baltazar was already leading her into the swaying mass of humanity.

A curse rumbled in Miguel's throat. He stood there alone, with his eyes riveted on the couple, and seethed with fury. Oh, he knew Baltazar would not try anything in this crowd, but clearly the gauntlet had been thrown.

And Karen... Had Baltazar known of her existence before tonight? If he'd been shadowing Miguel in New York, then he most assuredly had seen Karen.

It struck Miguel like a blow to his heart—the marks on her neck! If Baltazar spotted them—and he surely would—he'd believe her the easiest of prey; he would at the very least believe Miguel was using her nightly for sport!

Karen, Karen, what have I gotten you into?

He strained to see them in the swirling throng, his hands fisted at his sides. He could do nothing here, though, without creating a scene. And Baltazar knew he would not do that.

Five hundred years had come to this—Karen in the arms of his nemesis, Karen embraced by evil! Baltazar was a secretive and reclusive creature, originally a Viking, or so it was believed, and his berserk tendencies were always in evidence. He fed on crisis and human misery. Women, almost always women, because they could not resist his beauty and his charm. Oh, yes, it radiated from him; he loved women.

Baltazar could be fiendishly clever about those whom he chose for eternal life. Sometimes he chose randomly, the person's death a function of his gluttony, but at times he picked carefully, hunting far and wide, perversely choosing those with the purest of hearts, those who had much to give to humanity: a physician, an artist, a scientist, a priest.

Miguel watched, thinking desperately. He would not let this go on much longer. He *could* not.

But what a striking couple they made. Baltazar, so blond and fit and elegant, and Karen, her hair gleaming with golden highlights, as slim as her partner, her pale shoulder caressed by prisms of light, her gown sparkling as Baltazar swept her around and around the floor. At one point she was laughing as they twirled past Miguel, her eyes locked to Baltazar's, his arm supporting the slim arch of her back.

And then Baltazar was leaning close as the tempo of the music slowed, and he seemed to be whispering something into her ear, that shining curtain of her hair lying against his cold cheek. It seemed to Miguel that everything in the room was moving in slow motion, and the edges of his perception dimmed until all he saw was that single couple.

Baltazar finished whispering in her ear and slowly, slowly raised his head. Karen, equally as slowly, tipped her own head back and started to laugh again. Baltazar's eyes took her in, a hideously drawn out and thorough scrutiny, and then, as Miguel looked on in agony, the devil's stare fixed on those two marks on her neck.

Light began to glow in Baltazar's eyes. And as Karen dipped her head forward again, her gaze meeting her partner's, Miguel had had enough. He moved toward the dance floor, shouldering his way through the crowds. "Excuse me," he said to Karen, pulling her hand from Baltazar's. "We must go."

"But the dance isn't..." she began.

"Now," Miguel commanded.

"Miguel, Miguel," Baltazar said, grinning, his other hand still at her back. "Karen is quite correct. We haven't finished our..."

"It's over," Miguel said, his eyes on a level with Baltazar's. For a very long minute they stood like that, face-to-face, eyes locked. It took every ounce of strength in Miguel to keep from putting his hands around Baltazar's neck and squeezing, choking...for all the good it would have done. "Take your hands off her," he said and finally Baltazar did.

"Miguel," Karen said, embarrassed.

"Come." Miguel turned away, loathing Baltazar, loathing himself. Then Baltazar's voice knifed through the air.

"Oh, Miguel," he said, "I don't suppose you would care to join me for a drink in my cabin? Of course, Karen is invited, too."

Miguel froze. Slowly he turned back. "Please excuse us," he hissed.

"Ah," Baltazar replied, undaunted, "but I see that you've already partaken of refreshment." His gaze traveled leisurely to Karen. "Perhaps next time, then."

SOMEHOW MIGUEL STEERED Karen down the companionway, and somehow he got them to her suite and safely inside, locking the door, his hands shaking with the rage that refused to abate.

"Karen," he began, turning to her.

"Why were you so rude to that man? He said he knew you," she interrupted, obviously perplexed.

"Yes, we knew each other," Miguel said coldly.

"Then..." She frowned, and abruptly her eyes widened. She drew in her breath sharply. "Oh, my God, it was that man, the one in the painting, the one who..."

"Yes," he said, "it was him."

She spun away, raising a hand to her forehead. "Oh dear Lord, and I saw him earlier. At the post office. I thought he looked familiar." She hugged herself, her shoulders hunched. "I danced with him, I was... and he was so..."

"Yes," Miguel said.

"But why, what is he doing here?"

He told her that Baltazar was playing a kind of game with them, a game that could become dangerous, he added carefully.

"But Miguel, can't he be stopped? Hasn't anyone tried to stop him?"

"Yes, they have tried. He toys with them, then destroys them. He is very ancient and very powerful. I have tried myself, as I told you. We have fought in every way men can fight and then some. He cannot best me nor I him. At least that is what has happened up to now."

She raised her eyes to his. "But I'm here now, right? And that makes you more vulnerable, doesn't it? You have to worry about me."

"Yes," he admitted.

"Oh, God, he touched me," she said. She shuddered, still hugging herself, fear shining in her blue gray eyes, and the sight of her torture was a knife in his heart.

He knew he should not touch her, had sworn, cursed, made a thousand blood oaths that he would never touch her again!

But she was there, so frightened, and it was all his doing.

"Miguel," she said, "what are we going to do?"

He was beside her without knowing how he got there. He took her slim, pliant body into his arms, and he felt the warm quiver of her against him. He was trembling, too; her closeness made him into a demented thing, and he had to clench his jaw and give her comfort, only comfort.

"I will never let him near you, Karen," he said into her soft golden hair. "I swear that."

He stroked her neck with one hand, her bare shoulder with the other. Ah, the sweetness, the taste of her. He fought it down, but the hot scent of her blood filled him.

CHAPTER THIRTEEN

KAREN HAD BEEN ABLE to see little during the train ride from the port of Southampton to London because it had been dark. She'd only gotten an impression of a land very different from the one she'd left, a land green-and-gray and misty, divided by walls and fences, every small house or cottage or rowhouse on its own neat plot. Hedges and alleys, the backyards of Britain bordering the train tracks, smokestacks and streetlights and vehicles on the wrong side of the road, fading gradually into the solid old city of London.

There had been no side trips to Trafalgar Square or Buckingham Palace or the Tower of London—nothing, as dawn had been nearing and Miguel needed to be safely in his hotel room.

She sat now on her first day in England in her room adjoining Miguel's staring out the window toward the mighty Thames River that was mostly shrouded in fog.

The weather was miserable. Dreary. Cold. A light rain fell from a pewter sky and passersby on the street below were invisible beneath big black umbrellas. Not many people were out, either. The weather was too inclement. But there were plenty of cars and red double-decker buses and lorries, their tires hissing on the rain-soaked streets, and square, old-fashioned black cabs that looked as if they belonged in a Sherlock Holmes movie.

Dreary, she thought again, chilled, lonely and a little depressed as she stared over the bare tree tops and squat buildings toward the river.

She checked the time. Miguel had told her the sun set early here in the winter as they were farther north than New York City, and that he would rise by three-thirty this afternoon. He'd said, too, that he would then take her on a short tour of London and buy her a dinner of the city's best fish and chips—at a real English pub, of course, or whatever she desired. But somehow Karen's heart wasn't in it, and she wished they were in Finland already.

It was the waiting, the not knowing, that was beginning to eat at her. What if no cure existed? But she couldn't, she wouldn't allow herself to think about that. Cross each bridge when you come to it, she told herself.

She looked at the time again as the rain slid silently across her window and a bank of fog rolled in from the river. Two more hours before he'd rise. Two hours. So long. She'd slept earlier and wasn't the least bit tired. Only a little anxious. And she couldn't go out. Not alone. Not in a strange city. And what if that hideous creature Baltazar... But no. If he were in London, too, he'd be asleep, just like Miguel. For two more hours, anyway.

Karen rose and went into the bathroom, leaned her hands on the sink and studied herself in the mirror. She was different. It wasn't just the hair or the soft glow in her eyes. It was that loss of innocence that had seemed to radiate from her. Miguel had told her never to change, and yet she had. Together they had changed her. For the better?

She tilted her chin a little then and saw them—the fading marks on her neck. And she felt her belly clench at the knowledge of what they'd done. It hadn't been wrong. It hadn't! Nothing between them could ever be wrong. And if they never found a cure, she would let him, beg him to...

"No," she whispered, she couldn't think about that. The cure, that was all that mattered.

She left the bathroom and in her robe and slip went to the door that stood between her and Miguel. Instinctively Karen knew he wouldn't like it if she went in, sat by him. He wouldn't like it at all. Still, she turned the lock and then twisted the doorknob, anyway, just needing to look at him for a moment. It was awful feeling so lonely in this foreign city. And the weather really did have her down.

His room was dark, very dark, the heavy curtains pulled closed so that not a crack of that gray light squeezed through. But she could see him, stretched out on the bed in wool trousers and a dark brown turtleneck sweater, his hands folded just below his waist. She wished he'd awaken. She wished she knew what thoughts or dreams he was having, if any. There was so very much Karen wished she could share with him.

At first she just sat quietly in the chair near the bed. And she stared at him, his long shadowed figure so still he might have been dead. But he wasn't. And even though Miguel Rivera had told her he was not alive in any sense that she could comprehend, he was alive to her. Vital and subject to the same hopes and fears as she was; no matter what he claimed, he was very much alive with emotions.

She stared and stared at him, memorizing each darkly shadowed line and hollow, the way his hair waved over his brow, behind his pale ear. The dark line of his mustache. And, as she'd thought so many times before, she found him the most extraordinarily handsome man she'd ever seen. That he'd picked her. After five hundred years, having looked upon all the beauties of the world, Miguel had picked *her*.

A priest. Miguel had been a priest. She still could barely fit her mind around that knowledge, and she sat very quietly thinking about it. Miguel in his long brown hooded robes, his heart filled with goodness, his mind and soul so pure. And he'd never known a woman, not in that way. Never. Yet so many centuries later he was ready to know one at last. Her. It just seemed impossible, or perhaps destined somehow. And how unfair it would be for them to have come so very far seeking a cure and the chance to build a life together, only to have their hopes dashed. That simply couldn't happen.

Karen was not certain exactly why she finally rose and went to sit very carefully on the edge of the bed. She knew only that she was desperate to be close to him, to perhaps reach out and touch him very lightly. Surely that wouldn't hurt.

And so she did. She gently laid her hand over his cold ones and whispered, "I'm here, Miguel. I'll always be here for you, no matter what." And her heart swelled with love and that deep, forbidden yearning.

Karen knew it was wrong to go any further, and yet still she lay down on the bed beside him, her eyes wide, fixed on his face.

Did he know she was there? Could he sense her? Did he feel the same terrible ache in his belly?

She lay there motionless for a long time and let her fantasies run free, even though she realized he would be angry if he knew. It didn't matter. Nothing mattered but being close to him, sharing this bed, dreaming that he'd roll over and pull her against him, cover her face and neck and breasts with kisses—warm kisses—as his hands would stroke her, love her. To be one with Miguel in that way, to feel their bodies join...

Gently, carefully, Karen held her breath and ran her fingers along his side, down his hip, feather-light. And then she dared, her pulse racing, to touch him there, to feel with her fingers the bulge of him beneath his trousers. Her breath caught, and there was no shame, only that piercing desire to have him whole, mortal, and to share a passion that neither of them had ever known.

Karen lay there beside him for longer than she knew was wise. She languished there and dreamed her impossible dreams while outside the cold rain seeped from the sky and dusk began to gather.

MIGUEL'S EYES OPENED and sparked with knowledge, instant knowledge of Karen. She was everywhere around him, enfolding him, her scent, her warmth, her very aura.

He sat straight up in the dark room and felt her presence as if she were beside him. And he remembered. Her body stretched out alongside him, her hands on his, smooth and warm, trembling. Then lower, her touch, on his hip, his...

A terrible silent wail rose in him. Was she mad, coming to him like that? Didn't she know that he would awaken and feel her all around him, in him, probing the depths of his dark soul?

The memory of her sweet, coppery taste assailed him suddenly as if he had tasted of her only moments ago. Tasted the hotness of her and been denied fulfillment. And with that memory the hunger came swiftly. It came to Miguel as a predator, clawing at him; his arteries were threads of agony in his body.

He staggered to his feet, shaken, inhumanly cold, the thirst unbearable, the need for *her* draining his strength, twisting whatever rational thoughts he desperately tried to muster.

For a time he fought the monster within. He paced, tried to collect himself, but it was useless.

And then she knocked at his door.

"Go... away," he groaned, sudden fire blazing in his eyes. Karen. Just on the other side of that door. Karen. Stretched out next to him. The scent of her still on him, his clothes, his hands. He put his hands to his face and drew that irresistible scent into his nostrils, and his body cried out with a thirst he could no longer control.

"Miguel? Are you awake? Miguel? I thought I heard..."

"Go away! Damn you, go away!" he breathed, weak and yet possessing the strength to burst through that door and take her. Yes, he had all the strength in the world for that.

"Miguel, what... what is it?"

He stopped dead in the room, a shadow among shadows, and he stared fiercely at that flimsy wood, his eyes burning embers. "You fool," he rasped. "You fool, to have come near me!" And then suddenly he spun around, snatched up his long coat and threw open the door leading to the hall.

The last thing he heard was her cry, a sobbing plea to forgive her.

It was raw outside. Raw and raining, and the streets leading to the river were deserted. Miguel staggered down them, fog swirling around his legs, his eyes searching, searching, wholly unaware of the gathering of shadows that stalked him, moving alongside a warehouse only yards behind him, relentless.

Karen, Karen, Miguel's brain cried. What had he done to her, accused her of? Was this her fault? He was a fiend, too weak to destroy himself, too weak to resist the simple beauty of the only person on this earth who mattered to him! Karen. Her warm, lovely body beside his and he could do nothing, he could fulfill neither her nor himself. He could only hunger.

He moved along the river's edge, where the darkness concealed his misery, just as it dampened the din of the city. It was in this dark slipstream that he felt a certain freedom. It was almost as if he were viewing the world from behind smoked glass—he could see out, but no one could see in.

He strode along the old lanes and alleyways, searching for that inner safety that the shadows always granted him, but tonight no peace would come. He could still sense Karen all around him, and his accursed hunger only grew. It was futile, he knew, to fight it any longer.

He spotted the woman moving through the mist by the river's edge. She looked drunk. Swaying, stumbling, bumping into the side of a pier house, staggering on.

He followed, telling himself, promising himself, that this one he would let go—she'd done nothing save imbibe too much alcohol. Still, he followed, moving with the shadows, the curls of fog his silent vehicles. She came to a dockside pub and he watched, praying that she would go in, hoping she would not. He was torn, his thirst rising like a fever, when suddenly there was someone else there, also stalking the woman who stood, swaying, at the door to the pub.

The woman, sensing potential trouble, began to move along again, half looking over her shoulder, half tripping. And then the man who'd followed went up to her. When she put up a hand to ward him off and then let out a strangled yelp, Miguel moved in.

What became of the woman he neither knew nor cared. Surely she'd scrambled off, terrified, maybe never to touch a drink again. What Miguel did care about was the man. And as he sank down to the ground with him, the fog enshrouding them, he thought only of assuaging his need.

He fed. Quickly. And when he was done he lifted his head, felt the familiar sweet rush to his veins, languished in it for a long moment, his head tipped skyward into the rain as the ache inside abated.

Reason returned slowly and inevitably. Yes, the man still lived. And on the heels of that thought came the image of Karen, the memory of how he'd just left her there, alone, frightened. The words he'd spoken to her...

Miguel rose and pulled his coat around him, the warmth still singing inside him. Karen, he thought again. He had to get back to her, explain. But how could he explain? How could he tell her, describe to her the torment of her closeness, the all-encompassing need, his weakness? And he'd blamed her. It was unforgivable. If she ran away this very night he would not, could not, fault her. He was a monster.

Miguel hurried back along the riverbank, riddled with guilt, when he heard it, an unearthly sound, his name—*Miguel, Miguel.* The words came drifting along the fog. *You have not done a proper job.*

Baltazar.

As quickly as he'd rushed away from his victim, he returned, fear speeding his steps. By the time he got there, it was, as he'd feared, too late. Baltazar had finished the man off, his head lifted to the night sky, his lips bloodred.

"Oh, so tasty," Baltazar whispered, sated. "But surely not as delicious as the one you let go, the woman."

"You . . . did not . . ." Miguel ground out.

"No. But I should have. Women are so much more succulent. More like honey, wouldn't you say?" And he grinned a death's-head grin.

Miguel looked away, down at the man who was clearly dead. Slow, hot rage burned inside him.

"Have you ever killed, Miguel?" Baltazar said. "I doubt it. Alas, I did make an error when I selected you, a priest. And all the trouble I went to . . . Your mother, your sister, just to get you there."

Very slowly Miguel raised his eyes to his enemy.

"You mean, all these years and you did not know? How naive, my old friend, how stupid."

"You lie," Miguel said, desperate for it to be true. If he thought for a moment that somehow he'd caused the deaths of his family . . . "Tell me you lie!" he demanded, but Baltazar only laughed, and that was when Miguel sprang on him, and the age-old death struggle was played out once more.

They fought unlike other men, not with fists or feet or mere brute strength. Rather they came at each other with both their minds and their bodies, as if reading each other's thoughts, anticipating each other's moves, outwitting their opponent by ruse.

Their *danse macabre* was not an orchestrated ballet. It was primitive, bestial, two viciously cunning animals locked in mortal combat, each willing to tear the other's heart out.

Miguel fought harder than he ever had before, coming at Baltazar time and again with a killer instinct that amazed and frightened him. He used his wits to better advantage, too, though Baltazar had the greater strength. If their struggle resembled anything from this world it would have looked like two great jungle cats—one a tawny lion, the other a sleek panther—circling each other then striking, spitting, hissing, growling, locked in a tumble of fury.

It was exhausting. As the fog wrapped around Miguel's legs and he circled his opponent, he began to realize that once again there would be no victor. In the end, as they crouched and faced each other, Miguel knew it was indeed useless to go on, though he hid this knowledge from Baltazar's mind, instead sending out to him his hate and willingness to fight on forever.

It was Baltazar who finally gave a bloodcurdling laugh and then sprang off into the fog, his mirth echoing along the riverbank, striking terror into the hearts of those men who were about at that hour.

Miguel stood there overcome with exhaustion, staring into the fog after his old enemy until the sound of a siren reached him. And then it was his turn to go. He glanced down at the body of Baltazar's victim, felt a wave of sorrow and guilt, then he, too, left, his body racked with pain, the night seeming to swallow his hunched figure.

"Oh, my God," Karen breathed when he came through the door, his clothes torn, his face haggard.

But he told her it was all right. He sagged into a chair, drained, and told her only that he had met Baltazar and they had struggled.

"But..."

"It is all right, Karen," he whispered, his head bowed. "It will be fine in time. And the things I said earlier...blaming you. I was wrong to do that, and you must find it in your heart to forgive me."

But she waved that off for a moment. "Baltazar. Did you...is he...?"

Wearily, Miguel shook his head, and Karen sank down on the floor beside him, holding his hands, tears brimming in her eyes.

"Miguel, will he keep after you always? Even after we find the cure?" she asked, and he felt in his belly the fear that made her voice shake.

Now was the supreme effort, the big lie. *Forgive me,* he thought. "No, Karen, of course not. He will no longer be interested. I would present no challenge to him."

She believed him, he saw. She wanted to believe. Good. When, if, the time ever came to tell her the truth, he would do what he must. He felt tired then, defeated. Why had it never occurred to him before that it was impossible to take the cure while Baltazar was still at large? *Fool.*

"Are you still angry at me?" she was asking. "About what I did earlier?"

"Karen," he said, feeling the lovely warmth of her hands in his. "What you did, what you yearn for, is as natural as the rising of the sun. I know that. It is I who am to blame, who cannot give you the simple pleasures you deserve any more than I can watch the rising of the sun." And then carefully, a far-off look in his eyes, he pressed his lips to her forehead and whispered, "In five hundred years it is perhaps the one thing I have missed the most."

"What?" she breathed.

"The feel of that brilliance on my face, that warmth, Karen. To once more feel that . . ."

CHAPTER FOURTEEN

IT WAS, OF COURSE, dark in Finland when they landed at the airport. Dark and very cold, and there was snow on the ground. Miguel had arranged for a car to meet them, and it was waiting, motor purring, while the driver fetched their bags from customs. For once Karen was truly glad for the service Miguel took for granted, because she was very tired, exhausted, in fact. She hadn't slept, because she'd been so worried about Miguel, and now she had a whole new lexicon of things over which to agonize. Baltazar, the cure they were seeking, the awful, wrenching love she felt for Miguel, the impossibility of it all . . .

"Karen?"

"Um, oh, yes," she said, her head resting on the soft leather of the limo's back seat.

"Do you feel well?" came his voice from the warm darkness of the vehicle's interior.

"I'm fine, just tired," she murmured.

"Tired. You are sure? There is nothing else wrong?"

"Just tired, Miguel, really."

"We will be at the hotel soon," he said, "and you can sleep."

In answer Karen reached over and touched his hand, just once, lightly.

When they reached Helsinki proper, Karen's curiosity took over, and she looked out the window despite her weariness. The boulevards were broad, many of the buildings built in a formally beautiful nineteenth-century style of architecture as they got closer to the city center. On the airplane Miguel had told her that film companies often used Helsinki whenever they filmed Russian movies set in the past; the city certainly did have a weighty and somber central-European look. Despite the very late hour, there were still some people on the well-lit streets, although most of the bars and restaurants were closed, and there were cars on the wide avenues, especially Volvos and Mercedes. Helsinki had a prosperous look, no doubt about it.

"The Finnish people, you know, call their country Suomi," Miguel said. "Finland is only a name given to them by Sweden, who ruled the country for hundreds of years. The Finns are not of the Scandinavian race at all, although they've intermarried for centuries. They are racially akin to the Hungarians, and their language is similar, as well."

"Do you know Helsinki well?" she asked.

"I have not been here since 1940, and then the country was in the midst of a war against the Russians. It was a terrible time. The Winter War, it was called, and Finns dug up cabbages frozen in the ground so as not to starve."

"How terrible."

"Finland had a bad time of it then. They were forced to make a treaty with Germany against the Allies, all because of Russia, you understand, and when Germany lost the war, the Finns had to pay reparations to the Allies. But they did it, and succeeded in keeping Russia out. They are a very proud and stubborn people."

"And Yuri?" Karen asked quietly.

"A good...friend. One of the few. He fought in that war because he had principles, and he met a woman. I did not understand at the time, not at all. I thought he was foolish, talking as he did."

"Talking—how?"

"About his mortal woman, about wanting to stay and grow old with her. Insanity." Miguel bowed his head. "Or so I thought at the time."

"But you didn't stay, Miguel. Why?"

"I never stayed anywhere for very long. And I followed Baltazar, you see. When he left, I did, too."

"Where did you go?"

"Russia, the Soviet Union, actually. I followed Baltazar to Siberia, to the Gulags, where Stalin was murdering those who opposed him. The situation was ripe for a creature of Baltazar's habits."

"But you didn't find him?"

"Yes, I found him, several times."

She turned away and looked out the window, unable, unwilling, to imagine those meetings. She'd just seen Miguel return from one of them, and it was frightening how much it had taken out of him.

Their hotel was the Strand Intercontinental, a large, modern building near the seaport. It was done in the ultracontemporary design for which Finland was famous—sleek, clean lines, chrome and glass and pale wood, bright-colored, wildly patterned fabrics—and Karen thought that the brightness somehow must serve to dispel the endless dark of winter.

The decor did little to cheer her, though, as she waited wearily while Miguel checked in. She glanced around idly, noting the number of people still milling about, some walking in from the cold, many of them clad in elegant fur coats and hats. And that was when she noticed one particular couple, quite handsome, though there was something else...

Karen was certain that no one else in a million years would have noticed it, but the woman, a beautiful blonde with exquisitely white skin, paused, only momentarily, and made eye contact with Miguel. She then resumed walking toward the bank of elevators, but when she whispered something to her partner, he, too, made eye contact with Miguel.

They knew one another, Karen realized, and her heart began a slow pounding. Were they...?

Miguel had returned to her side, keys in hand. "I am sorry it took so long," he said. "I know you are tired." He began to move toward the elevators where a bellboy waited with their luggage.

"Miguel," Karen said, and she put a hand on his arm, stopping him. "That couple just getting on the elevator..."

"Yes?" he said mildly.

"You...you know one another."

For a long moment his eyes fixed on her, and then he said, "Yes."

"Are they..."

"Yes."

"Oh" was all she could say.

But before they began toward the bellboy again, Miguel said quietly, "It would be best if you say nothing more about this. Should we meet with them again, pay no attention. There are many of my...kind here in this northern land. It is the long winters, you understand, the darkness."

"Oh," Karen said again. "Oh."

They were shown to a suite, two bedrooms and a beautifully decorated living room, all blues and grays and swirling designs on the drapes and upholstered furniture.

Karen desired nothing more than a shower. Miguel, though, appeared distracted and said that there was something he needed to do. "I shall be back shortly," he said. "Lock the door behind me."

"You're going to find them," Karen said, looking up sharply from her suitcase.

"Perhaps," he allowed.

"You think they might know something about Yuri."

"It is a possibility."

"Oh, Miguel," she said, suddenly reenergized, "if they do know... If..."

But he put out a hand. "Do not get your hopes up, Karen. Just, please, make certain the door is properly latched, and I shall be back presently."

"All right," she said quietly, but gave him a hopeful smile, anyway.

While he was gone she showered in the spacious blue-tiled bathroom, letting the hot water flow over her for a long time, until the entire room was filled with steam. When she finally turned the water off and stepped out of the shower she had to open the door and rub on the mirror to clear the glass. She was peering at her reflection, her wet hair wrapped in a towel, when a swift blurred shadow appeared in the glass. She whirled around. "Miguel?" But there was nothing there, only the wisps of steam still floating in the hot, moist air.

"Miguel?" she said, but something in her already knew she'd get no answer. Her heart began a slow, heavy beat, and she wrapped a towel around her, forcing herself out into the bedroom.

"Miguel?" she tried again, her voice faint. Water pooled at her bare feet, soaking the carpet. "Okay," she said, taking a breath, "I know someone's here." Karen felt it then, a movement of air, as if something or someone had passed right in front of her. Goose bumps rose on her skin, and her breath came fast and hard.

It was him. Somehow he'd gotten in. It had to be Baltazar.

She stood stock-still, fear tingling along her spine. "I'm not afraid of you," she managed to say. "Why don't you show yourself?"

Again, that movement of air, a cool whisper against her skin. With all the courage she could muster, she turned around slowly, looking behind her. Nothing, nobody. Then slowly, slowly, she backed up against the wall and stood there, waiting, all her senses straining. And then she heard it, a noise out in the suite's living room, an almost imperceptible sound of something soft brushing against carpet, and her heart burst in her chest.

He was gone. She sensed it. She took a deep breath and forced her feet to move, across her bedroom, into the blue-splashed living room where the hothouse flowers in the beautiful Itala glass vase were shedding their petals. Then she was running to the door, fumbling with the handle. It was still locked.

When Miguel finally returned, Karen had calmed herself, had even tried to convince herself she'd imagined the whole incident. She'd dried her hair and sat in an upholstered, modernistic blue chair, bundled in a bathrobe, her legs tucked under her, reading brochures. He came in so quietly she almost didn't hear him. Her pulse leapt.

"Ah," he said, "I thought you might have been asleep."

"I was waiting for you."

He sat in a matching chair across from her. "You wished to hear what we spoke of, those others and I?"

"Yes. But first, Miguel, I..." She stopped, not wanting to upset him. Maybe she *had* imagined the whole incident. "Did they know Yuri?" she asked.

"No, they did not. However, they have heard of him. Rumors, whispers. From long ago. It may be that he did undergo some bizarre change, or so the tales go."

"Miguel, did you find out where they heard this from? Did you ask them for names?" she asked eagerly.

He held up a hand. "They were quite uncomfortable talking about it. And they knew nothing substantial. You must understand, Karen, that talk of a cure, of becoming mortal strikes fear into their hearts. It means death to them, age and sickness. They are not all as I am. You must know that the lure of eternal life, eternal youth, is too seductive for most. Even, sometimes, for me."

She sat there and studied him, this strange creature whom she loved. Sometimes she knew him so well it was as if they were two halves of a whole, yet sometimes he was incomprehensible to her. Inadvertently her fingers went up to her neck, to touch the fading marks as she considered what to say.

"Miguel, do you... are you truly willing to give up immortality? I mean, maybe you haven't thought about it enough."

He stood up as if it were not his own muscles propelling him, but some unseen force. He folded his arms and frowned, two vertical lines appearing between his eyes. "You ask me that, Karen? You ask me after what I have told you? You have seen me suffer, have you not?"

"Yes, but I . . . you have to be sure."

He turned on his heel and went to the window. He was quiet for a time, and when he finally spoke it was seemingly on another subject entirely. "When I saw this harbor last there were ships burning, explosions, men dying, blood. . . ." He pivoted toward her. "That was half a century ago. And twenty years earlier in France men died. In Africa, Japan, New Zealand, Peru. Wars, famine, pogroms, catastrophes. Five hundred years, and it goes on." He came close to her and looked down at her, his eyes hooded. "Enough. I have seen enough. I want an end, yes, to the loneliness and the horrors I must witness in every age. I want an end to the cravings that control me. Yes, Karen, I am sure."

She didn't say "What if we can't find the cure?" but she didn't have to; she knew he was thinking the same thing. The thought would remain unspoken between them, an unacceptable alternative. She was going to say something to him, something hopeful and loving, but he had stiffened and was focusing inward, as if a hidden voice had drawn his attention.

"What?" Karen asked. "Miguel, what is it?"

He didn't answer; instead he went back to the window and put his hand on the glass, his head bowed, concentrating. Then he turned and leveled his gaze at her, and she saw the glint of sapphire in his eyes. "He was here," Miguel said, his voice low, resonant, dangerous.

She froze, her hands clasped in front of her.

"He was here," he repeated.

"Yes," she whispered.

Emotions flowed across Miguel's face. Hate, fury, fear for her. He came close to her again, standing over her, his face set now, implacable. "Did he touch you?"

"No, Miguel, I wasn't even sure. I never saw him. It was just ..."

"He was here," Miguel repeated, "damn his evil soul!"

"How did he get in?" she asked, afraid of the violence of Miguel's emotions.

He said nothing, his face as hard and white as ice, but he went to the window and closed the lock, then yanked the drapes shut.

"The window," Karen breathed.

"There is a balcony outside," Miguel said. "I should have checked. I should have secured everything!" He whirled to face her. "You are never to be alone, do you understand? I will be with you every waking moment. Karen, do you hear me?"

"Yes."

He was pacing back and forth, agitated. He cursed in Spanish, then in some other language. She curled up in the chair, quiet, not wanting to incite him further.

"This time he has gone too far! This time I will finish him," Miguel muttered.

And that night, actually the early hours of the morning, when Karen retired, Miguel checked her room, her closet, her window, saw her into bed, stood at her door to shut off the light. "Sleep well," he said. *"Duerme bien."*

"Good night, Miguel," she said sleepily. "See you tomorrow."

The next day, as the sun made its low arc in the winter sky and Miguel still lay in his darkened room, Karen pored over telephone books for Helsinki and its suburbs, looking for the name Karlov. It was not there. He could live in another city, or he could have left the country, but if he'd been in Finland in the past, there would surely be a record of him somewhere. Finland was not a very large country, after all. She waited impatiently for the sun to set, which it did remarkably early this time of year; by two o'clock the sky was dimming, and Karen was dressed and ready to begin the search.

They had discussed the best way to go about this task. Miguel had already explained to Karen that the Finns were sticklers for keeping records of their citizens. There was an all-encompassing system of social security for everyone, which ensured that all Finnish citizens receive pensions no matter where they reside.

No one escaped the net of government record-keeping. Somewhere there would be information about Yuri Karlov—an address, a marriage certificate, a pension, a death certificate. Something.

They walked to the government building to which they'd been directed, a solid, imposing stone edifice. The office they were looking for read *Kasanelakelaitos* in Finnish, *Folkpensionsanstalten* in Swedish. National Social Insurance was the closest Miguel could translate it for Karen.

He spoke to the lady behind the counter in his limited Finnish, but the clerk's English was quite serviceable, so Karen could follow the conversation.

"Yuri Karlov," the clerk said, typing the name into her computer console. "I must tell you, sir, that it would take some while to locate records for 1940, if that was the last date Mr. Karlov resided here." She waited while names scrolled down her screen.

Karen held her breath. It seemed to take forever, but it must have only been minutes.

"No Yuri Karlov, I am very sorry, sir, not in these records. There is no one of that name receiving a pension."

Karen's heart fell. Miguel turned to her, his face showing neither hopelessness nor disappointment. "Shall we try elsewhere?" he asked in a smooth, uninflected voice.

"There are church records," the clerk said. "All births, deaths, marriages and divorces are registered there. It may be difficult to find one name, however.

If you knew his official number, it would help you in your search."

"Wait," Karen said, "could you try the woman? Miguel, what was her name?"

"I only knew her first name. Hilkka."

Karen turned to the clerk. "Please, could you try Hilkka Karlov?"

Again the woman tapped on her console, and they waited, Miguel absolutely immobile, Karen twitching with impatience.

Finally the woman looked up at them. "There is a Hilkka Karlov here, yes."

"Oh, my God," Karen breathed.

"She receives a pension."

Karen laughed with joy. "We've found her!"

"Perhaps this is not the same Hilkka," Miguel said.

"It is. I know it!"

"But there is no Yuri, no husband of this woman," he said.

"Exactly! Miguel, don't you understand? This is Yuri's wife, and Yuri must be . . ."

"Dead," Miguel said in a strange voice.

"Then he found the cure!" Karen cried. "Miguel, he found the cure!"

THEY DINED AT THE HOTEL, in the beautiful restaurant with its contemporary art collection. Rather Karen dined; Miguel was too distracted to even attempt disguising his lack of appetite this evening. He'd ordered only coffee.

"We'll drive up there tomorrow," Karen was saying. "It's only a hundred miles. Urjala. A village on a lake. We'll find her, Miguel, I know it." Her voice was full of determination. She was beyond hoping. For Karen the cure was a fact, nearly accomplished.

"Yes," he said, and the anticipation, the triumph, he saw in Karen's eyes made him even more anguished. Ah, the disappointment when it came would be that much worse. And even if, by some remote chance they did actually find this cure, how would he protect them both from Baltazar? How? In a puny mortal state, he had no hope of standing off his enemy. And Baltazar would like nothing better than to foil Miguel, take Karen from him—God forbid!—take her and possess her and . . . it was unthinkable. No, it could not happen.

Think, he had to think. How to finally vanquish Baltazar, how to tell Karen? How to tell her that because of him, her life—nay, something worse than her life—was in peril?

But she was talking again. "We'll rent a car. I'll drive. It's too late tonight, but tomorrow we'll leave as soon as you get up." Her words came quickly, piled one upon the other, and there was a frenetic light in her eyes. For him, all for him, this ceaseless energy of hers that radiated beauty. Could others see the new gleam in her eyes, the graceful movements of her hands, the sweet seductive curve of her mouth, the beautiful line of her pale brows when she frowned over some problem? Ah, *por Dios,* that it would all be dashed, and she would lose her exquisite innocence and her hope. Or worse...

"Karen," he said quietly, "it may not be as simple as you think. This woman may not be Yuri's wife, and if she is, she may not know anything about a cure. Perhaps Yuri was destroyed in some other way."

"No!" Karen said fiercely. "It *is* her, and she'll know. Oh, yes, she'll know. Don't you have any faith at all, Miguel?"

He tried to smile, a futile effort. "Not really, Karen. I lost it all, you know."

She looked at him for a long time, and he saw tears brimming in her eyes. Then she dashed them away with a hand. "No," she repeated, "I believe it's going to work out. I have enough faith for both of us, Miguel."

Being close to Karen was double agony. He wanted her ceaselessly, every moment. The whiteness of her neck, the way her golden hair swayed against her cheek, her pink earlobe, her small capable hands, the swell of her breasts under her blouse. He felt the cravings writhe inside him, and he repeated the mantra to himself: *I will not touch her, I cannot touch her.*

"Three hours or less, that's all it'll take, and we can find her cabin with no trouble. It's a tiny place. I looked on a map," Karen was saying.

She'd offered herself to him. He blinked, staring at her pink lips, at her throat as she swallowed a sip of wine. *Karen, you know not what you do to me.*

"Miguel, do you hear me?"

"Yes, I hear you. We will do as you wish. Of course we will."

"Miguel," she said, her gray blue eyes wide and so very earnest, "it won't be long. And then...everything will change. It will be so wonderful."

That it might be true! He considered for a moment, a split second, what it would be like to exist as a mortal. Loving Karen, sharing, raising a family, growing old together, small irritations, tragedies, maybe, pain and sorrow and unutterable joy. Life. And then he discarded the thought, and hopelessness enfolded him in its familiar shroud.

"Yes, Karen," he repeated, smothering the flames that licked at his innards, those bright hot yearnings that wanted her, all of her, flesh and blood and bone, to be possessed by him, now and forever.

In their suite she came to him, stood close, too close, her eyes inexpressibly sad. "I know how hard it is for you. I know how good you are," she said, and she put her small warm hand up to stroke his face. "It'll work out, Miguel. I know it will."

He drew back, not wanting to hurt her feelings, but afraid of his own reactions.

Her hand dropped to her side. "I love you, Miguel. Everything will be all right." Her voice was a gentle caress.

He stepped back farther. "Go to bed, Karen."

She sighed, her shoulders slumped. "I'll take care of the rental car tomorrow, Miguel. It won't be long now."

"And lock your door," he said.

"Yes, Miguel."

At dawn he lay in his darkened room, waiting for oblivion to overtake him. The sun was poised to rise in the cold gray sky of the city on the Baltic. The northern lights had ceased their dancing display. He lay there and probed with his senses. Yes, that presence...it was still there, close, too close. He could hear in his head Baltazar's mocking laugh, he knew Baltazar's intent, and he knew with certainty that Karen was in danger as long as Baltazar walked the earth. How could he protect her as a mortal? The thought churned in his mind until he was finally claimed by the darkness he sought.

They left Helsinki for the drive north just before four that afternoon. It was already full dark, and they were out of the city environs quickly as Miguel directed Karen from a road map.

She was trying to be cheerful, he could tell, and it was a valiant effort. "So I called home while you were asleep," she said. "I had to figure the time there, you know. Well, I got my mother and told her I was fine." She laughed then, and Miguel tried not to feast his eyes on the gleam of her teeth or her profile, the tiny blond hairs on her cheek made visible by another car's headlights. "And you know what she said? Why would anyone go to Finland in the winter for a vacation?"

"A vacation," he replied dryly.

"She asked about you," Karen said shyly, giving him a sidelong glance. "I told her you were the most wonderful guy on earth."

He stirred in his seat and turned his head as if he were watching the lights of the countryside go by. Ah, but she wounded him when she said things like that! *Family, mother-in-law,* words that pierced him to the heart. He did not belong to that world, he *could* not belong.

The drive was easy, the highway in good repair. The country was as Miguel recalled once they left the city— forests of evergreen and birch, hills, distant lakes. Fog lay in the low spots, drifting around tree trunks, lying over the black water of the lakes. A three-quarter moon threw shadows on the snow.

"Gosh, this reminds me of the Adirondacks," Karen said after a time. "When I was a kid, we went camping in the Adirondacks one summer. By a lake. It looked just like this."

"It is peaceful now," Miguel said. "It is hard for me to believe the war was fought here. It seems as if it were yesterday."

"It was more than fifty years ago, Miguel."

"And I am still the same, exactly the same as the day I left. Everything else changes, everything grows in its allotted pattern, blooms, dies. Everything," he said bitterly.

"Don't," she whispered. "Don't torture yourself. We're almost there."

He wanted to warn her. He wanted to say, "Karen, there is no cure, and if there was I could not dare avail myself of it before I destroy Baltazar." But he couldn't bring himself to do that to her. Not yet. Not until he had to.

Silence lay between them as they raced through the night. It sat heavily, breathing in all the air, all the hope.

"Well, we must be close," Karen said with forced cheer. "Look on the map, Miguel. How far is it?"

"Six miles, ten kilometers," he said.

"Oh Lord! My heart just gave a jump! We're almost there. Oh, Miguel." She dared a quick glance at him. "How well do you know this Hilkka? I mean, Yuri was your friend, but...do you think she'll remember you?"

"I do not know. I only met her once or twice."

"Did she...um, did she know you were...like Yuri?"

"Ah, yes, she did. She knew, and I made her very uncomfortable."

"But she loved Yuri."

"He thought so," Miguel said.

"Of course she did! They got married, didn't they?"

"One might surmise that."

Urjala was a collection of buildings, some picturesque log cabins from the old days, some newer, brightly painted houses. There was a lake like a black mirror, tall pines, clusters of white birches, sauna cabins built on the lake. Lights showed in windows, as if welcoming, beckoning them.

They asked the whereabouts of Hilkka Karlov at a gas station. The attendant only spoke Finnish, so Miguel got the directions.

"Well?" Karen said. "Well?"

"Yes, she lives here. Down by the lake."

"Oh, my God! Miguel, she's truly here! I don't think I really believed it."

Her innocence, the excitement she felt. He longed for a moment to share it with her, but refrained. No, he had other tasks to fulfill. Karen's agenda was not his. What he did not tell her was that the gas station attendant had recalled Yuri Karlov—he'd died six years before.

It had taken all of Miguel's self-control to remain calm when he'd heard that. So Yuri had succeeded, had grown old and died. He had found the cure, and he had lived his life out as a mortal man. His Hilkka was still here, nearby. And yet Miguel dared not even consider the ramifications. He could not.

Karen drove, following his directions, peering into the darkness, turning off the main road onto a long narrow driveway, covered with snow. The trees were close around them, casting moon shadows across the road.

"So, do we both go to see her? Or only you? Maybe the shock will be too much if we both go. I mean, she must be old now, Miguel. Does she speak English?"

Karen's questions came quickly. She hardly paused to draw breath. "I'm a nervous wreck. What if...?"

"There," he said, pointing, and Karen braked too quickly, sliding on the snow.

The small log cabin sat alone by the lake, a square sturdy building with a cheery glow from its windows and a question mark of smoke from the chimney that was quite visible in the moonlight.

Karen put a hand to her chest. "Oh, please, let her know what to do," she whispered to herself.

Miguel got out of the car and went around to Karen's side, opening her door. She looked up at him for a moment, then got out.

Together they stood facing the house, and without speaking they began walking across the moonlit snow that crunched coldly beneath their weight. Halfway there he felt Karen's hand touch his, then clasp it tightly, and even through his fears for her, his quandary over Baltazar, he considered the possibility that something might occur here tonight, a diverging of the paths, a choice, a difficult choice, but still...

He reached the cabin door, stood there, feeling Karen at his side. He raised a hand and knocked on the plank door, once, twice, loud in the nighttime stillness. They waited, together, and he felt Karen's hand trembling in his. A minute crawled by, then another. Finally there was a faint shuffling, a rustle from inside, and Miguel caught the scent of blood, old, slow-moving blood.

The door swung open, the light an elongated rectangle laid down on the snow, heat in his face, the sound of a fire crackling. A woman stood on the threshold, her face scored by lines, her gray hair pulled back strictly into a wispy bun. Her blue eyes were sharp, though, and took them in with no surprise, only a deep, weary worldliness.

She remained there studying them, and after a long minute she finally nodded and said, "I've been expecting you for a very long time." And then she held the door open for them to enter.

CHAPTER FIFTEEN

KAREN AWAKENED with a start and that disorienting sense of not knowing where she was for a moment, then she realized that she was home, in New York, in her own bed. She remembered now—she'd left Miguel's at dawn when he was asleep, and come back to her apartment to catch a few hours' rest, and because her nurse's uniform hung in the closet and she needed it.

She rose quickly, adrenaline pumping through her veins. Today was the day. Then she frowned. Miguel had been so strange last night, ever since they'd returned, in fact. She would have thought he'd have been happy—nervous, maybe—but happy, looking forward to what he'd told her over and over he coveted...a mortal existence, life. And yet now that it was within his grasp, he was distracted, decidedly unenthusiastic. It was as if he really didn't want to be cured.

She fixed herself some coffee and paced barefoot in her apartment, thinking, sipping from the mug. Could he have changed his mind? Could he? Now that the cure was imminent, had he decided not to go through with it?

No, she couldn't believe that. He suffered so. She knew his torment as if it were her own; she knew he loved her and wanted a life with her. She knew that.

Or did she?

Well, Karen had her duty to perform. She and Miguel had gone over the plan a dozen times. He hated the idea of stealing, but there was no other way: it wasn't possible to buy blood.

She dressed in her nurse's uniform and tried to calm down. She wouldn't get caught—she simply couldn't, because Miguel's entire existence, their existence together, depended on her now. It was a weight on her shoulders, but she could handle it. Hadn't she handled dozens, hundreds, of crises in her time? If something went wrong at the hospital today, something came up that they hadn't anticipated, she'd handle it.

Karen pinned her hair back with barrettes and checked her appearance in the mirror. She looked like her old self, and today that was good, no one would remember she was supposed to be on vacation. And it was possible she'd run into someone who knew her.

She took a taxi to the hospital, the big, oversize purse she'd bought sitting on the seat next to her. It was a bright, cold January day, and the sunlight on her shoulders dissipated her tension. Soon, she thought, soon Miguel would be able to feel the warmth again. God willing. Soon.

Paying the driver a block away from the hospital, Karen stepped out into the brisk air and breathed deeply. She'd gotten out a block early because the last thing she wanted was to draw unnecessary attention to herself. It was daytime, and she hadn't worked a day shift in over a year, but she could only hope there would be no one on duty who would know her face and question her presence.

Karen entered the hospital through the employee door in the rear, near the service entrance. There were delivery trucks crowding the alley, men pushing dollies of cases of food and linens and hospital supplies. Two nurses walked past her and merely nodded as she headed to the locker room, where she hung up her coat.

She was ready to begin, her purse under her arm, when the door swung open. In came Julia Martin, who'd once been Karen's supervisor. "Why, hello... Karen, isn't it?" the woman said.

"Hi, Mrs. Martin," Karen managed to say past the sudden dryness in her throat. "Nice day."

"Yes, it is. So good to see the sun again. Cold, though, real cold."

"Sure is," Karen said, pushing open the door. "Well, good to see you."

"You take care," Julia Martin said, and that was that.

Karen got off the elevator with two orderlies on the fifth floor. She wasn't afraid of getting caught in the blood bank—she had keys to it. What she was afraid of was that someone was going to notice the purse she was carrying. That part was odd. She and Miguel had discussed this, but there was no way around it. None.

Once she was out of the blood bank no one would notice her bag. Nurses were always carrying their purses when coming on shift, heading to lunch, going off shift. No problem. But entering the blood bank with one was against the rules.

She went to the ladies' room three doors down from her destination and waited. As planned. And, as planned, it wasn't long before a Code Blue call came over the speaker system. A Code Blue meant that there was a life-threatening situation somewhere on the floor, and nurses and doctors scurried to respond. It was the perfect time for Karen to make her move. When the inevitable call came, she pushed open the rest room door and walked purposefully and swiftly to the locked door, inserted her key and went in.

Thank the Lord it was empty. Of course, they'd planned a cover story if Karen should need one. But as it was, she was safely by herself and worked quickly, taking five units of blood and the necessary IV apparatus, stuffing it all into her bag.

Karen's underarms were damp by the time she stood at the elevator doors, waiting. Her bag seemed too heavy and her cheeks were flushed. She was swept by sudden guilt, even though she and Miguel had agreed that there was no other way to restore his life. He'd even promised to donate a new, badly needed wing to the facility whether or not the cure worked, but Karen still felt like the worst of thieves.

It's for a good cause, she kept reminding herself, it's to save a life.

The elevator finally came. It was crowded, and a doctor dressed in his surgical greens was pressed right up against her purse. He knows, Karen thought desperately, he could feel the blood units against his arms!

But of course he didn't, and soon Karen was headed down the corridor toward the nurses' locker room, her knees rubbery.

Too easy, she kept thinking. It was going along too easily.

She got her coat, hoisted the heavy purse over her shoulder and left, passing a nurse whom she didn't recognize, merely nodding as she headed toward the rear exit. And that was when she ran into Dick Freeman.

"Whoa, there," he called, hurrying up behind her. "Hey, Karen, what on earth are you doing here? Thought you took a vacation." He held the door open for her.

Karen was faint with anxiety. "I...ah..." What was her cover story? Oh, God!

"What, did they call you in or something? Hell, half the staff is out with the flu," he said. "I got called in myself."

"That's right," she managed to say as he kept pace with her across the parking lot. She didn't even know where she was going.

"You want to grab lunch at Eddie's or something?" Dick asked.

"Ah, no, thanks," Karen said, the cold air stinging her flaming cheeks.

"Well," he said, nodding, "my car's over this way. You want a lift somewhere?"

"Um, no, thank you."

"Say," he persisted, "you feeling okay? You look a little flushed."

"I'm, ah, getting a touch of the, ah, flu myself," Karen muttered and then took off in the opposite direction, the purse so heavy on her shoulder that she prayed the seams wouldn't burst.

IT WAS THERE THE MOMENT Miguel opened his eyes that evening. And he knew it had been there all along; he simply had not seen it—the way to defeat Baltazar.

He rose, buoyed by this knowledge, amazed that it had taken him five hundred years to see it. But then, until the possibility of a cure had presented itself, there had been no reason to see it.

Yet on the heels of the hope that leapt in his chest came sudden sadness, a sense of remorse. He had spent the entire return journey to New York completely absorbed in the dilemma—how to vanquish his nemesis once and for all before attempting the cure. And because he had been preoccupied and afraid to confide in Karen, he had withdrawn from her, offering little help as she outlined her scheme to procure the necessary blood.

She had not appeared to notice his distance, however. She'd gone on and on excitedly, the hope in her radiating from her very pores. And he had been a cad. Now, here she was putting herself in peril, and he'd only been able to mumble something about being careful when she'd left for her apartment to try to get a few hours' rest before going to the hospital.

Miguel heard the chimes of the clock. Six in the evening. She was late. A pang of fear for her struck him—had the plan worked? If anything were to happen to her...

He instantly thought of Baltazar again. Now that he knew how to destroy Baltazar, he was easier in his mind, but it was still unspeakably dangerous for Karen to be alone outside of this house at night. And Baltazar must suspect nothing about this attempt at a cure. That was imperative. If he even sensed it, there was no doubt in Miguel's mind that he would try to get into Miguel's house and thwart their plans by any means possible. Yes, it was imperative he suspect nothing, for the one thing Hilkka had warned of repeatedly was the weakness that would overcome Miguel. He would not be able to protect Karen, and they were going to have to be very, very careful.

Where was she?

He dressed and went below, all too aware that darkness had fallen over the city some time ago. He'd warned her that if nothing else she must be back here by dusk!

Anxiety gripped him, and he went out into the night, standing at his wrought-iron gate, honing his senses. But it was impossible to sort out the many signals that assailed him. The one thing he was certain of: Baltazar was nowhere nearby.

But then, neither was Karen.

He waited. And waited. It wasn't until nearly six-thirty that a taxi pulled around the corner and Karen stepped out, hoisting a large bag onto her shoulder.

"Miguel!" she said, surprised. "Is something..."

"Where have you been?" he demanded.

"Waiting for a cab. It was rush hour. Miguel, has something..."

But he only waved off her question, took the heavy bag from her and led her inside.

It was the worst of bad luck that Baltazar had picked this time and this city to come back into Miguel's life. Then, Baltazar following him to Europe... It struck Miguel that perhaps Baltazar had already sensed something was afoot, and that was exactly why he'd been following Miguel.

"Are you or aren't you going to tell me what's wrong?"

"Nothing. There is nothing wrong. I was anxious that you were out after sunset. I told you how dangerous it could be."

"Well, nothing happened, and here I am safe and sound. And, Miguel—" she smiled widely "—I got it. You're holding it."

"What?" he said.

"The bag in your hand. That's it."

Miguel looked down at it, felt its weight, and suddenly he was overcome by the odor of blood, rich, coppery blood. "Yes," he breathed hoarsely, making a supreme effort to hide from Karen the instant thrill that swept him. "Everything went well, I take it," he said, forcing down the urge to open the bag, to look upon the plastic containers of ruby liquid.

Karen took her coat off, and he saw that she was wearing a white nurse's uniform, white stockings and shoes. Over her breast was pinned her name tag: Karen Freed, R.N. A nurse... Abruptly the image of white-robed sisters of mercy came into his head, women fearlessly aiding plague victims, women on battle-fields. His Karen was one of those dedicated souls. A rush of emotion shook him, so strong that for a time he forgot what was in the bag he held. And he could lose her, he might have to live on without her. No. He must be successful this night, and then he would give himself over to Karen.

"It was easy," she said, and he knew she was boasting a little.

"No one saw you?"

Karen shook her head. "I don't know if I was lucky or clever, but I got away with it. I didn't feel very good about it, though, Miguel. I've never, ever, taken any-thing from the hospital before. There are nurses who do, though, and..."

He took the bag and placed it on a table, stepping away. "You must not feel guilty, Karen. Even if I should not survive this cure."

"No..." she began.

"Even if I do not," he went on, "I have instructed my agent to see that the new wing on the hospital is erected."

"I don't want to hear about you not surviving, Miguel," she said firmly. "Half the battle will be your believing, your faith that you will make it."

A slow smile gathered at the corners of his mouth. "Karen the Nurse talking."

"That's right."

"It seems I will have little choice," he said.

They went together into the library, where Miguel built a fire. He knew how anxious Karen was to begin, anxious and nervous, too. As Hilkka had told them, there were no guarantees, no second chances. Yuri had barely survived the ordeal; there were others over the centuries who had not.

Miguel was not concerned about that, though. Not yet. And now he had to put her off, leave her here alone. How he despised himself for placing himself and Karen in this situation. And how he hated to have to delay again. In five hundred years he had never done anything so reprehensible as involving a mortal in his perverted life!

He still knelt by the hearth, feeling the heat of the flames as the kindling caught. An ember spat out onto the carpet, and he picked it up with his bare fingers, not even hiding his ability to do so from Karen. Then he stood, dusted off his hands and looked at her. Yes, her excitement was on her face, flushing it, and in her eyes. Dear Lord, he would disappoint her so badly.

"I think we should begin," she started to say, squaring her shoulders.

"Karen," he said carefully, "I do want to do this, believe me. I have no fear, and I trust you completely. There is something, however, that I must do before I attempt this cure. You will have to trust me."

The light fled her eyes. "What are you saying?"

"Only that I have a task to accomplish that could not be done if I were mortal or weakened by this process."

She stared hard at him, and then abruptly her chin came up. "Baltazar," she breathed. "You're going to..."

Miguel put a silencing finger to his lips and moved toward her. "I will say no more," he told her, and against his better judgment he pulled her to him and held her close, his mouth in her hair, his nostrils drinking in her scent, a wild and heady combination of blood and woman and cold, fresh air. "Trust me," he whispered, "as I trust you," and then he released her and went to the hall, fetching his coat.

"How long will you be gone?" she asked from behind him, a catch in her voice.

"I cannot say."

"Oh, God," she said, "Miguel, you won't..."

But he would hear no more. "This must be done. Now, stay here, Karen, in the sanctuary of the house, and I promise I shall return as soon as possible."

"Miguel..."

It was too late, though, for words. He merely touched the silken softness of her hair and then left, going out as the dark creature he was this last time, his form swiftly swallowed by the night.

KAREN DOZED FITFULLY in the big leather chair in the library. She couldn't really sleep, but she was too tired to do anything else. The only light came from one lead crystal lamp on the desk, a circle of light that left the corners of the room in shadow.

She dozed and jerked awake more times than she could count, and every time she woke with a start her heart would start pounding. She was frightened, so afraid for Miguel. He hadn't admitted it, but she knew he was out there somewhere tracking down Baltazar. She knew it as surely as if he'd told her.

No wonder he'd been so quiet, so distracted, putting her off. She saw it now. Sitting in the dim library with only a few red embers glowing dully in the fireplace, the clock ticking in the entryway, she understood. He had to take care of Baltazar before he became mortal. That was it.

Oh, Lord, he might be fighting with Baltazar right this minute!

She curled up in the chair, her legs under her, hugging herself and staring at the light. She listened for Miguel's step, the opening of the front door. All she heard was the creak and groan of the old house, the pop of a dying ember, the clock, the damn monotonously ticking clock.

What if he never came back? What if Baltazar destroyed him completely? What if they fought to a draw and Miguel refused to take the cure until he could win? Another five hundred years?

She dozed again, dreaming in confused snatches. Miguel lying somewhere with his enemy standing over him, triumphant. She jerked awake, cold, frightened. Miguel. But he wasn't there.

She rested her head on the back of the chair, closed her eyes, tried to relax. Her neck and shoulders ached with tension. She rolled her neck to loosen the muscles, took a deep breath. Miguel would come back; he simply had to.

Her eyes flew open, and she knew she'd been asleep again. But this time something had awakened her, something...

"Karen," he said from across the room.

She flew up out of the chair. "Miguel! Oh, my God, I was so worried!" She went to him, searching his face for answers, for signs of a struggle. "Where were you?"

"I was in the city," he said. "Some last-minute matters to attend to. As you can see, there was nothing for you to be concerned about."

She put her hands on his arms and looked into his eyes. "I was so worried. Miguel, please don't do that to me again." She felt his gaze on her, his eyes boring into her, and she flushed, knowing how he wanted her.

Then he moved back from her and averted his eyes. "It is near dawn, Karen."

"Oh, yes," she said, waiting for him to say something, explain why he'd been gone all night, what he'd been doing. Waiting for him to tell her he could not take the cure after all.

But all he did was step close to her, put a hand, a cool, smooth hand, on either side of her face and look long and deep into her eyes. "I am ready now," he said, his voice haunting, reaching down into her and resonating there. "I am ready for whatever the future may hold."

THE SUN STRUCK the bare branches of the trees in Riverside Park, reached further to touch the roof of Miguel's corner brownstone, slid lower down the squared-off stones, the black shutters, the iron grilles, the shrouded windows. A narrow bar of light knifed through an opening in the drapes at the bedroom window, picking out the colors in the oriental rug, the striped fabric of a chair, the deep garnet red of the bedspread.

Karen had pulled a chair up to the bed where Miguel lay. She watched him as he entered his state of unnatural sleep. His body was absolutely still, his eyes closed. No hint of life remained in him, no movement, no rise or fall of the chest, no furtive emotions tugged at his features. She studied him long after he was asleep, the slim length of his body under the spread, his elegantly handsome face, its lines clear and sharp, his brow, the curve of his nose, the dark line of his mustache, the faint smudge of whiskers on cheeks that he never had to shave. He was so pale, so cool. She laid a hand on his chest. Nothing, no beat, no movement of any kind. He was so beautiful, like a marble statue carved by the hand of a master. And he was her responsibility now. He could do nothing to help her—he'd relinquished all control to her. She had to justify his trust, protect him, take care of him, bring him through this ordeal.

Hilkka had told her how ill he'd be, how weak and vulnerable. He could die; Yuri had almost died. In fact, it had in the end shortened his mortal life.

"But it was worth it?" Karen had asked.

"Yes, yes, it was worth it," Hilkka had replied.

Karen rose from the chair and stood over Miguel, precisely like a surgeon at the operating table ready for the first incision. She took one last loving look at him as he lay there, drew in a deep, cleansing breath and went to work.

If Miguel could have seen her, he would barely have recognized his sweet Karen in the capable, taut-faced nurse who hovered over him, fixing the IV needles in his arms, draining on one side, ready for transfusion on the other. Deftly she taped the needles to his skin. He was almost ready now.

But first... Karen took the tiny bottle she'd carried from Finland and held it up to the light. An amber liquid filled the vial, a herbal infusion Hilkka had given her, the secret ingredient Yuri had found in ancient Egyptian writings in the British Museum, recorded in hieroglyphics that he was able to translate. For Yuri had been alive when they'd been written.

Very carefully Karen opened the vial—God forbid she should spill it!—and was instantly assailed by a strong odor that was completely unfamiliar. She sniffed it, wondering if that was foxglove she smelled, maybe some eucalyptus, mixed together with half a dozen other scents. Trained only in modern medicine, her first inclination was to be skeptical—but then, hadn't the ancient Egyptians concocted a method of embalming that was so powerful it had preserved bodies for five thousand years? And who knew how long those beautiful, ancient kings would have lain in that amazing state had modern man not disturbed their tombs.

No, Karen wasn't going to take this lightly at all. Even with every modern advance in medicine, they still didn't have the wondrous knowledge of those ancient peoples.

After a moment she carefully poured the liquid into the unit of blood she had ready, fixed the tube into the IV needle in Miguel's arm, a task she'd done countless times, so many times she could do it without thinking. But this time it was different—oh, God, so different.

There was only one thing left to do. Karen shut her eyes tight, whispered a prayer, then released the clip that held back the blood. She watched, holding her breath, as the red liquid flowed down the transparent tubing, down, down, through the needle, into Miguel's arm.

She watched him like a hawk, bending over him, laying a hand on his forehead from time to time, checking, adjusting the flow of blood.

Hilkka had described what could happen, what *would* happen, but it might not occur until the second transfusion, or possibly the third. Altogether there could be more than ten transfusions, a pint each night until she'd given him at least five quarts of blood. A larger man would require more, depending upon his weight, but Karen had figured on five. Time would tell.

After a while she sat in the chair by the bed, and in the dim light of the curtained bedroom she watched the blood drip, drip, into Miguel's cold white body.

THE NEW YORK UNIVERSITY coed was in heaven. She'd been attending classes for more than eighteen months at the excellent Greenwich Village school but had met only two boys with a maturity and sophistication that attracted her, and both of those fleeting romances had flared and fizzled quickly.

Sue was a pretty girl, and intelligent, with long raven black hair and Oriental features she'd inherited from her mother. Men were drawn to her exotic looks, though until last night Sue had always found flaws in the men that vied for her attention. Either they were too arrogant, too controlling, or, most often, they were too married. She'd almost given up hope of finding Mr. Right at college, figuring she'd just finish her education and begin a career, and maybe then she'd meet the perfect mate.

That was last night.

Tonight, Sue was walking on cloud nine.

She'd been heading home after her 8:00 p.m. biology class when she'd met him, the most wonderful, charming, handsome man she'd ever seen. Sure, he was maybe ten years older than she was, but who cared? Sue had dropped a couple of books while crossing West Ninth Street, and suddenly he'd appeared, asking if he could help, and instantly she had known she could trust him. There was just something about him, a gentlemanly quality, something. And then, in the light of a street lamp she'd seen him and her heart had swelled. He was, in Sue's estimation, an absolute replica of the young Robert Redford. No doubt about it.

He'd bought her coffee at a local café, the nicest, most debonair man she'd ever met.

If Sue had been forced to describe him, she would have said he was charming and deliciously sexy, though he seemed not even to be aware of it. They sat dining at a swank, intimate sushi bar, and Sue couldn't believe her good fortune. Maybe her karma was right, maybe all the stars in the heavens had lined up in perfect symmetry—it didn't matter. Sue only knew that life was suddenly very wonderful and very romantic. Was it possible to fall in love after only a few hours?

They walked after dinner, despite the brittle night. He seemed to enjoy it, although when he took her hand his was terribly cold.

"You're freezing," she said, laughing, happy, her insides melting each time he held her gaze with those beautiful blue eyes that seemed to mesmerize her. God, he was gorgeous! And smart and sophisticated. European, he'd said, of Nordic descent. He had a slight accent. A banker or something, who traveled a lot. He must be wealthy, Sue had guessed, because his clothes, though casual, were exquisite.

They talked while they strolled the darkened, cold streets of the Village, and Sue began to see and hear only him, as if they were the only two people alive in this huge metropolis. And then he said he'd like to invite her back to his place—a Madison Avenue address—but if Sue didn't feel right about...

"I'd like that," she said, so mature, no games. And mentally she congratulated herself for her selection of underwear, black lace, garter belt, the whole nine yards. But she wouldn't think about that, not yet. And wouldn't it be marvelous if they spent an evening at his apartment and he didn't even come on to her? He was that sort of man, she knew, and she'd wait.

"Oh, darn," he said when they climbed into a taxi.

"There's a chore I simply must do tonight. I don't know how I could have forgotten. It will only take a few minutes, but if you want, I can go alone and perhaps we could get together tomorrow."

"Oh," Sue said. "I can tag along. I mean, if you don't mind."

"Of course not." And he directed the cabby to an address on the Lower East Side, explaining to Sue, "It's a shabby neighborhood, I'm afraid. But a client of mine who's presently in Madrid is very interested in this old building, and I promised I'd give it a look before tomorrow. It won't take long."

"I don't mind," she said, and he bent and brushed her neck with his lips, whispering that she was an angel.

He let the taxi go, which was odd, she thought, but the notion was only fleeting. The truth was, Sue was excited. She'd never been in this section of New York, and it had an air of danger to it—run-down, collapsing buildings, huge vacant lots littered with dirty snow and trash, a sleazy bar on the corner. Somehow it all combined with the new experiences she was having and a new, worldly man. She was positive he could take care of himself anywhere. And that titillated her imagination.

"Awful place," he was saying as they entered the abandoned building, pushing aside a broken-in door. "Perhaps I should have taken you home."

"It is kind of...gross in here," Sue said, shivering, trying to adjust her eyes to the sudden blackness. And, oh God, was something scurrying over there? "Is your friend, the businessman, going to tear this down or something?"

"But of course," he said, taking her arm, leading her up a rickety flight of stairs. "Don't trip," he said kindly.

Sue followed, not liking this place at all now. And why did he have to check it out if the man was going to raze it? Oh, well, she thought, clinging to him, following him up, up.

The room took her by surprise. There were candles, which he lit, seeming to know just where they were located.

Sue was eyeing the place, disgusted, wanting only to get out of there. Even the candlelight that flickered on the walls seemed tarnished, she was thinking, and she never saw it coming, the shadow that slid across the floor behind her, slowly, growing, and the long-fingered hand that reached out to extinguish the candle beside her.

BALTAZAR FINGERED the delicate, lacy black thing that covered Sue's bosom. My, but women wore the most sensuous clothing, he thought, his fingers gliding up to her throat, so white, so creamy, the two holes still oozing blood. He stroked her bosom, feeling nothing but the texture of the lace, and leaned over, licking at the holes, his body racked in ecstasy.

"Oh, Sue, Sue," he groaned against her, "there was too little of you. And now you are drifting away from me." He shrugged eloquently, then lowered his head, sinking into her, sucking, his body going rigid with delight as he felt the small, slow pulse of her still beneath his lips; then that beat, beat, slowed even more, became faint against him, and finally it was gone.

He sat up, his mouth rimmed in scarlet, his eyes blazing, fire coursing through him. A deep moan welled up from his soul and hung in the cold air. So good, so good. Was it good for you, too, Sue?

After a time Baltazar cleaned himself in the bathroom, changing his shirt and sweater. And then he went back into the shabby room and stared at the lifeless thing, sweet Sue. Last night when he'd chosen her, he'd thought she would have lasted much longer, but then, even with all his powers, it was impossible to know. And now she'd disappointed him, and he was going to have to lug her over to the East River and dump her. Such a waste of time. To make matters worse, he was not yet filled. Almost. But he could feed again. Ah, well. And if he did, if he decided to drink once more this night—after all, the night was young— then he most certainly was going to select someone with more staying power. Someone like . . . Karen.

Yes. Karen. She had been floating in and out of his dreams for weeks now. Miguel's woman. The fairest of all women. Goodness and innocence radiated from her, the notion unbearably sensual to him. When he'd danced with her aboard the ship, held her so close, his thirst had been liquid fire in his veins.

Ah, Karen, so ready to be plucked. And she'd let Miguel have a drink or two, hadn't she? That one had staying power.

Baltazar shoved Sue's body aside and sat on the mattress and thought about that. Miguel and his woman. He'd followed them across the sea, to London, Finland—why had they been to Finland?—and back again. He'd trailed them out of pure curiosity, to see if Miguel, after so many, many years, was going to create a mate for himself. But he hadn't. He'd only taken little sips from her. Why? What was that accursed priest up to?

Well, Baltazar thought, grinning, the candlelight playing on his beautiful waxen face, he could always ask Karen. Lovely, sweet Karen.

He put his head back and allowed the memory of her scent to fill him, to kindle his cravings. Yes, he decided, Karen might be just the one to tell him what Miguel was up to. So, it was all very simple—he'd have to pay her a visit.

CHAPTER SIXTEEN

MIGUEL FIRST SAW the pale light in the room as another facet of his terrible confusion. It couldn't be, therefore it was not, and yet it was. His head swam with malaise, his body ached, betraying him in all ways. Light, he thought, and not from a lamp.

He closed his eyes and drifted back into a state that was neither wakefulness nor sleep; certainly it was not the familiar darkness he'd known when at rest for the past five centuries. He drifted in that murky sea, his consciousness punctuated by cramps and waves of unfamiliar discomfort as the sun made its winter arc over the city, and then, late in the afternoon, when sunlight still bathed the city, he awoke again.

He turned his head on the pillow, feeling something akin to fear when he saw that the room was still too light and that there were needles in his arms. And then he saw Karen through that strange, shimmering haze. She was sitting near the window, her head fallen to one side. She was asleep.

Miguel must have sunk back into that abyss again, because when he was conscious again the room was very dark and Karen was standing over him, her face serious, adjusting the IV tube and the bag that was attached to the bedpost above him. Through the mist of his vision and his delirium, Miguel's eyes fixed longingly on the plastic bag, the ruby liquid filling the tube. He wanted to groan, to hide his eyes, but he was too weak, too confused.

Blood, he thought, the sticky metallic feel of it a memory on his lips. Shouldn't he be thirsting for it, craving?

He tried to say something, but sudden nausea gripped him, and then he was vomiting, his head hanging over the side of the bed, Karen's hand on his brow while she held a pan for him.

"It's all right, it's normal. You *should* be getting sick," she said soothingly. "Remember what Hilkka told us."

He retched until he was certain his insides would rip apart, and still, each time he tried to collapse back onto the bed, the nausea rose and took him over.

"Go on, Miguel," her sweet voice kept urging, "be as sick as you need to be," and somewhere in his brain he had a flash of memory—his mother holding his head while he was sick. He was a boy. It was five hundred years ago—the last time he'd vomited.

When Miguel was done he rolled onto his back, licked strangely dry lips and passed out. The next time he came to it was nearly dawn and a wild panic seized him. "No!" he cried out, trying to sit up. "No! I cannot be awake for sunrise!"

And Karen was sitting beside him on the bed, pressing him back down, placing a cooling rag on his brow. "It's all right," she said over and over. "You awakened yesterday, Miguel, you already saw the light of day. You remember? It's all right.''

He did remember! But no, it had been a dream, an illusion, surely he had not been conscious during the day, he thought as terror ripped through him.

He ached all over. Only this pain was not craving or need. It was real physical pain as the ancient Egyptian poison worked on his cells, destroying, allowing others to awaken, cells that had lain dormant all those years. At moments the ache was excruciating, causing his sight to blur with white spots. At other times he passed out, welcoming the familiar oblivion of blackness.

But all the while Karen was there, at his side, wiping his brow, fetching a blanket when he shivered uncontrollably, moaning between chattering teeth, "I am so cold! I cannot bear the cold!"

Every waking moment he was aware, too, of the metamorphosis of his senses. Karen's voice. It seemed to come from the haze, soft, soothing. Her touch. It was as if an angel were laying healing hands upon his burning flesh. And when the cold overcame him, she was warm, so warm.

He opened his eyes once and saw a bar of light lying on the carpet, and he thought crazily that it was the most amazing sight—a bar of sun.

Smells were peculiar. His bedding, his hands, Karen. They came at him with a new, different sharpness from that which he had known, and then they would recede.

"Is this reality?" he asked her once.

The crisis came on the third day of his changing. He imagined that Karen had told him he was running a temperature—a temperature for him, that was. And then she was trying to get him up, but it was too hard.

"Miguel, we have to get you cooled down," she said. "It's too soon. Can you understand me? You're too warm, it's like a fever, but . . ."

No, he did not understand. He knew only that somehow he was on his feet, the needles gone, and she was supporting him, leading him toward the bathroom.

"Too weak," he groaned. "Leave me alone."

"I won't let you alone!" she said fiercely, pulling at him, dragging him. "Miguel, you listen to me, damn it, you will not die! Now move it! Help me get you in here. You've got to get cooled down."

They managed somehow, and he was aware of sitting in the bathroom, Karen tugging at his shirt, the shower running. And then he was naked. There were oily droplets of moisture—perspiration?—all over him and she was half steering him, half leading him, into the shower, getting soaked herself, holding him up.

"Help me, Miguel," she said, and he tried, leaning his fists on the cool tiles as the water streamed down his back. Cold, cold water. Not since the monastery had he felt cold water.

And then he was back sitting on the closed toilet, towels wrapped around his nakedness—a woman had just seen him naked—and she was rubbing him, drying him, his hair, chest, lower, her hands on him, quick and professional. He felt it, too, when she touched him there, and he was amazed, stunned—to have any feeling whatsoever down there.

He was dressed in fresh pajamas and in bed again, the blanket over him, the needle back in his arm. He blinked, wondering if this weren't all a dream, and then his entire body seemed to be seizing up, as if someone had put him in a vise.

He curled up in agony. "Oh, God! Karen! What is happening!"

She was there in an instant, her hands trying to relax the cramps, her voice reaching him. "It'll pass, Miguel. Don't fight it, relax, relax. There, that's better."

And he did relax, but only when he passed out.

Karen later told him that on that night he'd almost died. Although he had no memory of it, she said that he screamed almost the whole night, alternating between fever and chills, cramps that drew him up into a fetal position and seizures in which he stopped breathing for a minute at a time. But all Miguel felt the following morning was incredible weakness: every fiber of his being felt as if it had been beaten.

"Karen," he whispered, licking his lips, trying to open his eyes.

"I'm here" came her voice, and he was sure there was a sob in it. "I'm right here."

It was Karen, too, who made him sit up that afternoon. He twisted his head away from the light that leaked in the window and said he could not, he was too weak. But she kept at him, telling him that they had to keep the blood circulating through him, they had to wash the poison out.

"You need to try to get on your feet," she told him. "Hilkka said..."

"To hell with Hilkka," he groaned. "I cannot. All my strength is gone! Is this what a mortal endures!"

"You aren't there yet," Karen said firmly. "And you won't be unless you do what I tell you. Now up, onto your feet. Do it."

He did. But, dear God, his limbs were shaky. He was no longer a being of easy strength but instead a weak sapling of a man. He would rather have died! Yes! To be so weak was unbearable.

She made him walk then. One step. Two. Karen supporting him. And then she let him sit in the chair by the window. "Don't be a difficult patient," she said, forcing him to sit up. "Miguel, the weakness will pass. But you have to help me. You have to help yourself. You wanted to live, you swore you wanted to live out a normal life. So, try, damn it." And then she moved toward the pulls on the curtain.

Panic rose in him. "No," he said, shaking. "No. I cannot do it. Not yet."

"You have to. Hilkka said you had to look into the light. It's only for a second." Her hand poised on the pull.

"Hilkka," he moaned. "Old wives' tales. I cannot. Why must I...?"

"She said only a little each day once the crisis passed. You heard her say it."

So weak, he was so weak. Why must Karen torment him so? Didn't she know that to look into the light would kill him? God! What a coward he was! But he didn't care. He simply could not...

She pulled open the drapes.

For a long moment Miguel stared at the world outside—a world bathed in sunlight—stunned, his blue eyes wide, blinded with the enormity of that light, and he cried aloud, a moan rising from deep within. He slumped over, covering his face, feeling as if his flesh were sizzling.

She drew the curtains shut and was at his side quickly, cradling his head against her belly, whispering, "It's okay, it's all right."

He could not tell her, he could not speak. As the pain finally ebbed he searched his mind desperately for words to describe what had just happened, but none could be found to tell of the sight that still filled his vision. The sun. He'd just had a glimpse of that fiery orb. The sun! After five centuries. Dear God, the sun.

He slept that night, restlessly, as if his body were rejecting him. He dreamed, too, of terrible things, and he awoke with a wretched sense of loneliness until he saw Karen in her chair, dozing, and he knew he was not alone. He recalled the sun then, the image of it, a big orange ball, fixed in his mind. Karen had made him look upon it. Without her he never could have done it. He felt craven and spineless, wondering what new tortures awaited him. And yet he had looked upon it and survived, the life-giving sun that he hadn't seen since that day so many many years ago, the day he'd gone in search of the murderer Baltazar.

Miguel lay there in his quiet pain and remembered that creature. He remembered, too, that were he not to survive this cure, Karen would be in deadly peril from Baltazar, with no one in the world to protect her. It was up to Miguel to live. He had to live. It was the only way to stop that monster. The only way...

It was just before dawn that Miguel became cognizant of Karen leaning over him. He did not open his eyes, he was too feeble. But when she leaned down and gently pressed her lips to his—so warm—and something unfathomable in him quickened, Miguel knew that he could endure the pain. For where there was pain there was life.

FOR KAREN THE ENSUING days seemed to run together. At times she thought she was in hell—seeing torment on Miguel's face, feeling his pain as if it were her own, and she felt fear, fear that she was going to wake up from one of her fitful naps and find him gone, dead. Maybe she never should have talked him into this.

And then there were the times that he was nearly conscious and gripped her hand, forcing a smile to his cracked lips, licking them, whispering that she was an angel. Those moments were sheer heaven, and she'd think: he's going to live. Oh, God, he's going to live!

She worked as the professional that she was, but she called often on her "gift," asking a higher power to give her strength, to allow that strength and will to flow into Miguel's body.

The blood ran out on the sixth day. She sat on the bedside while he slept restlessly, and she worried. Hilkka had told them that the transfusions could stop when his body temperature reached ninety-five degrees. Well, it hadn't. And now they were out of the life-restoring fluid. It seemed, then, that there was only one thing to do.

She tried to awaken him. "Miguel, I have to go out for a couple of hours. Miguel, can you understand me?"

But he was still delirious, saying, "Go if you must... I will merely await you. Would you like a fire built? Are you cold?"

She left him. She didn't like it one bit, but she needed to get that blood. Just this one last time. Either he would be cured or he'd slip back into his shadow world. Or... He still could die.

Karen did have to admit to herself that breathing the fresh air, getting away from his eerily silent house, revived her. She needed a break, though she would have preferred something less stressful. But she steeled herself, the image of him lying so helpless in that dark room spurring her on, and she entered the hospital.

The trouble came in the blood bank. And, as she'd feared, it was over the big purse she carried.

It was an older, seasoned technician who questioned her. He entered the blood bank, scaring her half to death, and immediately eyed her bag. "Hey," he said, frowning. "You know having that in here's against the rules." He squinted then, staring at her name tag. "Karen Freed, huh? Well, who's your supervisor?"

Oh, God, she thought, this was it. A flashing image raced through her mind—administrators, police, jail. No, she couldn't let that happen. *Think.*

"Well?" he said.

She launched in, her pulse racing. "You know," she said, trying not to swallow, "you guys really tick me off. I was on my way to lunch, and someone down on two asked me to run this errand first. So I forgot my purse. Big deal. Half of the staff's out sick and we're scrambling as it is. You could at least thank me." She glared at him.

He glared back. And then his expression softened. "Well," he said, "I guess it's all right. This once, anyway. I know we've been real shorthanded in the lab, too. I didn't mean to..."

"Forget it," Karen said, shouldering by him. "I'd better get the supplies or that patient will die. Excuse me." And she went to work, finding the IV kits and units of blood, taking her time, her heart still pounding. By the time she was done, he had gone. She quickly stuffed the supplies in her purse, then beat a hasty retreat, whispering a prayer of thanks. And when she got back to the brownstone she found Miguel sleeping peacefully. Another prayer of thanks.

It was a rough week that followed. Often he seemed to be teetering between two worlds, and Karen wondered which one would ultimately claim him. He was awake for hours now during the day, sometimes quietly, sometimes thrashing with painful cramps. She held him against her and stroked his brow, willing him to heal, willing strength and hope into her touch. And then she'd ease his head back onto the pillows and just watch him.

It was on the twelfth day that she noticed the first signs of true change. It seemed a miracle, but she swore she could see a hint of color in his cheeks. She quickly took his temperature—it had risen to ninety-five degrees. And then she saw them: whiskers. There was the beginning of a dark growth on his chin. Dear Lord, she thought, her heart singing, had his body made the choice of mortal life?

The next day, she was able to get him into the chair by the window again. When she drew open the curtains he groaned so painfully at the sudden, blinding light that she quickly closed them. He simply was not ready for prolonged exposure to the sun. But Hilkka had said he must slowly begin to take in the sunlight or all their efforts would be for nothing.

Karen moved him to the library the following day. As with any patient, no matter what the illness, she knew it was important to get him up and moving despite the pain. And the change of scenery wasn't going to hurt. She made him comfortable on the sofa, though he barely seemed aware of his environment, and she built a fire, because he complained constantly of being cold.

That night she tried to feed him. Water only. But he quickly threw it up and sank back weakly onto his pillow. Okay, she thought, they'd try it a sip at a time.

Eventually—if he truly was going to survive this—he'd hold it down.

By day sixteen Miguel had taken in almost eight ounces of water over a two-hour period and not once vomited. That night she gave him a little chicken broth—her mother would be so proud of her, Karen thought, amused—and he held that down, too.

At eleven that night he awakened, and for the first time in weeks, it seemed, he was more alert than delirious.

"My God," he said, rising to a sitting position, a look of amazement on his drawn features. "I think I... I have to..."

"What?" Karen said, going to him.

But he said no more. Instead, to her amazement, he staggered to his feet and, using the backs of chairs and the walls for support, he somehow managed to make it to the hall powder room.

Karen followed, hiding a smile. And she waited while he went in, closed the door, and then returned, gripping the doorframe weakly, his eyes glistening with moisture as he tried to control his emotions.

"Karen," he said in a whisper, "I... Do you know how long...?"

She let herself smile then. "I can imagine," she said, and then she helped him back to his bed in the library, aware of his shock, his emotional response, his embarrassment. He was, after all, a man of impeccable propriety. God, how she cherished that in him.

The next day, a warm late January day, Karen took him outside. He leaned weakly on her shoulder, his color ashen, but his growing beard evident now. He only spent perhaps thirty seconds in the sun, wearing the sunglasses she'd brought him, but he did it. The following afternoon he managed a full minute with the strong rays on his face before he ducked his head, put the sunglasses back on and asked to go back in.

A bubble was growing in Karen, a bubble of hope and joy and so much love she was afraid to examine it too closely. On the day that Miguel spent nearly ten minutes outdoors on a wicker chair in his weedy garden, she finally allowed herself to bask in that joy, and she told herself that they had done it; together they'd restored his life.

It was that night, however, that her bubble burst. She'd been in the kitchen, fixing soup, when she saw it, a shadow moving through the garden outside, and she knew, knew as sure as she was standing there, that *he* was out there.

Her heart stopped. It was Baltazar, stalking them, trying to find out what Miguel was up to.

Karen had thought that Miguel had taken care of him that night he'd gone out. She'd truly thought...so what had he done, then? She could hardly march into the library and confront Miguel about it. He was all but mortal now, and completely powerless. That puzzled her—why would Miguel have taken the cure when he must have known Baltazar was still a threat? Had Miguel only thought he'd dealt with the problem?

All evening she was haunted by questions. Miguel never, ever, would have taken the poison and the transfusions if he'd known Baltazar was still here.

Or... Did Miguel have another plan? Karen desperately wanted to ask, but Miguel was still too weak, barely able to walk without her help. Not yet.

Miserable and afraid, she was unable to sleep a wink until dawn crept over the city. Her worry did not abate, either, until that afternoon when she'd helped Miguel out to his chair in the sun, sunglasses on, a blanket around his shoulders, and he took her hand.

"Karen," he said, looking up at her, "how can I ever repay you?"

She gazed down at him. "Just... let me be with you," she said, no longer the nurse but again the shy girl.

"Forever," he said, a whisper. "And someday, God willing, I will be able to... to be the man you deserve."

"You will, Miguel," she said. "I know you will." And she held his head to her stomach, embarrassed at the tears in her eyes.

It was Karen's idea to take the taxi to her apartment that afternoon. Actually, as she explained to Miguel, the trip was a necessity. "My rent's two days overdue, I need my clothes, my mail... But you'll be fine for an hour alone, I know you will."

He didn't like it, and insisted that she be back before dusk. "Promise me," he said, struggling against the weakness.

"Of course," she said, and she didn't ask him why she had to be back.

"Before dusk," he said with more strength than he'd shown in weeks.

"I got you," Karen said, and she gave him a thumbs-up.

The first thing that went wrong was the fender-bender that the taxi got into. But Karen checked the time as the drivers exchanged insurance information and driver's license numbers. It was okay. Not great, but she had plenty of daylight left.

"Stupid..." the cabby said, swearing up a storm when they were off again.

"Just hurry, please," Karen broke in, ignoring his tirade.

And then her landlord waylaid her in the hall. "Yo there, Miss Freed," he called, opening his apartment door, coming down the hall, reeking of beer. "You can't just march yerself in here, missy, without paying your rent, and expect to get away with it. Who the hell do you think you are? Who the hell do you think pays the bills around here? Not you, that's for damn sure."

Karen sighed. There was no point mentioning the fact that when the heat or hot water ran out it took days to restore them, or that the rent was already higher than any other comparable building in the area. Why argue? "I'll get your check. That's where I'm headed, in fact."

"Oh, yeah? And I suppose you'll run it right down."

"Yes, I will." She checked her watch impatiently, aware of the dusk gathering in the hall.

"Maybe I just ought to go on up there with you."

"That's not necessary," she said. "Now, if you'll excuse me..."

Between the accident and her encounter with the landlord, Karen had lost a half hour of light. She raced up the stairs, dropping her mail, catalogs slithering from her hands, and swore, a sense of urgency making her break out in a cold sweat.

Clothes, she thought when she was inside her apartment. But first she had to write that idiot the rent check. She flipped through her check register, wrote in the figures, and then her eyes lifted desperately to the windows. It was twilight. Oh, God!

She rushed, scribbling the check, telling herself she was being silly. He couldn't possibly get here so quickly after the sun had set. And how would he know where she was, anyway?

Get a grip, Freed, she told herself, snatching up an envelope and sealing it. That was when she felt a sudden draft of ice-cold air.

Karen froze, the envelope in her hand. It was as if the atmosphere of the room had suddenly changed, and she could feel evil in the very air that she breathed.

No, she thought frantically, please, no, and with every ounce of courage she possessed she turned slowly around. Her heart stopped.

"Sweet, sweet Karen" came his voice, drifting on that wave of evil, and he seemed to glide toward her.

She backed away, her knees buckling, until the wall stopped her. A scream of terror lodged in her throat.

"Oh, Karen," he whispered, standing so close she could see the shades of blue dancing in his eyes, the incredible marble smoothness of his skin. "Karen, what have I ever done to make you fear me so?" And he reached up and stroked her cheek with the back of his hand. It was hideously cold. "So warm," he breathed, a man, a being so extraordinarily handsome that the terror quickened in her. "And Miguel, where is my old friend tonight? Did he let you go out alone? Tsk-tsk."

She tried to speak, instinctively knowing that he was feeding on her fear. But no words could get past the dryness in her mouth.

"Come now, Karen," he went on relentlessly, his body against hers, his face so close, so close now. "Has the cat got your tongue?"

And then, with that icy hand still against her cheek, he nudged her head to one side. She closed her eyes, the blood beating madly in her veins, and prayed for courage.

"Ah," he breathed, "they are still on you, Miguel's marks of love. Does he love you, Karen?"

She licked her lips. "Yes," she murmured.

"And you think he is truly capable of love? But of course you do. So sweet, so innocent." And then, with the back of his hand still holding her head to one side, he drew his mouth along her jawline, then lower, his tongue now on her neck, licking her. "Um," he whispered, "I can taste you, Karen. Honey. Did Miguel tell you that you taste of honey? Did he tell you he was once a priest? What has Miguel told you?"

"Everything," she whispered.

He licked her again, a sigh coming from deep within him. "And what is our mutual friend up to these nights? I have not seen him in the city."

"But you stare in his windows," she said, her stomach coiling in revulsion, every cell in her cringing from him.

"Aren't you the clever one. Is this why Miguel is saving you, for your cleverness? Indeed, I admit I am most puzzled by his behavior. By now he should have sucked you dry, Karen, *ma belle*. Why hasn't he?"

She wouldn't answer, and she could feel the change in him. Frustration?

"What is Miguel doing in that monstrosity of a house?" This time he put his teeth against her.

Karen's heart beat furiously, and it took a strength she never knew she possessed to stand there stock-still and not fight him. Oh, he wanted her to fight, to scream and cry and call out Miguel's name. She knew that. *Oh, God, give me the courage to defy this demon!*

"Tell me," he said, drawing back his head, catching her eyes. "Tell me what it is you and Miguel are up to. Surely you are not playing house with that priest." He grinned wickedly.

She drew in a ragged breath and looked into those ice blue eyes. "Why don't you ask him?"

He was deathly silent for a moment. "Are you playing a game with me, Karen?"

"Not at all."

He considered that. "Ah, but I think you are. I think you hope that I will spare you."

"Why should you do that?" she ventured.

"I may have my reasons," he said, and she could feel his hesitation. He wanted her, yes; his eyes were blazing with the need, but he also wanted information and an audience—Miguel.

"So take me," she said.

"Oh, I most assuredly will. But I truly wish you'd show some resistance, Karen. This is too easy."

"I can't fight you."

He bared his teeth. "And Miguel. I want to know why he is closeting himself in that house. Is he coming here, Karen? Is he?"

"How should I know?"

His hands were on her shoulders now, and he pushed her against the wall, hard. "Do you think Miguel would enjoy the spectacle of my possession of you? Should we wait till he comes? Is he coming, Karen?"

She clamped her lips shut, and that was when he struck her.

"Fight me, damn you!"

She said nothing. And then he pushed her away from him, disgusted. "Where is he?" he demanded.

She still said nothing.

"You are a weakling," he ground out. "And Miguel is a fool! You think that puny priest loves you, but where is he? Where is he now? Why has he let you come here alone?"

"Figure it out for yourself," Karen said, and it seemed for a long, terrible moment that he was going to spring on her and sink his teeth into her, but he didn't.

He only glared at her furiously, cold fire spitting from those eyes, and then he hissed, "You will be mine whenever I say, whenever I want, and that revolting priest will witness it! I swear it to you! Tell him that! Tell him he cannot trick me!" And suddenly, as if by magic, he was gone.

For a very long time Karen stood there against the wall in the ice-cold room and stared at the space he'd occupied. Then she let out a ragged breath and thought that he must have gone out quickly through the door she hadn't bothered to lock in her hurry.

As her breathing quieted and rational thought returned, she realized that she'd been lucky this time. He'd never let her go again. And if he somehow figured out what was going on with Miguel, he wouldn't hesitate to enter the house and have his way.

She had to tell Miguel. Warn him.

Then, as she stood there thinking, she realized that she couldn't possibly tell him. Not in the state he was in right now. It was up to her, then, up to her to keep that fiend from finding out, up to her to keep them both alive.

CHAPTER SEVENTEEN

MIGUEL CURSED his weakness. Even climbing the stairs left him short of breath. His body had become a prison, a feeble, putrid thing that controlled both him and Karen. Centuries ago he had forgotten illness of the body, pain, wrenching nausea, sweating, voiding, coughing, itching. Breathing.

He was over the worst, or so Karen told him. He barely recalled those days in bed, only her face, calm and reassuring, and her hands that gave him blessed relief—for a time.

It was one-thirty in the afternoon. The sunlight spilled in through the tall front windows intermittently because there were clouds, fluffy white clouds that did not hold moisture. Yet it was cold out. And how he felt the cold now!

Impatience ate at him; unjustly, he knew. Karen had taken the afternoon to visit her parents. He realized he couldn't expect her to spend every daylight hour with him, but he was unreasonably jealous of the time she spent elsewhere.

God knew she'd spent enough time with him already, hardly sleeping, caring for him in every way when he was helpless. Bathing him, feeding him, holding his head when he vomited. And now that he was better she had the right to have some time to herself.

He looked out the windows again. The light, the shadows, the colors. People strolling by on the sidewalk, cars, delivery trucks, the bustle of a normal day. Clouds sailing across the sky. Blue, a blue sky. Bare-branched trees revealed by a space between buildings, the trees of Riverside Park.

Five hundred years since he'd seen such splendid things!

He sat for a time in one of the leather chairs, marshaling his strength. He was going to surprise Karen this afternoon. He was going to take a shower and shave. Yes, shave. His beard had started growing again, and when he saw himself in the mirror he recalled the bearded monk he had been. A sad-eyed, gaunt monk.

Miguel took the stairs slowly, like an old man, his lungs going in and out, in and out, like a wheezing bellows. Frustrating and inconvenient, but he would grow used to it. Karen had assured him he would.

When he thought of her he felt a warm melting in his belly, not the awful hunger he'd known before. Ah, that was a relief, the most important thing, really. She was safe now. She was safe from him, although not from Baltazar. She'd been careful to be in his house by sundown every day since the time she had made him so nervous when she had been late getting back, but still he worried. Baltazar must suspect something by now, must be planning some hideous confrontation. At night.

He reached the landing and drew air into his lungs. He was better each day, certainly. Soon he would be ready to execute his plan. Very soon.

The bathroom. He'd had little use for it previously, but Karen had stocked it with toothpaste, soap, deodorant, shampoo. The scents were so strong, overpowering, yet different from before. He was beginning to live in a whole new world.

He took his clothes off. His ribs showed, his skin was pinkish, not white as it had been. It felt rough to the touch, warm and rough. Alive. He turned on the shower and adjusted the temperature as Karen had shown him. The water felt good, warm and clean. He washed his hair. Soap got in his eyes and stung. He had so much to learn, things he'd forgotten or never known.

He turned the water off and stepped out onto the rug, experiencing water dripping, the air touching his skin with cold, goose bumps rising, prickling, water running into his eyes, burning. The towel? Ah, this human condition required so much diligence.

Miguel looked into the mirror over the sink. It was fogged up, so he opened the bathroom door and watched steam swirl out, but cool air came in and made him shiver again. He wrapped the towel around his loins and studied his face in the mirror: his hair was too long, there were new lines, and his cheeks beneath the dark whiskers were sunken.

"Miguel," he said to himself, "you do not look well, not at all."

Karen had bought a package of disposable razors. She'd shown it to him and told him she'd shave him when she had time. No knife or straight razor anymore. No, now they were plastic "safety" razors. Easy to use, she'd said.

He lathered soap on his face and took one of the bright yellow razors, examined it. Simple. He raised it and stroked it against his skin. The hairs pulled, the blades scraping across his cheek. At his chin he felt the razor catch, stop, and there was red blood on his skin. *Dios*.

Downstairs he heard the front door open. "Miguel!" Karen called. "I'm back. Where are you?" And he heard her footsteps, the rustle of her coat as she took it off, the thump of something she put down. "Miguel?"

"Up here," he said.

Her footsteps on the stairs were light and full of energy. She stuck her head in the half-open door. Her cheeks were pink from the cold, and she wore a pale blue sweater. She was radiant.

"Oh, my goodness," she said, "you're bleeding!"

He put his hand up, and it came away red. "It's nothing, a nick."

She grinned at him. "You cut yourself shaving," she said proudly, as if he'd done something commendable.

"I need practice."

She took the razor from him. "Sit down, there, on the side of the tub. I'll shave you."

"I wanted to surprise you."

"You did. Marvelously. But I'd prefer you not to lose any of the blood I've so laboriously pumped into you. Now, sit."

The feel of her hands on him was so fine, tickling, sending arrows of almost painful delight through him. She soaped his face. "You should have shaving cream. I forgot. Or an electric razor. I could get you one."

Biting her lower lip, she put one hand on the top of his head and with the other she ran the razor swiftly and efficiently across his skin, rinsing the blade in the sink. It took no more than two minutes, and he was curiously let down when she was nearly done. It was the feel of her against him, her deft hands, one thigh touching his left side, a breast brushing his shoulder. He found that he could not ignore that firm swell against him, and despite his weakness, he felt heat in his loins, a pulse that was attaining a mind of its own. He had no idea whether to be embarrassed or proud or whether or not he should inform Karen of this awakening within him. He sensed, though, that this heat in him, this life, was best kept private for now. One thing of which he was certain, however, was that he was not ready for that particular act. No. He must be fully recovered, because if he were not, he might somehow fail her, and of all the changes he had undergone these past weeks, this was the one he was growing to fear.

"There," she said, laying aside the razor, "all done." Miguel recognized her nurse voice.

She was patting his face with a warm, damp wash rag. He put his hand up and closed his fingers around her wrist. "Come here," he said, his voice rumbling, unfamiliar to his ears, and he pulled on her wrist. She was close then, her eyes shining, her pink lips parted. She put her hands on his shoulders to brace herself and closed her eyes. He kissed her carefully, breathing in her scent, which was different now, no longer cloying and coppery, but fresh and alive.

"Miguel," she said against his mouth, "you *are* feeling better." She sounded surprised and thrilled and expectant, and her voice was a contented purr.

They drew apart and looked at each other. A hush filled the bathroom, and Miguel could sense the unfamiliar beating of the organ in his breast grow stronger. He put a hand on his chest, feeling it.

"Are you all right?" she asked in alarm. "Maybe you should lie down. You're cold. Miguel . . ."

"Is this what I must expect from a mere kiss?" he asked lightly.

She flushed. "Oh."

"You are so beautiful," he said.

"And you're freezing. Please get dressed," she said in her efficient nurse voice. "I'm going to start fixing dinner. I got some groceries, and my mother gave me some leftover pot roast."

"Shall I grow to love your mother's pot roast?"

"You might just have to, Miguel." And she went downstairs.

They ate a meal like real people, sitting at the kitchen table, not the huge, sheet-shrouded dining room table, and talked like ordinary folk, the light outside dying as they ate. Miguel chewed slowly, tasting, smelling. Each mouthful was a new discovery.

Karen talked idly, and he listened. He felt better, weak but better, and he was content for the moment.

"They keep asking about you," she was saying. "I make excuses. They know I'm living with you, because I'm never at my apartment."

"Are they angry about that?"

She shrugged. "No. My mother is so glad I've got a man she doesn't care what I do."

"I will meet your family," he said. "Soon."

"You'll need a few more units of blood for that," she said dryly.

"I am not afraid. Not with you." He chewed a piece of meat and swallowed. "I will tell your mother I like her pot roast."

After dinner they sat in the library. Miguel got cold easily, so they lit a fire in the hearth. He was in one of the big chairs, and Karen sat on the floor at his feet, legs curled under her, her back against the chair, and he rested his hand on her shoulder. They were quiet together, not needing to talk. Miguel felt the heat of the flames burnish his face, smelled the smoke. His body was a constant source of sensation, and Karen's presence heightened his perceptions. He sat, thinking of the long, long nightmare from which he was awakening, staring into the flames.

"You must be tired," she finally said, turning to look up at him.

"A little."

"Let's go to bed, then. You need your rest."

She slept next to him now, having gotten into the habit when he was so ill and she needed to care for him. They didn't discuss it, and she didn't press him. It was unspoken, but when he was stronger, when he was totally well...

He lay next to her in the darkness, feeling her heat, hearing her breathe, and he thought about what was coming. Baltazar. He tested his strength, flexing muscles, breathing. *Dios,* but his recovery was slow!

It would come, though, the time was approaching. He lay there and felt the oddness of his body, the twitches and tickles and air rushing in and out, a yawn erupting.

Yes, the time was near.

KAREN AWAKENED to Miguel's hand on her breast and his lips on her collarbone. She turned and snuggled against him. "Good morning," she murmured.

He put his arms around her and held her close, saying nothing, and she felt such complete contentment she could not have put it into words. They were together, and the cure had worked. Miguel was on the mend, and they loved each other. As for the other—Baltazar—she would not think of him now. She'd put him from her mind and enjoy the moment, for it was daylight, and he couldn't bother them.

She felt Miguel's body, the whole length of it, against her. He was warm now, and his face had lost its smooth, waxen look. He was too thin, and in his fine silky black hair there was a streak of gray at one temple, but, oh, how she loved him!

He shifted, and against her thigh there was a stirring and something pressing into her. She held her breath and lay still. Could he...? But suddenly he rolled away from her and sat on the side of the bed. She reached out a hand to trace his backbone. "It's all right," she whispered.

"It is not all right," he said.

"You've been so sick. It's only natural."

"Do not patronize me, Karen."

"I'm not. Miguel, believe me, it will happen."

"When?" he asked hoarsely.

"Soon." She pulled on his arm. "Come back to bed. It's cold."

He did, lying on his back, a hand behind his head. He was very quiet.

"Did we just have a quarrel?" she asked.

"No, because I am not angry with you, only myself."

She raised herself on an elbow and regarded him gravely. "You're not sorry you took the cure, Miguel, are you?"

"No, never."

"Do you wish you'd never met me?" She ran her fingers down his bare chest.

"*Por Dios*, no! How could you think that?"

She leaned down and kissed his lips. "Soon," she whispered.

They had the conversation over lunch at the Russian Tea Room. It was Miguel's first daylight outing.

"I am keeping you from your work," Miguel said over coffee and pastries. "I have been thinking about that. I am well enough now that you could return to the hospital."

"Not yet," she said.

"I am a burden to you."

"Oh, Miguel, you're not. I've never been so happy in my life. I'll go back when you're entirely recovered, okay?"

"You must work during the day, though. The night is for others."

"Don't even think about it now. We'll talk about it later."

"You will not be able to put it off forever," he said. "You should have your own life."

She put her hand on his where it lay on the table. "I have no life without you."

That afternoon he took her to meet his agent, whose office was in a restored building on West Twenty-first Street.

"Why, Mr. Rivera," the agent said, rising from behind his desk, "what a pleasant surprise. I honestly can't recall when you last visited the office. Sit down, sit down."

"Mr. Hagel," Miguel said, "I wish you to meet Karen Freed. I would like to set up a power of attorney for her and add her name to my signature cards and the title to my house.''

''Miguel!'' Karen said, shocked. ''You don't have to do that. I mean . . .''

''Karen, I have been planning to do this. Do not interfere.''

''And, ahem, what is Mrs., uh, Miss Freed's legal status, Mr. Rivera?''

Miguel looked at her, his eyes meeting hers, a solemn expression on his face. ''She is my betrothed.''

Karen's heart leapt. She couldn't speak for the lump in her throat. Tears came to her eyes. ''Miguel,'' she managed to say.

''Your fiancée,'' Mr. Hagel said. ''My congratulations, Mr. Rivera, Miss Freed.''

They spent the better part of an hour arranging everything, and Karen was so embarrassed she could barely speak a word. She was positive this elegant-looking agent of Miguel's thought she was a fortune hunter, and of course he had to believe Miguel was a complete fool. It wasn't until they were back out on Twenty-first Street that she felt she could breathe again.

''He thinks I'm after your money,'' she said, dying inside. ''I wish you'd warned me. I wouldn't have let you do that. Oh, Miguel, I'm so . . .''

But he only smiled indulgently. ''Karen, Karen,'' he said, tipping her face gently up to his. ''The man knows, as obviously you do not, that my holdings in New York are a mere fraction of the fortune I have amassed. If today you were embarrassed, you had best brace yourself."

"Miguel," she said, horrified. "You aren't to put my name on another thing. I mean it."

"Of course, whatever you wish," he said.

That afternoon, for the first time since he'd been ill, Miguel went up to his studio and attempted to paint. Karen left him alone, knowing he needed time to himself. She took the opportunity to tidy up, to vacuum the floors with the new Hoover Miguel had had delivered. And she thought, as she worked, that everything was so perfect, so wonderful. Too perfect. Life couldn't remain like this, a constant happy ending. No, she had to be realistic, and no matter how much she and Miguel loved each other, problems would crop up. Oh, sure, she knew that. But for now...

It was a few days later when her prediction came true.

"I have to go out," Miguel said that morning.

"Oh, where?"

"An errand, that is all."

"I'll go with you," she said.

"No, Karen. I have to do this alone."

"Miguel..."

He smiled to reassure her, but it didn't reach his eyes. "You are not to worry, my dear."

Her heart caught. "You're lying to me, Miguel," she said. "I can tell. You're going to do something...."

He laughed, a false laugh. "Do not be silly. You are overprotective, a tyrant."

"Miguel, please, I'll go with you. You're not entirely well yet."

"I am perfectly fine." He came close and kissed her on the lips. "You have seen to it that I became a man, Karen, so let me be one."

"Oh, Miguel..." But he was right, and there was nothing she could do.

He put on his coat, wrapped a scarf around his neck, a red cashmere scarf she'd bought for him, and leather gloves.

She busied herself in the kitchen, her heart thudding, unable to bear the thought of what he was going to do. And then it occurred to her why he'd made all those legal arrangements, putting her name on everything. He'd thought it all out, so that if he... Oh, God, he was not coming back!

"Miguel!" she cried, running to the front door, where he stood, one hand on the knob. "Don't go! Stay here!"

He smiled. "You are foolish to get upset over a simple errand, Karen."

A simple errand.

He left then, walking down the white marble steps, along the flagstone path, through the wrought-iron gate to a waiting taxi.

There was no thought, no coherent decision, on Karen's part as she grabbed her coat and her purse and flew out the door, running to the corner, chasing after Miguel's taxi, which turned south. She stood there desperately waving her arm for a cab, watching the bright yellow vehicle that carried Miguel grow smaller and smaller.

A cab stopped, thank God, and she burst in, breathless, telling the driver to hurry. "See that cab up ahead?" she said, leaning forward, pointing.

"Yeah, lady. I know, follow it and there'll be a big tip in it, right?"

"Yes, yes! Hurry!"

She leaned forward the whole time, her hands on the back of the front seat, her eyes glued to Miguel's taxi.

"You lost him!" she cried once.

"Take it easy, lady. He just turned onto the avenue. No problem." And her driver careered around the corner just as the light turned red behind them.

Downtown they went, across to the East Side, the neighborhood changing from commercial through shabby residential to abandoned warehouses, boarded-up tenements.

It was bright out, sunny and clear, and Karen had to squint. Her cabbie put on his brakes suddenly, and she jerked forward.

"Sorry. He stopped up there," the cabby said. "I figured you don't want him to see you."

She peered out through the windshield. Yes, there was Miguel getting out of his taxi; she could just see the bright red of his scarf. His cab pulled away, and he was left standing there on the deserted street, in front of a condemned brick tenement.

"Thanks," she breathed, digging in her wallet, thrusting some bills at her driver. "Is that enough?" But she was halfway out the door before he could answer.

She walked briskly down the street to where Miguel had stood a moment before, her heart pounding so hard she felt weak. Shielding her eyes, she looked up at the building, an ugly structure with filthy windows, mostly broken, some boarded over. Someone had put a sign on the door: Danger, Do Not Enter. Trash had blown into the corners of the recessed doorway.

Karen swallowed, stepped over some boards and pulled on the tilted door. It opened. Inside, the building was dark, and she had to wait for her eyes to adjust to the gloom. She didn't question why Miguel had come here; her mind wasn't really working. She only knew she had to be there. She had to help him.

Quietly she closed the door behind her. The darkness frightened her, and the awful smells of mold and urine and decay assailed her senses. She listened. Yes, Miguel's footsteps on the stairs, climbing.

Karen started up the stairs. She knew what was up there. And she knew how Miguel had known of this place—he'd found it that night he'd gone out before starting the cure. He'd been planning this all along, just waiting until he was well enough. He'd kept it from her, too, although she should have guessed. There would be no peace for Miguel until he met his nemesis one last time—in the light of day.

Of course.

Up she climbed, cobwebs brushing her face with shadowy fingers, rats scurrying, scratching. Doors were broken, hanging on hinges, missing altogether. Miguel's footsteps stopped. Karen froze. A door creaked open. She moved quickly, quietly, toward the open door through which a pale rectangle of light spilled onto the stained floor of the hallway. She knew who, what, was in that apartment. She recalled the coldness of the monster's tongue on her neck, and shuddered.

She crept up to the door, peeked in. Miguel stood there, looking down at a filthy mattress and the figure that lay so still upon it. She could see Baltazar clearly, and even in his trance an aura of evil came from him. His face was so smooth, so young, unreal in its perfection, his blond hair lying close to his skull, his long white hands clasped over his chest.

A strangled sob escaped from Karen's throat, and Miguel whirled. "God in heaven!" he breathed. "Karen!"

"I had to follow you, I had to. I was so scared," she whispered.

He stepped quickly to the doorway, took her arm in an iron grasp and pulled her out into the hall. "Go," he said fiercely. "Leave this place! You cannot imagine the danger!"

"It's daylight, though," she breathed. "Isn't he..."

"He is powerful, Karen. I cannot be sure. You will leave!"

Karen straightened and gently pulled her arm from his grasp. "I won't go. I'm staying. You can't do this alone."

Miguel leaned against the wall, wiped cold sweat from his brow. "Karen," he groaned, "you do not know what you say."

"Yes I do. Look at you, you're still sick."

"Damn you, Karen." He put an arm out, barring her way. "Stay here. Do not enter this room. Obey me." And he went back inside.

Karen bit her lip, twisted her hands nervously, then stepped to the open doorway. Miguel was pulling at the creature's arm, struggling. She knew that he would have been able to do the job effortlessly when he was a revenant, but now he was weak. She could hear his labored breath, the body dragging across the floor. She drew in a deep lungful of musty air and stepped into the room.

Miguel stopped for a second, turning a black look on her. "Go away, Karen," he said, panting.

"No," she replied, and she grabbed Baltazar's other arm and bent her back, pulling at him.

They got him out the door, down the corridor. He was a dead weight, surprisingly heavy. Karen couldn't bear to look at his face. The stairs, four flights, lay ahead of them. Miguel took his arms, Karen his legs, and they started down. It was so horrible, a sick thing they were doing, but she couldn't consider that, not now.

She struggled with the weight on every step, and she knew Miguel bore most of the load. Then she dropped a leg, and it thumped hollowly on a step. She was bending to pick it up again when her eyes flew to its face, and her insides turned to ice. His eyes were slits, partially open, full of hate, gleaming with evil.

"Miguel!" she cried, and he turned and saw, but he kept on, one step at a time.

They reached the first-floor landing. Only one more flight. He was so heavy. Karen's arms and chest ached, but she was afraid to stop, to look at him again. What if he really woke up?

They stopped on the landing for a moment to rest. Horror clawed at her. Baltazar's eyes opened; his mouth stretched into a feral grin. "Oh, God," she sobbed, "hurry!"

But Miguel was having trouble getting hold of an arm. It moved by itself, out of his grasp! Then he recovered it, and Karen stumbled, faster and faster, slipping, missing a step, almost falling, gasping for breath. The creature was so heavy, as if it was deliberately making itself more dense to thwart them.

They burst outside, and Karen could feel the monster buck as she dragged at one leg, desperately pulling him along the ground.

"He moved!" she gasped. But Miguel said nothing, only pulled their captive doggedly, foot by foot, along the broken pavement in front of the tenement, to a vacant lot next door.

It was hard to hold on to him now. He struggled, writhing, convulsing. Karen dropped his leg once; it kicked at her. She ran around and took an arm, and they went on, only a few more yards. Through a break in a chain link fence, now on snow that made him slide more easily. His torso twisted.

They dropped him in the dirty snow in the empty lot where used hypodermics and broken glass littered the ground and papers flapped against the wire fence. The winter sun glared down. And then they stepped back and stood side by side and watched the monster.

A thousand curses poured from his throat, though his lips didn't move. Karen put her hands over her ears. His body arched up until it rested on its heels and head, until they could hear its spine crack. The fire shot from his eyes, and they widened, glaring, while the babble of a hundred tongues erupted from him. Then the fire dimmed, his eyes closed, his arms flailed and thrashed. A scream tore from his throat, weaker now. Smoke rose from him, and he seemed to wither, to lose mass, even as his body squirmed and kicked. It was unspeakably horrible. He shrank, still smoking, until there was nothing but leathery skin and bones, and then even those turned to dust, a man-shaped blot of dust on the snow.

"It is done," she heard Miguel say in a deathly quiet voice. He put his arm around her shoulders and looked up into the noonday sun. "It is done," he said again.

CHAPTER EIGHTEEN

OUTSIDE MIGUEL'S brownstone it was mild, the late February sun thawing the earth. Golden sunlight streamed through the attic windows and the newly installed skylight and warmed Karen's shoulders.

She squirmed on her stool. "Can I at least get up for a minute and stretch?" she asked.

But he only frowned, going back to the canvas he was working on, his concentration total.

"Miguel, I'm stiff as a board. And we have a ton to do this afternoon. You have to meet with the hospital board at three, the architects at four...."

"Your new wing will still be built if I am five minutes late," he said distractedly.

"*My* new wing? I suppose there'll be one of those plaques at the entrance. Donated by Karen Freed, ER Nurse. Right."

"Karen Freed Rivera y Aquilar, as of forty-eight hours ago," he said, wiping a palette knife with a rag. "I cannot seem to get this shadow correct."

"You're not used to the light yet. Give it time."

"I paint worse than an amateur."

"You're doing great." She shifted a little, her neck cramped, and could feel him frown at her. "Sorry.

Anyway," she said, "put *your* name on the plaque, Miguel. I'd die a thousand deaths if anyone saw mine there."

"You must get used to the notion of your wealth, Karen."

"Right. Sure. But indulge me just this once. I still work there part-time, and I'd be so embarrassed."

"Ah!" he said, palette knife in hand, poised over the canvas. "I do believe this is close."

"Can I see it yet?"

"No, not yet," he said, looking so concerned, that Karen laughed.

"You mock my efforts?" he said dryly.

She loved her new Miguel, although really he was not so different from the old one. A bit less silent, less moody, more spontaneous, but still the same man she'd adored from the first. Each day of his recuperation had seen them grow closer, discovering new things about each other. He was a man with a heavy burden removed from his shoulders, and he had told her everything about his life, so much that she couldn't take it all in.

So much was changed, yet one thing remained the same, looming larger as the days went by. They loved each other in all ways but one, that one way that defined the human condition.

Oh, Miguel tried very hard to pretend there wasn't a problem, but it stood between them, and they both played an elaborate game, the object being to save the other unhappiness.

Last week they'd gone to Brooklyn, in the new Volvo he'd bought for her, because, he'd pointed out, it was reputed to be a safe vehicle. She really was a poor driver, he'd noted cautiously, and unused to driving in the traffic. She'd told him he ought to get a license himself if he didn't like it, and how would it have looked to her parents and their neighbors if they'd driven up in a limo?

"It would appear that I take excellent care of my fiancée," he'd remarked, shaking his head at her.

Still, the entire family had been in awe of Miguel, utterly charmed by his impeccable manner and speech and the obvious affection he had for Karen. Then the fateful moment had arrived when they'd all sat down for dinner and Dorothy served her pot roast. Miguel had taken his first bite, chewed slowly and thoughtfully, swallowed and declared that it was superb, equal to any he'd tasted in the capitals of Europe. After that he was, for better or worse, one of the family.

They'd married quickly and quietly at the courthouse two days ago, exchanging vows and simple gold wedding bands. To Karen the moment was as thrilling and as magic as a royal wedding, and when he'd kissed her gently in front of the judge, she'd never known such happiness.

Karen had been certain they would work things out at last on their wedding night.

They'd gone to a little French restaurant for dinner that evening, and it had been so romantic, the champagne, the flowers Miguel had had delivered to their intimate table, the way their eyes had met over each mouthful of food with a secret knowledge. Yes, Karen had thought. This was going to be the night.

"To my bride," Miguel had said, raising his wineglass, his sapphire eyes dancing in the candlelight. "To the most beautiful woman on the face of the earth."

At home he'd undressed her, and she him. His hands, his touch, his breath on her nakedness had been sweet torture. They'd lain on the bed, clasped in each other's arms, and Karen was breathless with expectation. So in love, so very much in love she was deliriously happy. But then something had happened; it seemed such a small thing when Miguel had poised over her and she'd instinctively tried to guide him, but apparently that was all it had taken to diminish his manhood.

He'd rolled off and come to a sitting position on the side of the bed, his head in his hands. "I am no husband," he'd said, and then he had risen to his feet, snatching up his robe and stalking out.

Her wedding night. *Their* wedding night, and she'd ruined it. She'd cried herself to sleep.

The next day, yesterday, Karen had realized that with his new condition, with mortality, came all the strengths and weaknesses, all the follies and glories, of mankind, and she knew that he wasn't going to feel truly male until he could perform that one simple, basic function. And now, today, the act—or, rather, the lack of it—hovered over them like an avalanche ready to break.

"You can stand up now," he was saying, cleaning off his brushes, the knife, studying his morning's work. "I dare say," he began, then corrected himself. "I mean, I don't think I'll ever be a truly great artist, Karen." And then he smiled at himself. "Oh, well, it's the pleasure I get from the act of painting that counts, not the fame."

"Right you are," Karen said, stretching, watching him, her heart swelling just as it had the very first time she'd seen him. She'd never, ever, get tired of watching Miguel.

They had a late lunch in the garden, which was still bare, but the sun was marvelously warm.

"I will never grow used to the sun," Miguel said, stretching his legs out, tilting his head back. His mannerisms were purely human now, purely male.

"Maybe you'd like to move to someplace warmer, you know, like Arizona or Florida, where there's more sun," Karen suggested.

"It is something to consider. A second home." He smiled in his new way, with real humor. "And I will take up golf."

Karen shook her head, grinning. "Golf."

"And why not? As a boy I was quite athletic."

"Tennis," Karen said. "I always wanted to play tennis."

"Certainly."

"Quite a life you have planned for us, Miguel."

"I hope so. I want you to be happy. Ask for anything you want, whenever you want it."

"You spoil me. I don't really want much, only you."

He turned his face from the sun, and his expression grew serious. "The one thing I have not given you," he said quietly.

"You've given me everything, Miguel," she said, sorry she'd inadvertently brought up the sensitive subject. "Please don't..."

"Not quite everything." He stood, looking down sadly at her, then walked inside, leaving her there.

"Damn," Karen whispered, tears stinging her eyes. Had they gone through so much only to come to this?

Karen was a modest woman. Although at work she dealt with the human body in all its naked and most basic functions, in her private life she'd always been shy and careful of proprieties. And so she had been with Miguel. She'd felt instinctively, and correctly, that he was a modest person himself. And then, of course, he had been a priest. And because of their natures, their upbringings, she was as incapable as he of talking over their troubles. She looked at the door he'd just passed through and sighed. What was wrong with the two of them? Well, she thought, tonight, somehow, they would have to talk, work this out.

That afternoon they made both appointments at the hospital and went home, satisfied that Miguel's money was being spent wisely on the wing, but when they arrived back at the brownstone there was a message for Karen—she was needed at work.

"Oh, no," she said. "Miguel, I'm sorry. But until the new girl is trained... Promise you'll get dinner?"

He smiled indulgently. "I promise. Now go and change and work your magic with the patients. I'll await your return."

"I love you," she whispered, and then rushed to change into her uniform, thinking only for a moment that this was the night she'd planned on working things out with Miguel. She pulled on her white panty hose and thought, coward.

It was a long night. And Karen didn't get home till almost dawn. She was tired, and as she quietly let herself in and tiptoed along the hall the last thing she expected to see was a light still on in the library.

She peeked in. He'd waited up for her.

Miguel looked up from the book he was reading, and then slowly, pensively, he closed it, his eyes fixed on her.

"I'm so sorry," Karen began.

"Do not be," he said quietly. "I needed the time to think." Still his eyes were riveted on her. "You see," he went on, and he laid his book aside and rose, "I have not been entirely honest with you, and I have been sitting here getting up my nerve, as you would say."

"To do what, Miguel?"

"It is a delicate subject."

"Oh." She stood there, knowing, afraid. Oh, God, she couldn't say the wrong thing.

"Yes."

"Miguel..." She swallowed. "I...I want you to know that it's very common for people to be...ah... nervous the first time."

"I fear being . . . inadequate."

And then she hid a smile. "There's something you should know, then," she said, her hands still in his. "It's always this way the first time. Men and women, well, they want to be perfect for each other. You understand?"

"You are saying... You are telling me that you, also, are afraid?"

"Well, nervous, yes. Sure." She lowered her eyes. There was a long, anxious moment, and then she felt the warm pressure of his hands.

"Let us go upstairs," he said softly. "Let us go to bed." And Karen would always remember that first time, the slow walk to the second story, the way Miguel closed their bedroom door and turned slowly to her, the love in his eyes and the beating of her heart. And then, as he stepped up to her the light in the room quickened, and all she saw before closing her eyes was a bar of mother-of-pearl brightness from the window as it moved across his face. Then there was only Miguel. Forever.

HARLEQUIN SUPERROMANCE®

WOMEN WHO DARE
They take chances, make changes
and follow their hearts!

Premonitions
by Morgan Hayes

Psychic Alessandra Van Horn can't bring herself to use
her abilities—not since the night she witnessed the
brutal slaying of the man she loved, a Manhattan police
detective killed in the line of duty. Now, a year later, she's
living in a small city in upstate New York, building a
career as an illustrator. She's finally put the past behind
her...until Detective Sam Tremaine shows up, asking
for her help.

The last thing Ali wants is to get involved with another
investigation—and another policeman. But there's
something about Sam that makes her reconsider. Ali can
only hope that the past isn't about to repeat itself!

Watch for *Premonitions* by Morgan Hayes.
Available in February 1995,
wherever Harlequin books are sold.

Take 4 bestselling love stories FREE

Plus get a FREE surprise gift!

PRESS RELEASE

Houston, Texas:

Texas media magnate Martin Foster is stepping down as head of the Foster Entertainment Corporation. In announcing his plans yesterday, Foster stated that one of his children—each of whom currently manages a Foster TV station—will take over. Whichever one achieves the greatest increase in station ratings will inherit control of the network. As a result, media watchers expect the next few months to be "unusually exciting."

Share the excitement! Let Lorna Michaels take you to Texas. Join the Foster family as Ariel and Chad vie for control...and look for love.

The Reluctant Hunk by Lorna Michaels. Harlequin Temptation #523. Available in January 1995 (Ariel's story).

The Reluctant Bodyguard by Lorna Michaels. Harlequin Superromance #633. Available in February 1995 (Chad's story).

Wherever Harlequin books are sold.

 HARLEQUIN®

LORNA-M

HARLEQUIN SUPERROMANCE®

Where the Heart Is
by Patricia Keelyn

Nick Ryan was Maddie's first love. But when he married
another woman, Maddie left her hometown of Felton,
Georgia, and never looked back.

Sixteen years later, Maddie's come home. Nick is a doctor
now...and a widower with a teenage son. But Maddie has
no intention of getting involved with him again. She's
returned to Felton for a completely different reason—she's
going to have a baby.

Where the Heart Is by Patricia Keelyn is available in
February, wherever Harlequin books are sold.

NML-2